An English war hero must unlock the secrets of an Irish beauty's heart…

Named for the heather in her native Ireland, botanist Erica Burke dreams of travel—somewhere she won't be scorned for her scientific interests. Instead, a storm strands her with cool and commanding Major Tristan Laurens, the Duke of Raynham.

An unexpected heir, Tristan is torn between his duties as an intelligence officer and his responsibilities as a duke. A brief return to England to set his affairs in order is extended by bad weather and worse news— someone is after the military secrets he keeps. Could the culprit be his unconventional Irish guest? He needs to see her journal to be sure, and he'll do what he must to get his hands on it…even indulge in a dangerous intimacy with a woman he has no business wanting.

Erica guards her journal as fiercely as she guards her heart, fearing to reveal a side of herself a man like Tristan could never understand. But though she makes Tristan's task infernally difficult, falling in love may be all too easy…

Also by Susanna Craig

Rogues & Rebels Series
The Companion's Secret

The Runaway Desires Series
To Kiss a Thief
To Tempt an Heiress
To Seduce a Stranger

The Duke's Suspicion

A Rogues & Rebels Novel

Susanna Craig

LYRICAL PRESS
Kensington Publishing Corp.
www.kensingtonbooks.com

LYRICAL PRESS BOOKS are published by

Kensington Publishing Corp.
119 West 40th Street
New York, NY 10018

All Kensington titles, imprints, and distributed lines are available at special quantity discounts for bulk purchases for sales promotion, premiums, fund-raising, educational, or institutional use.

Special book excerpts or customized printings can also be created to fit specific needs. For details, write or phone the office of the Kensington Sales Manager: Kensington Publishing Corp., 119 West 40th Street, New York, NY 10018. Attn. Sales Department. Phone: 1-800-221-2647.

Lyrical Press and Lyrical Press logo Reg. US Pat. & TM Off.

First Electronic Edition: October 2018
eISBN-13: 978-1-5161-0402-4
eISBN-10: 1-5161-0402-1

First Print Edition: October 2018
ISBN-13: 978-1-5161-0403-1
ISBN-10: 1-5161-0403-X

Printed in the United States of America

To the doctors and nurses who kept me—and my writing dream—alive.

Acknowledgments

You know you've assembled a great support network as an author when you find yourself thanking the usual suspects. My heartfelt gratitude to Jill Marsal; Esi Sogah and the team at Kensington/Lyrical; the members of The Beau Monde chapter of Romance Writers of America, especially Bill Haggart, for thoughtful feedback and helpful information on military matters; Amy Hay and Cynthia Tennent, for their insights and sage advice; and last, but never least, my husband and daughter, for their grace, patience, and love in helping me survive much more than the usual deadline panic this time around.

Chapter 1

As dark clouds rolled over the Cumbrian sky and thunder rumbled in the distance, Erica Burke discovered she had made a serious error in judgment. Several errors, in fact.

The most serious error, obviously, had been leaving her journal inside the inn where they had stopped to rest the horses. She was often forgetful. *Careless*, other people called it. But in truth she cared a great deal. Losing her journal would have meant losing months of work, losing the record of every botanical observation she had made since coming to England.

It would have meant losing a piece of herself.

To be fair, though, she would never have left her journal at a posting inn if she hadn't been traveling. So hadn't the real error in judgment been agreeing to accompany her sister? True, a lady often took a female companion on her wedding trip, a custom grounded in the assumption that the activities and interests of men and women, even newly married ones, were entirely separate. But Cami's insistence on Erica's joining her had had very little to do with convention. And as far as Erica could see, her brother-in-law, Lord Ashborough, had only one interest: his new bride. The only activity in which he wanted to indulge was... *Well.*

With a wary eye toward the sky, Erica hopped from the coach without explanation and hurried back across the filthy inn yard, blaming the sudden wave of heat that washed over her on the exertion. She had been promised the chance to explore the plants and flowers of the Lake District, and she was determined not to be put off by the occasional moment of embarrassment, or by the knowledge that her presence was entirely extraneous. Her only concession had been to ride in the baggage coach on occasion, with Mr. Remington, Lord Ashborough's manservant, and Adele. Try as she might, Erica could not bring herself to think of the French girl as "Lady Ashborough's maid." It would have required her to concede that Cami was now a lady, and not simply her overbearing elder sister.

On the threshold of the inn's dining parlor, she was forced to reevaluate her assessment once more. A group of rowdy young men now filled the table at which she and her party had been seated only moments ago. Avoiding as best she could the men's eyes, hands, and voices, Erica pressed forward to retrieve what was hers. Perhaps the most serious error had been leaving Lord Ashborough's mastiff, Elf, in Shropshire with the new vicar and his wife. Elf was neither fierce nor especially brave, but even half-grown she was enormous, and Erica had no doubt that her mere presence would have sufficed to forge a path through the room.

On the bench closest to the window sat a man with greasy dark hair. If the sight of him thumbing idly through the pages of her journal had not blanketed her vision in a red haze of anger, she might also have noticed his red coat. His militia uniform.

"Kindly unhand my journal." Though she spoke quietly, she thrust out her hand, palm upward, so forcefully that the muscles of her arm quivered.

He did not rise, and a lazy smile revealed rather mossy teeth. "What have we here? An Irish rebel—?"

The words sharpened her senses, brought the moment into vivid relief.

As if observing her own actions from a great distance, she watched her hand sweep the journal from his grasp and then swing back. The sturdy leather binding—no delicate lady's commonplace book, this—struck along his jaw, effectively wiping the grin from his face.

One of his fellow soldiers guffawed, and suddenly the noises and odors of the room rushed back to full force, threatening to overwhelm her. Her narrow pinpoint of focus expanded from his uniform, grimy from travel and frayed around the collar and cuffs, into a swath of chaos. Clutching her journal in one hand and her skirts in the other, she ran from the room.

Hitting him had been yet another mistake. She could not even say what had prompted her to do it. Her distrust of soldiers? His disdain for Ireland? Perhaps a bit of both. Oh, why could she never seem to control her temper, her impulses? Was he following?

Outside once more, she paused only to scan the inn yard for Lord Ashborough's coaches. But the yard was empty. Perhaps around the corner? No? Well, surely that was his carriage, standing by the church…

Oh, no. *Now* she understood her most serious error. When she'd discovered her journal missing, she'd hopped from the baggage coach without telling Mr. Remington to wait. He must have assumed she had decided to ride the rest of the way with her sister. Erica's absence would likely not be noticed for hours.

She was stranded.

She could almost hear Cami's voice telling her to wait right where she was. But Erica's hasty reaction to the soldier's sneer had rendered this village's only lodging less than hospitable.

Regrettably, she had a great deal of experience with crises. Most, like this, of her own making. And sitting still had never been her preferred method of coping with any of them.

She furrowed her brow, trying to recall the map in the guidebook. People came from all over Britain to visit the Lake District. There would be signposts to Windermere. Surely even she, with her notoriously poor sense of direction, could find it. With another glance at the threatening sky, she began to walk.

What was a little rain?

For the first mile or so, she watched the clouds tumble toward her, listened to the peals of thunder as they swelled and grew, seemingly born of the earth as much as the air. Mud from an earlier rain dragged at her hems and sucked at the soles of her walking boots. At the second mile, she gave up the roadway in favor of the grassy verge. Cold, thick drops began to fall, speckling her dress and face. Hardly had she managed to stuff her journal into her pelisse when the sky opened and water poured down in sheets, whipped by the wind like clothing on the line, blinding her.

Something sharp snagged at her skirts, jabbed at the chilled flesh of her thigh beneath. The hedgerow. A flash of lightning showed her a gap in its tangled branches, barely wide enough for her to pass through. And a little way beyond it, an abandoned-looking stone cottage. Would its roof provide shelter? She could not tell until she reached it.

Head down, she pushed onward. The wind snatched at her sodden bonnet. Nearly strangled by its ties at her throat, she scrabbled with numb fingers to loosen them. Once free, the bonnet whirled into the storm and was gone.

The twenty yards standing between her and her goal seemed to take almost as long to travel as the two miles she had already come. At last, its stout slab door stood before her. Here, in the shadow of the low building, the wind still lashed, but it no longer threatened to carry her away. As she leaned her head against the door to fumble with the latch, she felt a movement. Not of her own making. Not the rumble of the storm, either. The door swung inward and she collapsed onto the dirt floor at the booted feet of a stranger.

The cottage was not abandoned, after all.

Even a cursory glance told her these were not the sort of boots generally worn by cottagers, however. The supple leather was not muddy or scuffed as it would have been if the man were a laborer or had recently trudged across the open field. Perhaps he had been traveling on horseback. Or perhaps he simply had been wise enough to take shelter before the rain began.

Without speaking, he stepped around her to shut the door, muffling the storm's noise and closing out its murky light, casting the single room into near darkness.

Oh, God. This was it—her most serious error in judgment. *Ever.* Erica scrambled to her feet and whirled about to face him, her rain-sodden skirts slapping against her legs. But he was already moving past her again.

"Wait there." His voice was pitched low, audible beneath the storm.

Gradually, her eyes were able to pick out his shape, now on the far side of the small room. A narrow seam of light formed a square on the wall behind him—a window, blocked by wooden shutters. She heard a rattle, a scrape, a hiss. Flame sparked to life in his hands then became the warm, flickering glow of a candle.

"That blast of wind blew it out," he explained with a glance past her at the door. Was it her imagination, or was there an accusatory note in his voice?

The candle lit his features from below, giving them a sardonic cast. Impossible to tell whether he was handsome or plain, dark or fair, young or...well, his voice, his ease of movement, certainly did not suggest an old man. And he was tall—taller than Papa. Than either of her brothers or her brother-in-law. Taller even than Henry...

Oh, why, in this moment, had she thought of Henry? But so it always went, her mind flitting from one idea to the next, fixing on precisely the things she ought to forget, and forgetting the things she ought to—

Her journal!

With a shudder of alarm, she slithered a hand between the wet, clinging layers of her pelisse and her somewhat drier dress and pulled the book from its hiding place. As she hurried toward the light, the man drew back a step. With the candle between her and her journal, so the stranger could see nothing but its binding, she turned the book over in her hands, then thumbed through its pages to assess the damage. The leather cover was damp; rain had wetted the edges of the paper here and there. It would look worn and wrinkled when it was dry, but so far as she could tell, the journal's contents were miraculously unharmed. A sigh of relief eased from her.

When she laid her journal on the tabletop, the candlelight once more threw itself freely around the room. The stranger was looking her up and down, his expression both incredulous and stern. A familiar expression. Cami wore it often in Erica's presence.

Of *course* she looked a mess. Who wouldn't, under these circumstances? Icy rivulets ran from her hair down her face, and beneath the howl of the wind, she could hear the steady patter of water dripping from her skirts onto the floor. If this were a scene in one of those novels her sister denied reading, the hero would probably invite her to strip off her drenched clothing and dry herself before the fire. Something shocking would likely follow.

But there was no fire. And this man showed no intention of acting the part of a hero.

As if to confirm her thoughts, he shook his head and folded his arms across his chest. "What in God's name are you doing out in a storm like this?"

* * * *

When Major Lord Tristan Laurens asked a question, he expected an answer. He certainly did not expect the subject of his interrogation to bristle, fling a lock of wet hair over her shoulder—spraying him with rainwater, almost dousing the candle—and reply, "I might ask you the same."

Unblinking, she faced him across the table, communicating quite clearly that if he was waiting for her to bend first, he might wait forever. He had some experience coaxing information from unwilling sources, and he knew better than to begin by barking at them. But her arrival had caught him off guard. He had never liked surprises.

The silence that stretched between them was eventually broken by her fingers drumming against the cover of the book she'd unearthed from her bodice. She radiated a nervous kind of energy that refused to be contained. When another moment had passed, she plucked up the book, tucked it against her breast, and began to move around the room. Its narrow compass, crowded with ramshackle furniture, prevented her from pacing.

Or perhaps the predictable, orderly, back and forth motion of pacing was anathema to this woman.

She put him in mind of a bedraggled spaniel, with her slight build, rapid movements, and curling hair hanging limply on either side of her face. Though, admittedly, far more attractive than any spaniel he had ever seen. The precise shade of her red hair was difficult to determine under such dim and damp conditions. He tried to imagine what she might look like bathed in the warmth of a shaft of sunlight but gave it up as a bad job. Sunlight was unlikely to be granted them anytime soon.

When her wandering feet brought her within arm's length of him, he held up one hand in hopes she might cease. Her jerk of surprise made him wonder if she had forgotten his presence entirely.

"The storm doesn't show any signs of abating. Perhaps we ought to begin again." He made a crisp bow. "Tristan Laurens."

Her gaze raked over him, and for a moment he thought she meant not to respond. "Mr. Laurens," she said after a moment and curtsied.

Ought he to correct her? At the very least, he might have introduced himself as "Major Laurens," as he'd not yet resigned his commission. "Lord Tristan" was entirely incorrect now, of course. Both Father and Percy were gone, had been gone for some time. Still, it felt strange to think of himself as a duke, stranger still to call himself "Raynham." Men of seven and twenty did not usually acquire new identities in quite so abrupt a fashion.

In the end, he let her assumption stand. After the weather cleared, they would go their separate ways, and his rank would be irrelevant.

Her fingertips danced over the book she was holding. "Miss Erica Burke."

"Erica?"

It was not a given name he had heard before, and her inclusion of it hinted at the existence of an elder sister who generally took precedence as "Miss Burke." Her Irish accent was distinct but not unpleasant. From Dublin, if he had to guess. And his guesses were usually correct.

"*Erica* is the Latin word denoting the genus to which several common species of flowering shrubs belong."

She must have given a variation of that explanation many times; it had the air of a rehearsed speech. So she knew at least a bit of Latin and a little botany: the marks of what passed for an educated gentlewoman. Then again, she might be a bluestocking.

Or something more unusual, and more interesting, than either.

His surprise at the explanation must have been evident on his face, for she continued, with a little grimace of resignation, "Heather. It means 'heather.' My father named his children using Linnaeus's *Species Plantarum* as his guide."

Though mildly curious about the names with which her siblings had been saddled, he focused his immediate concern on the fact that her family had let one of their number out of their sight. A young woman wandering about alone faced dangers far greater than a little rain, especially in a time of war, when so many were desperate.

Having learned his lesson about speaking sternly, however, he dipped his head in a nod of greeting. "It is a pleasure, Miss Burke, to meet someone else who has known the travails of having been named by an eccentric father. Mine was a student of the Arthurian legends."

That confession brought the twitch of a smile to her lips, quickly wiped away by a crack of thunder that shook the tiny cottage. "Oh, will this storm never end?" She began once more to move about the room, like a caged bird flitting from perch to perch.

"It will, of course." He tried to speak in a soothing tone, though it was not something he'd often had occasion to use in the army. "But I think we must resign ourselves to the fact that darkness may fall before it does."

"You mean, we must spend the night? Here?" A panicky sigh whooshed from her lungs as she sank onto a wooden chair. "Oh, when my sister discovers I'm missing, she'll be furious."

Furious? Not worried?

Seizing the opportunity, he righted her chair's partner—though they matched only in being equally rickety—and seated himself near her. "You are traveling with your sister? How did you come to be separated?"

"We—my sister, her husband, and I—are bound for Windermere. Their wedding trip. There are two coaches in our party, and I believe the occupants of each must have thought me safely aboard the other. But I had—" She leaped up again, fingering the leather-bound book.

Dutifully, he got to his feet, as good manners dictated. He had not been away from polite society long enough to forget everything he'd learned. "I'm sure she will be too relieved at discovering you are safe to upbraid you."

The candle's flickering light painted her face with shadow. Was she amused? Skeptical? "It's quite clear, sir, that you do not know my sister."

"No. I do not believe I have that pleasure."

She laughed, a rather wry sound, and sat down again. So did he. A moment later, she was up, trying to peer through the narrow crack around the shutters. "How long will it take for them to reach Windermere?"

"They were driving into the storm," he answered as he rose. "Several hours, perhaps, for although it's not a great distance, fifteen miles or so, the roads in that direction are prone to flooding." She turned from the window and a wrinkle of concern darted across her brow. "I expect they stopped somewhere along the way to wait out the rain," he added, trying to reassure her.

"Oh." Once more, she sank onto a chair. This time, he remained on his feet—wisely, it turned out, for she soon resumed her erratic wandering. "But then, mightn't they have returned to that village a few miles back, expecting to find me? I have to go."

"Absolutely not."

The commanding note brought her to an abrupt halt. Her mouth popped open, preparing to issue an argument.

"I will personally see you safely reunited with your sister as soon as possible, Miss Burke." Already he feared he would regret making such a promise. "In turn, you will not put yourself at unnecessary risk."

She pressed her parted lips into a thin line and sat, nearly toppling the chair with the force of her frustration.

This time, she stayed seated long enough that he began to think of returning to his own chair. Hardly had his knees bent, however, when she uncrossed her arms and laid one hand on the edge of her seat to rise. His awkward position—somewhere between sitting and standing—must have caught her attention, for she waved him down with her free hand, the one not clutching her book.

"I know it's the custom for a gentleman to stand when a lady does, but you'll do yourself an injury if you try to keep up with me." Three of her quick steps put the breadth of the deal table between them. The candle lit her face, revealing a scattering of freckles. "I've never been noted for my ladylike behavior, if you hadn't already guessed. So why should you worry about acting the gentleman? Not that I doubt you *are* a gentleman, Mr. Laurens," she added hastily, looking him up and down where he stood. Color infused her cheeks. "And I certainly hope you will not take my thoughtless remark as a license to—to—"

"Miss Burke." He stepped into the river of words, hoping to divert their course. "You may rest assured, I *am* a gentleman. You're far safer in here than you would be on the other side of that door."

Her nod of acknowledgment was quick, a trifle jerky, and he realized she was trembling. Now that the heat of the blush had left her face, he could see more clearly the bluish cast of her lips. "Come," he said, moving both chairs closer to the table, closer to the meager warmth offered by the candle. "Take off that soaked pelisse."

That order sent another flare of uncertainty through her eyes. But after a moment, she laid her book on the table and attempted to comply, though her fingers shook. The dress beneath was nearly as wet in patches and clung provocatively to her curves. He took the sodden pelisse from her hands and quickly turned away. On a rusty hook near the door hung his greatcoat. After making a simple exchange of wet garment for dry, he returned to her side.

Once enveloped by his greatcoat's length and breadth, she allowed herself to be guided to a chair. "I'm afraid I dare not build a fire," he explained as he took the place across from her. "The chimney looks on the verge of collapse." Indeed, some of its uppermost stones had tumbled down through the flue into the firebox. They lay glistening in the candlelight as rain trickled over them and damp air seeped into the room.

The candle gave at least the illusion of heat, though he knew, and she must too, that it would not last until dawn. It was only September. They were in no danger of freezing to death. But it promised to be a miserable night.

"You should try to get some rest," he urged.

For once, she did not argue. Laying one arm on the tabletop, she used it to pillow her head. With one finger of the other hand, she traced the tooled leather binding of her book. "Thank y-y-you," she stuttered through another shiver masked as a yawn. "It has been a tiring day."

"Yes," he agreed automatically.

Except he wasn't tired. He'd ridden a good distance since morning, it was true, but today's exertion was nothing to what he had known in recent years. If it wasn't fatigue that had prompted him to take shelter when the storm clouds rose, then what was it? Major Lord Tristan Laurens would have spurred his horse to a gallop, outrun those clouds, and made it home before nightfall, no matter how tired.

Raynham, on the other hand, was not so eager to reach Hawesdale Chase.

Crossing his legs at the ankle, he leaned back in his chair and prepared to pass an uncomfortable few hours. Rain continued to fall steadily, though the thunder now rolled farther off. Erica's restive hand at last fell still, but even in her sleep, she still guarded her book. It made him wonder what was inside. Already the candle's heat had begun to dry her hair, transforming its tangled waves from rusty brown to polished copper. He had no notion of what had become of her bonnet, or even if she had been wearing one at all. She had no gloves, either, and her nails were short and ragged. *I've never been noted for my ladylike behavior*, she had told him, with only the merest hint of chagrin. He did not envy the sister who had been charged with her keeping.

Yet he could not truthfully say he was sorry for an excuse to stay put a few hours more.

Chapter 2

Half awake, Erica bolted upright. Pain stabbed through her neck and down her back, driving away her drowsiness. Where—? Why—? Her eyes fell on the sleeping form of Mr. Laurens, slumped in his chair, chin resting against his chest.

Oh.

Sunlight poured in through the cracks around the shutter, illuminating the dingy room, with its cracked plaster walls and broken furnishings. It was a wonder the cottage hadn't collapsed around them while they slept. The light picked out the features of Mr. Laurens's face, too, considerably less timeworn than their surroundings. Why, he wasn't much older than she, certainly not thirty. His tawny hair caught the sun, while a day's growth of darker beard shadowed his square jaw. Not a bad-looking face, but she refused to think of him as handsome. No one who took such obvious delight in giving orders could ever be appealing to her.

Silently, she stretched her stiff muscles—another unladylike habit for which mother frequently chided her—and let his greatcoat slide off her shoulders as she picked up her journal and rose. If the storm was over and the sun was shining, then she must make her way, either back to the village or on toward Windermere, and hope her sister never asked where she had spent the night.

She managed to lift the door latch without rattling it. This was hardly the first morning she had arisen early and been eager to get out of doors. Leather hinges creaked and the bottom of the door dragged through the groove it had worn into the dirt floor. A quick glance over her shoulder confirmed that Mr. Laurens slept on, however. A little wider, and she could slip through. She'd just snatch her pelisse from the hook, and—

"Miss Burke?"

"*A Thiarna Dia!*"

Molly had taught her the oath. Not deliberately, of course. Erica had managed to pick it up after years of startling the family's housemaid in the kitchen. And on the stairs. And, on one particularly memorable occasion, at the back door, as Erica was sneaking in from an early morning stroll and Molly was stepping out to empty the slops.

"You cannot be thinking of leaving, Miss Burke?"

She could hear an edge of annoyance in his voice. The same voice that yesterday had snapped, "*What in God's name are you doing?*" Well, he might have made a plan for when and how she'd leave this cottage, but she had never agreed to wait around for his help or protection. She didn't need either one.

Determinedly, she turned back to tell him so. And discovered him standing just inches away now, one hand on the partially open door, blocking her way. Her pulse quickened. Did he mean to keep her prisoner? What would she do if he slammed the door shut and latched it?

Instead, he swung it wide, ducked under the lintel, and stood with his arms crossed behind his back, filling the opening. "Just as I feared."

Curiosity got the better of her, though she was forced to peer around his shoulder to satisfy it. The sight that greeted her eyes was breathtaking. In the way a swift blow to the stomach might take one's breath away.

The cottage had been built on a little rise. If it had not, they might have been standing ankle-deep in water. Ponds had formed in every hollow and dip. The roadway on which she had intended to walk to Windermere was now a river of mud. Wind had stripped the autumn leaves from the trees. They floated over the ground in spills of tarnished gold and blood red, leaving bare, wintry branches to scratch at the sky like ghostly hands. And though the sun shone down mercilessly on this scene of devastation, on the western horizon, dark clouds were gathering. More rain was on its way.

"Still determined to strike out on your own this fine morning?" He did not glance her way as he spoke.

"I—"

Oh, why hadn't she bothered to learn a few more Irish curses? She could've used them now, for this was a fine mess. For once, it seemed unlikely her sister would catch her in it, but she could not take consolation in the thought. What if Cami had discovered her missing, turned back to find her, and been trapped—or worse—by the storm and its aftermath?

"*A Thiarna Dia.*"

This time, the words took the form of a whispered prayer.

"Well," said Mr. Laurens, "I can see just one solution."

"And what would that be?" She could see only water.

He turned from the door. Reflexively, she stepped out of his way, though he did not seem to notice. He moved as though he was used to people clearing a path before him. She fought a childish impulse to stretch out one toe and trip him.

"I have a house not three miles east as the crow flies," he said. "We can reach it before that storm cloud does, if we make haste."

Her mind bounded like a hare, chased from one question to the next. How could they travel safely through all that water? But if they stayed put, with no food and no way to build a fire, how long could they survive?

And if his own home stood so near, what had possessed him to stop here? The last, of course, could not be asked. Even she understood that. They were, after all, almost perfect strangers. Still, curiosity itched at her, a rash she was desperate to scratch—worse, even, than the day she'd thrust an ungloved hand into a patch of leaves and found stinging nettles hiding beneath.

Fortunately, before the question could form on her lips, he strode across the room to collect his greatcoat. "My horse is stabled in the lean-to at the back of the cottage. You'll ride. I'll lead her, so as to guide her through the worst dangers. If we stick to the higher ridges, we should reach Hawesdale by midday."

Her fingers closed once more on her pelisse. "Hawesdale? Is that the name of the town from which you hail? Perhaps there's an inn there where I can wait for the weather to turn. I would not wish to—"

"Hawesdale is the name of the house. Hawesdale Chase." He shrugged into his greatcoat. "No inn, I'm afraid. Not even much of a village. You'll have to stay with me."

She tried to take some comfort in the fact that he sounded no more pleased by the prospect than she felt. "You are very generous, I'm sure. But I couldn't possibly." In twenty-three years, she had broken almost every rule of ladylike behavior her mother had laid down. Now, she'd spent the night with a gentleman, unchaperoned. Under duress, it was true. Perhaps that made it a forgivable offense. But she dared not continue in that error, just in case.

She'd never worried over her reputation, and she wasn't worried about it now. She only knew that crossing certain lines would ensure she was packed home to Dublin and never allowed to leave the house again. And no one had ever become a highly regarded botanist by sitting in a drawing room, drinking tea and embroidering cushions. For more reasons than one.

Then again… One glance took in the humble cottage and its furnishings. No, she didn't relish the possibility of staying here alone. "Unless, of course, you happen to have, ah, a sister at home?" The presence of another lady would lend sufficient respectability, surely. "Or…or a wife?"

Something about the question made his lips twitch, and she could not decide whether it was with humor. "I do have a sister at home, as it happens," he said as he gathered his horse's tack from the corner of the room and picked up a tall beaver hat she had not noticed before. He made no attempt to settle it on his head; its crown would have brushed plaster from the crumbling ceiling. "And a mother—my stepmother, to be precise. But no," he added as he ducked once more through the door. "I do not have a wife."

Her body greeted his words with an unexpected tingle of awareness that traveled down her spine and through her limbs, into the very center of her being. Why on earth should she care whether or not he was married? And yet, some parts of her seemed very interested in the information.

Or perhaps she'd taken a chill. The cottage *was* very damp. Unhealthy, even.

Tugging her wrinkled pelisse over her equally wrinkled dress and swiping a tangle of hair from her eyes, she followed him out the door.

* * * *

To Tristan's relief, the lean-to stable had weathered the storm. Lady Jane Grey, a steady dapple-gray mare he'd purchased for the journey, pricked her ears forward at the sound of their approach. Last night, he'd emptied the manger of musty straw and scattered it on the stable floor. As he led her out this morning, he could see the bedding was still dry. Lady Jane might well have passed a more comfortable night than he had.

"Do you ride, Miss Burke?" Even without turning, he knew she stood no more than a step away. He had been listening as she squelched through the mud behind him.

"Yes."

"Very good." A shudder passed along Lady Jane's withers as he laid the damp saddle cloth on her back. He ran a hand down her neck to steady her. "Though we haven't the proper tack for a lady, I'm afraid."

Miss Burke stepped forward to stroke the soft velvet of the horse's nose. "I'll manage if she can."

Would she sit astride? A certain sparkle in her honey brown eyes convinced him she was no stranger to it. He had a sudden vision of her with her skirts hiked to her knees, showing off well-turned calves to match the shapely figure he'd glimpsed beneath her rain-soaked dress last night.

When he could no longer pretend to busy himself with cinching the girth, he turned back to Erica and held out one hand. With obvious reluctance, she laid ice cold fingers across his palm. His first impulse was to cover them with his other hand, to chafe some warmth into them. Instead he shook his head. "Your book first, please. I'll stow it in the saddlebag. You'll want both hands free."

"Oh." She snatched her fingers back. "Of course."

After tucking her book safely among his things, he laced his fingers to form a step and hoisted her into the saddle. One hand gripped his shoulder and was quickly gone. To his relief—certainly not to his disappointment— she hooked her right knee around the pommel rather than throwing that leg over Lady Jane's back. He saw no more than one muddy ankle boot before her skirts swept into place and fully hid both legs from view once more.

She took up the reins just as he gripped them beneath Lady Jane's chin, at the base of the bridle. The horse tossed her head to express her displeasure at their tug-of-war.

"It seems she knows who's really in charge," Erica said.

Did her voice always carry that mischievous note? Tristan leveled a look over his shoulder, one that had quelled more than a few impudent junior officers.

It had no visible effect on her, however.

"*I* am in charge, Miss Burke," he said then. "Make no mistake about that." After nearly ten years as an officer, command came naturally to him. "Now, the reins, if you please—or frankly, even if you don't please. Because I don't fancy waiting about for those clouds." He jerked his chin in the direction of the steadily darkening western sky.

Whether it was his words or the weather that persuaded her, he could not be certain. But with a toss of her own head, she surrendered the reins and contented herself with two fistfuls of Lady Jane's mane.

Well, she didn't lack spirit, he'd give her that. He had always valued spirit and enthusiasm in the men he had commanded. Perhaps Miss Burke's unconventional streak would prove to be an asset.

One must always have hope.

The ground was slick, spongy in some places and rocky in others. The ridge of higher ground that ran between the cottage and Hawesdale Chase appeared unbroken from a distance. In reality, however, it was made up of many small hillocks and an equal number of little valleys. Both his boots and Lady Jane's hooves fought for purchase. Every step was a gamble.

On one particularly sharp descent, the horse locked her forelegs and refused to take another step. With a firm grip on the reins, he stepped ahead to show her it was safe. "Forward, Lady Jane." The mare gave no sign of having heard.

Erica shifted slightly in the saddle, leaned over Lady Jane's neck, and whispered in her ears, which twitched forward and back as she took in the words. Then, to Tristan's amazement, the horse took three wary steps down the embankment and followed him through a newly formed stream and up the next hill.

"What did you say to her?" he asked when they were safely on higher ground.

"A lady never tells, Mr. Laurens."

"I thought you weren't a lady, Miss Burke," he teased.

Her spine stiffened. "I was referring to the horse."

Forcing a laugh, he took one stride forward. Somehow, however, his boot never met the ground. Instead, his other leg slid from beneath him and he found himself on his arse in the mud, skidding down the slope. Miss Burke, damn her, had the foresight to twitch the reins from his grasp so that Lady Jane did not come tumbling down after like some awful parody of a child's nursery rhyme. And to add insult to injury—for the slope was dotted with sharp rocks—when he splashed to a halt in the ditch at the bottom, his hat fell off and was swept away on the water.

"Mr. Laurens!" There was laughter in her voice, he felt sure of it. "Are you harmed?"

"Don't—"

—*dismount.*

But the order had not left his lips in time. She was already on the ground. Her boots soon found the same slick spot, and faster than he could shout or she could scream, she had slid and tumbled her way down and nearly landed in his lap.

Alas, some part of him whispered devilishly, *not nearly enough.*

Such wayward thoughts ought to have scattered when she began to laugh. That outlandish sound ought not to have made her more attractive yet. A proper lady, at least those among his acquaintance, would have been either frightened or mortified by their predicament.

For her part, Lady Jane gave a snort and began to amble away. He watched the horse go. "What's that phrase of yours, Miss Burke?"

A frown of incomprehension notched her brow. "Do you mean *A Thiarna Dia?*" Her freckles stood out dark against the sudden rush of pink that streaked across her cheeks. "But it's…well, it's blasphemous, you know."

As he hoisted himself to his feet, he felt cold mud slither beneath his clothes and settle into every crack and crevice. "Not blasphemous enough."

Though he held out a hand to help her rise, she sprang up unaided, unfazed by the fall. With a flick of one wrist, she shook out her skirts, spattering his ruined boots with more mud. "Oh, I'm sorry. I didn't think before I—" Her expression turned rueful. "My sister would say I never do."

For a moment, the smile slipped from her face and she stared past his shoulder. Not with longing, as one does when imagining a place of respite at the end of a journey. But steeling herself against reproach, as if she had been chastised often and expected to be again.

He was a soldier. He'd had intimate acquaintance with dirt. And cold. And aches in places well-bred people did not mention. "What possible difference could a little more mud make, Miss Burke?" he said, trying to reassure her. Never mind that this was not the appearance he had planned to make at his homecoming.

"Well, the rain will likely wash some of it off," she said, dispelling her momentary despair with a shrug, tipping her face toward the sky. The morning sun had given way to first to clouds, then to heavy mist, which had shifted over the last quarter hour to a steady drizzle. When she met his gaze once more, she had tacked her usual stubborn expression back in place.

Now, however, he could guess that something else hid just beneath the surface. Something softer and less sure. Experimentally, he held out an arm, expecting her once more to refuse his help. But after a moment's hesitation, she threaded her hand lightly around his elbow.

When they reached Lady Jane, she caught the reins in her other hand and kept walking. Before he could offer to help her back into the saddle, she said, "It's better this way, don't you think?"

"Safer, yes." No sense in risking another fall, for either horse or rider.

Walking arm in arm was not without risk, however. Though the pressure of her hand was slight, he could feel himself being drawn ever so slightly off his usual course nevertheless. He had always been the straight arrow, the plumb line. But from the moment this woman had been blown into his life, she'd been tugging him off-balance.

Determined to regain his center, he squared his shoulders and lengthened his stride. He was an army officer. For God's sake, he was a *duke!* Neither wind, nor rain, nor a copper-haired sprite would stay him from his duty.

"Miss Burke, I think it's time I explained—"

"Please tell me that's Hawesdale Chase." Though they spoke at the same time, he heard the weariness in her voice.

Below them, nestled in a grove of poplars, stood a red brick house with tall, narrow windows and a chimney at either end, from which ribbons of smoke unfurled like the faintest traces of pencil sketched against a slate sky. A respectable manor by almost any standard, and compared to the cottage in which they had sheltered, a mansion.

He drew a deep breath. It was not that he hesitated to speak the truth, but rather that the truth was complicated. "In the time of the Tudor kings, that was Hawesdale Chase, yes. Intended as an autumnal retreat. A hunting lodge, as the name implies. But when the estate passed from that family, another house was built and claimed the name."

"Your house. Is it near?"

"Not quite half a mile away. This one now serves as its gatehouse."

"Gatehouse?" She tipped her gaze upward but did not meet his eyes. "Then Hawesdale Chase must be quite large..."

"See for yourself."

He directed her attention past the gatehouse to the denser woodland behind it, divided from them by what was, on any ordinary day, a picturesque winding stream. The ground was thick with freshly fallen foliage. Only a few leaves now remained to filter the view. Above the bare branches, the rolling landscape rose to grander heights, not quite mountains. Nestled at the foot of those rugged hills stood a sprawling mansion, the fever dream of some Jacobean architect whose love of pierced work, scrolls, and other ornamentation had known no bounds. The most charitable compliment Tristan had ever been able to pay the house was that it was almost symmetrical.

Still, wreathed in mist and shadow, it was a striking sight, and Miss Burke seemed to be forcibly struck by it.

"I—I don't... Are you—?" She looked from Hawesdale to him and back again, nostrils flaring. "Are you the...the steward or...or the housekeeper's son, or—?"

"I'm afraid not, Miss Burke." The wry smile that curved his lips was only partly in response to her reaction.

Mostly, he was remembering the day he had overheard Cook telling one of the new kitchen maids what seemed to be common knowledge among the staff: *"Her Grace, God rest 'er, were that desperate to give His Grace another son. A spare, so to speak. When the years rolled by with no babe in sight, folks did say she took comfort in the arms of another man..."* At those words Cook's smoke-roughened voice had dropped to a whisper, and Tristan had had to hold his breath to hear the rest. *"'Tis not for me to*

*say, o' course. But there's little enough of the old duke in Lord Tris, to be
sure. An' the head gardener did leave his post thereafter...*"

Whether the rumor that the late duchess had consorted with the gardener
was true, and whether the second son of the Duke of Raynham in fact
belonged to another man, only his mother could have told him for certain,
and she had died too soon after his birth to tell him anything. His brother
Percy, eleven years his senior, had been unapproachable on matters of far
less import; Tristan could never bring to himself to ask about sordid gossip.

After that day, he had taken the only prudent course. He had walled up
every weakness he imagined inimical to the son of a duke. He had refused
to indulge in behaviors that might invite speculation. And he had followed
rules, rather than breaking them, as boys—and men, and even, it seemed,
some women—were wont to do.

Ultimately, he had consoled himself with the knowledge that, if the
story *had* been true, the man who called himself his father surely would
have disowned him, or at least betrayed his disdain in some word or
deed. Instead, he'd willingly granted Tristan's request to purchase him
an officer's commission. He and Tristan were alike in neither appearance
nor temperament, it was true. But really, what did it matter? Tristan was
not next in line for the dukedom.

Until he was.

"*That* is your house?" Erica demanded, bringing him back to the present
moment. "And I suppose all this"—she gestured feebly with her free hand
toward the woods and the hills—"is also...yours?"

"Yes. Every step we've taken today has been on my land."

Her hand slid from his sleeve. "You mean...the cottage—?"

"Once housed the estate's head gardener."

"Then you are—you're a—"

"A duke." He felt strangely as if he ought to bow when he said it, as one
did when making a proper introduction. And he might have, if not for the
mud and the rain and the fact that they had already spent a night in one
another's company. "Raynham, for my sins."

If her hands had not already been white with cold, her fierce grip on
Lady Jane's reins would have stripped the color from her knuckles. "You
misunderstand me, Your Grace." Her amber eyes swept boldly over him.
"I was going to say, you are a coward."

Chapter 3

And a liar, Erica wanted to add, but a rare flash of self-preservation kept her tongue in her mouth. *Tristan Laurens*, indeed! Although…

At the wedding ceremony joining her sister to the Marquess of Ashborough, she'd learned one thing. Noblemen were saddled with a long string of names that were almost never used, not even in the family. Vaguely, she'd wondered whether such a man might even forget a few of them. Perhaps the Duke of—what was it he'd said? Ah, yes. *Raynham*—had a similar litany that included the name *Tristan*. Tristan, whose father had been fond of the stories of King Arthur and his knights…

What rubbish!

Over the plodding steps of the mare, who followed her dutifully though the reins had fallen slack in Erica's hand, she heard the splash-stomp of a man's booted tread. "A *coward*, did you say? Explain yourself, Miss Burke."

Did he ever *ask*? Plead, cajole, beg? She would hear him barking out orders in her sleep tonight.

"And if I won't, Your Grace? Ah, but I forgot. Your sort considers it a matter of pride to answer an insult. Or is it a matter of *honor?* Oh, dear. Will you challenge me to a duel, then?" She whirled on him so fast she nearly lost her footing in the mud. "Before you speak, you ought to know my younger brother taught me to shoot, and I almost never miss."

She tried to convince herself he didn't look like a duke, standing there covered head to toe in mud, overlong hair plastered to his brow and neck, rain tracing glittering tracks through the scruff of his beard. Yet even through the dirt, his bearing radiated power, authority, control. As did his eyes, which at this distance were black and hard as mica chips. "*You almost never…*" he repeated, incredulous. "Stop spouting nonsense, Miss Burke. If you can."

As he spoke he continued to stride toward her, and on the last three words he stopped just inches away. Perhaps his eyes really were black. At the moment, not even a sliver of color rimmed his flared pupils. His breath formed little puffs of steam in the chilled air, putting her strongly in mind of a cartoon sketch of a raging bull.

The fingertips of her free hand drove into his breastbone. "Only a coward would have kept his true identity a secret. Did you imagine if I had known who you were, I would have used last night's unfortunate circumstance to my benefit? Let's see…a young woman, stranded overnight with an eligible gentleman…ought I to expect an offer of marriage?" At that, his jaw actually fell open. "Silly me, I thought only to shelter from the storm. And for that matter," she went on, lifting her fingers for the satisfaction of thrusting them forward again with the next point, "why on earth were you there to begin with? You might have reached your home easily before the heaviest rain began to fall. Only a coward would have chosen that tumble-down shack over the risk of getting wet."

"Have a care, Miss Burke." In a flash, his hand came up and pinned hers flat to his chest. A wall of muscle and bone leaped to life under her touch. Were pampered, privileged noblemen usually so wonderfully… hard? "I am—"

But whatever he was remained unspoken. Lady Jane stamped and snorted, heralding the arrival of another set of footsteps.

"Raynham? Is that you?" The man spoke with a strong Scottish accent that carried through the rain as he trudged up the hill from the direction of the gatehouse. He was neatly dressed, bespectacled, and carrying an umbrella.

"Mr. Davies." The duke dropped his hold on her hand and leaned forward to extend his in greeting. "What brings you out in this weather?"

The man stopped a few feet from them and bowed his head crisply; he made no attempt to shake hands. After holding his own position a moment too long, the duke jerked himself upright, as if a fishhook had caught him in the spine. "Her Grace asked me to keep a lookout," Mr. Davies said. He looked to be her father's age, or thereabouts. His clothes, his complexion, everything about him bespoke the sort of person who performed his most important work behind a desk. And everything about his current demeanor suggested he toiled behind that desk at the behest of the man standing before him. Even the rain seemed to make him nervous. He fumbled with his umbrella as if weighing whether or not he should surrender it to the duke.

For a moment, silence fell among them. Mr. Davies glanced at her once out of the corner of his eye but gave no other indication of noting her presence. He seemed to be waiting for the duke to decide whether she merited an introduction.

She dipped into a curtsy, a shallow one. Anything deeper might send her toppling once more into the mud. "I'm Miss Burke," she said, mustering all the dignity she could.

"Oh, er, pleased to make your acquaintance, Miss Burke," the gentleman stammered and bowed again. "Walter Davies. Raynham's man of business." His gaze flicked over her once before lighting somewhere in the vicinity of the duke's chin.

"I found Miss Burke sheltering in the gardener's cottage. An unhappy accident separated her from her family, with whom she was traveling to Windermere."

"'Tis fortunate you rescued her, sir."

Tristan—she would *not* go on thinking of him as "the duke"—accepted Mr. Davies's praise with a stiff nod.

As neither of them showed any sign of consulting her opinion on the matter of the supposed "rescue," she cleared her throat, drawing both sets of eyes her way. "I wish to be reunited with my sister," she said. "At the very least, I must get word to her, to let her know where I am."

"But the rain and the flooding have likely made that impossible," Tristan interjected smoothly. "I fear the best we can do at the moment is to send a messenger to Endmoor to leave word for her family when they are able to return there."

Mr. Davies nodded his agreement. "Of course, Your Grace. I'll see to it that a lookout is kept in the village for...for the Burke family, is it?"

Tristan looked at her expectantly.

"Yes—er, no." For a moment, she had forgotten her sister's newly acquired title. "My sister is Lady Ashborough."

"Lady Ashborough?" Mr. Davies exclaimed. "The authoress?"

Erica nodded. "The same, sir."

Tristan looked from one to the other in open incredulity, but Mr. Davies did not seem to notice. "Oh, *The Wild Irish Rose* is delightful. I'm no' sure I can bear it until the next installment is released." In his excitement, t's began to drop from his otherwise proper speech. "I dinna suppose you know...?"

"Whether Lord Granville is the villain he seems? Even if I were so fortunate as to know the story's outcome, I would not dare reveal it, sir. My sister would—" She hesitated. Cami was going to have her head, either way.

"Of course, of course." Mr. Davies nodded, disappointed but resigned. "You may rest assured, Miss Burke," he said, "that my son will do all in his power to find her and to set her mind at ease."

"I would advise him to go on foot rather than risk a horse." Tristan quickly reclaimed control over the conversation with that commanding tone of his. She doubted he ever offered mere advice. "And tell him to take the eastern path, through the wood. The main road appeared to be under water."

"I'm not surprised to hear it, Your Grace. Some of Her Grace's guests told quite a harrowing tale about the state of the roads. And that was well before last night's rain."

"Guests?" The echo of that single word hung on the air long after the steam of his breath dissipated.

"Aye," said Mr. Davies, though the affirmation rose like a question, and his lips gave a nervous twitch. "She planned a grand welcome for you—and here I've gone and spoiled the surprise."

"For which I can only be grateful, Mr. Davies. The surprise would be all hers, and not a pleasant one, were I to step into the drawing room looking like this."

Mr. Davies dared to give a rusty laugh. "Aye, Your Grace. That it would."

Despite his claim of gratitude, however, Tristan still looked vaguely unsettled by the other man's revelation. He dipped his head once more, a sign Mr. Davies evidently read as dismissal, for that gentleman at last jumped into action.

"Very good." He bowed sharply, nearly poking them both with the spines of his umbrella. "I'll send Kevin out straightaway. Miss Burke is welcome to wait here for any news." The enthusiastic glimmer in his eye foretold a few more questions about the plot of her sister's novel if she accepted his invitation.

Without looking at her, Tristan offered Erica his arm. "I will not impose upon you, Mr. Davies. I made a promise to Miss Burke. She is my...responsibility."

That hesitation. She felt certain he'd been about to say "my *problem*."

Except she was neither his responsibility nor his problem. Not *his* in any sense.

She glanced toward Mr. Davies, but even if he wished to, he obviously believed he dared not contradict his employer. Why was Tristan so determined to take her to Hawesdale Chase? His behavior smacked of something more than simple hospitality.

Then an earlier question jostled its way to the forefront of her mind: Why had he stopped at the cottage to begin with? It was as if he didn't want to go home alone. Or perhaps he didn't want to go at all. What awaited him in that enormous, ornate mansion? A sister, he'd said. And a stepmother. Was that all? With five siblings, Erica hardly knew what solitude was. Loneliness, however, was another matter entirely.

An unexpected—and no doubt unwarranted—ache of sympathy coiled within her, and she knew it would find its release in ill-advised words if she did not give it some other outlet. She had to move.

Pinned between Tristan's outstretched arm and his horse, however, she had few alternatives. Suppressing a tremor that had nothing whatsoever to do with the icy rain, she lifted her hand and settled it on the sleeve of his greatcoat.

* * * *

When they arrived at the stable block, Tristan found it full of horses and the mud-spattered carriages belonging to his stepmother's guests. Grooms stood in a knot near the back, and for a moment, no one broke away to take his horse. At last the huge hand of James, the head groom, caught a passing boy on the shoulder, nearly bringing him to his knees. "G'on wit' ye, Dick." The boy righted himself, tugged at his forelock, and scampered forward to take Lady Jane Grey's reins.

A cold reception, no question, and though different from Mr. Davies's strange obsequiousness—as a child, Tristan had played with the man's son, for God's sake—he could not help but wonder whether the behavior stemmed from the same source. Distrust. For a duke who ought never to have become one.

Fortunately, Major Laurens could fall back on the rank he had earned. He had years of experience in establishing his authority and maintaining proper order.

"James," he barked to the head groom. "You'll look after my horse." Not waiting for an answer, he turned to Miss Burke, who stood beside him in the pungent warmth of the stable, breathing quickly. Her rapid stride for the last half-mile had given Tristan no excuse to check his own. "Come. We'll go to the house," he said, though he did not relish facing anyone in his present condition.

Her bare hand lay pale against the darker sleeve of his muddy greatcoat, highlighting the dirt under her nails. What a pair they made. What would his guests make of such a display?

"Are you displeased with your stepmother?" she asked, catching unexpectedly at the thread of his thoughts and withdrawing her hand from his arm.

"I am..." He reached for Davies's word. "Surprised."

Oh, how he despised surprises. And he was about to escort the living embodiment of one into his home.

If only he had not given in to the impulse—not sentiment, surely—to stop at the abandoned gardener's cottage. But he had, and so had she, and he could not, in good conscience, have abandoned her there. Still, he might easily have avoided bringing her here. A man of sense would have accepted Davies's offer to keep her. And he was nothing if not a man of sense.

But this morning, he had not acted like one. Perhaps a part of him had hoped, in a most ungentlemanly fashion, that her appearance would distract attention from his own. The better part of him, however, had begun to suspect that something interesting lay beneath Miss Burke's rough exterior, like an unpolished gem...

His mind tossed aside the cliché. She had more in common with a challenging bit of code. The cultured voice, the educated mind, a well-made dress—if one overlooked the filth. Almost certainly a young lady of good breeding, despite her protests. So why did she resist the label so strenuously? And if he succeeded in cracking the code, would he uncover something dangerous after all?

Almost instinctively, he ushered her toward the servants' entrance near the kitchen garden. As a boy he'd made frequent use of it on escapades not unlike this one.

Until sneaking past the kitchen had lost its appeal.

"Now," he said as they moved quietly along the empty corridor, "we shall enlist the help of Mrs. Dean."

The housekeeper was not, however, the first to greet them in the servants' hall. A dark-haired girl, the very image of her father, peeked from a doorway, squealed "Tris!" and barreled toward them, throwing her arms around his waist, heedless of dirt or damp. "Is it really you?" Her voice was muffled against his coats. "It's been weeks since your things arrived. I was afraid I'd—" She hiccupped around a sob. "I was afraid you'd never come."

"Vivi." He laid one hand on the back of her head and wrapped the other around her body, her shoulder blades sharp against his palm. Her slight figure shook and trembled against him.

His sister had entered the world when he'd been almost fifteen. The bond that had sprung up between them had surprised everyone. Most of all himself. On school holidays, he'd spent hours in the nursery simply watching her. When she'd grown old enough to toddle, she had gamely followed him everywhere, and he had never complained. The morning he had descended the stairs wearing his first scarlet uniform, she had beamed up at him through tears streaking down her cheeks. During the years far from home, her ill-spelled, rambling letters had given him hope.

"Don't cry," he murmured, stroking her hair. Months had passed since the accident that had claimed Father and Percy, months in which the news had traveled over land and sea to reach him. He was surprised to find her grief so raw. Twenty-five years her senior, Percy had been all but a stranger to her. And if Father had sometimes been distant to Tristan, he had been largely indifferent to his only daughter.

Still, Vivi was young and had always been sensitive. He held her until she pushed away and looked up at him. A welter of emotions crossed her pinched, tearstained face. Grief. Guilt—over the secret of this ridiculous party, perhaps. But he was relieved to see she had not lost all her good humor, either. "Phew," she said, wrinkling her nose. "You smell like a wet sheep, Tris."

"A wet sheep, eh?" He swept her up into his arms and spun her around before returning her to her feet. "And just how would you know? Have you been going about in the rain sniffing sheep?" She dissolved in a fit of giggles.

The severely clad figure of Mrs. Dean came sweeping down the corridor at the sound. "Hush, Lady Viviane. You'll have only yourself to blame if Miss Chatham hears that screeching and finds you here." The sight of him sent her rocking back on her heels. "Why, if it's not Lord Tris—" He caught the flicker of a twinkle in her eyes. But before he could speak, she shuttered her expression and curtsied deeply. "I beg your pardon, Your Grace."

His arms ached to sweep the housekeeper into a boisterous hug too. Propriety held him back. He thought of his cool reception from Davies and in the stable. Now, more than ever, it was time to behave like the son of a duke.

Correction: like the duke himself.

He stiffened and held his sister at arms' length. "Lady Viviane, may I present Miss Burke, who was stranded in the storm."

Erica dipped into a curtsy made ungainly by the weight of her sodden skirts. "I don't know if I smell like a wet sheep, but I certainly feel like a drowned rat."

Vivi's uncertain stare shifted into a smile; inwardly, he winced. It was one thing for a girl of twelve to say such outrageous things...

"What's this about hiding from your governess, Viv?" he demanded sternly. He was responsible now for his sister's upbringing. He was her guardian. It was his job to prevent her from turning into a hoyden, and Miss Burke was hardly a suitable role model.

Vivi turned saucy, dark eyes on him. "I can't help it if she's—"

"Will I take Miss Burke to the south wing with the other guests, Your Grace?" The Mrs. Dean of old would never have interrupted her master. But he had the distinct impression she was doing it for Vivi, trying to turn the conversation away from his sister's misbehavior.

And it worked, though not quite in the way she had intended.

"Oh, Mrs. Dean," Vivi cried out, "now you've ruined the surprise."

"Mr. Davies told me already, and even if he hadn't, I'd have known something was afoot. The stable is full of strange horses," he pointed out. "May I ask how I came to be hosting a house party?"

"It's not a house party," she insisted. "It was meant to be only dinner. We expected you sooner. But the storm came instead. Now the vicar and his wife are stuck here. Along with Sir Thomas and Lady Lydgate. And Captain Whitby too, though he wasn't exactly invited." Vivi's voice dropped slightly from its usual exuberant pitch, as if sharing a secret. "I think he was simply passing through and wanted to get out of the rain."

"David Whitby is my oldest friend. He doesn't need an invitation."

"Oh, and Miss Pilkington, of course," Vivi added. "With her parents."

"Miss Pilkington?" he repeated absently. His stepmother had no doubt felt obliged to include the clergyman and his wife. The Lydgates were near neighbors, old friends. But why on earth had the Pilkingtons been invited to celebrate his homecoming?

Percy had had an understanding with Caroline Pilkington, though no formal announcement of their betrothal had ever been made. Years had passed under the quiet assumption that his brother would eventually do the necessary. After all that time, Miss Pilkington must be teetering dangerously near the edge of the shelf. A pity she had been kept waiting so long with nothing to show for it.

"I expect you'll want to get cleaned up before she sees you," Vivi added, wrinkling her nose once more. "Or smells you."

"Oh?" He was only half listening. Without waiting for further orders, Mrs. Dean had motioned to Miss Burke to follow her down the corridor. Good God, but he hoped the housekeeper would at least find her another dress to wear, and soon. Something clean. Something suitable.

Something that didn't cling quite so distractingly to her limbs with every step she took.

He forced himself to focus his gaze on his sister. "And why is that?"

"Because I overheard Lord Easton Pilkington tell Mama he expects you to keep Percy's promise to their daughter."

Chapter 4

Mrs. Dean led Erica briskly down corridors and up staircases. The first impression of Hawesdale Chase was not an illusion. The place was vast. The housekeeper was saying something about the west wing, the dining room, a ballroom, but Erica hardly heard her. Her mind was still back in the servants' hall.

Erica had two brothers and she loved them both. But she had never looked at either of them with the naked devotion she had seen in Lady Viviane's eyes. Nor, in her estimation, was it wise to do so. Brothers were, when all else was stripped away, only men. And adoration gave men a dangerous degree of power.

"The family apartments are in the east wing," Mrs. Dean was explaining when she dragged her attention back to the present. "You'll be here in the south…with the other guests." She paused and turned toward Erica. "You'll be thinking the family doesn't know what's seemly in a time of mourning. It's just—oh, dear."

Mourning? Guilt needled Erica like a thorn. *Of course.* She should have realized. That explained Lady Viviane's tears and black dress.

"It's just the rain," Erica supplied as her mind frantically tried to piece together the bits of conversation that had flown among Tristan, his sister, and the housekeeper. She had not considered that his father might have died quite recently.

"Aye, miss." Mrs. Dean resumed walking, though her pace had slowed. "'Twas clarty then too." *Clarty?* Erica's expression must have betrayed her ignorance, for Mrs. Dean was quick to explain. "Muddy, messy. Rained like anything the day of the accident."

"The...accident?" Erica struggled to make sense of it all, though she knew her tangled brain would never keep everything straight. Mourning etiquette. The floor plan of a ducal manor. Already details were skittering away. Who was Percy, who'd made some promise Tristan was expected to keep?

"The Duke of Raynham was killed in a carriage accident with his elder son, Lord Hawes. Oh, a terrible thing it was." Mrs. Dean shook her head. "'Course, one must expect rain in the spring of the year."

Erica's thoughts sprang up like weeds in an unkempt garden, impossible to contain once they'd gone to seed... Seed. Springtime was the season for planting. But it was autumn now. The leaves were falling from the trees. Trees. Family trees.

Inwardly, she shook herself, trying to regain focus. An accident had claimed Tristan's father and brother no more than a few months ago. He'd come into his title unexpectedly—and reluctantly, if the inheritance had come at the price of losing his father and brother.

"No wonder he was hesitant about returning home," she murmured to herself.

But Mrs. Dean had heard. "He would have been here sooner, but he was abroad when the accident happened, miss," the housekeeper said, her round notes of her broad northern accent suddenly clipped.

Erica's thoughtless remark had snuffed Mrs. Dean's loquaciousness as completely as a gust of damp wind put out a candle. They passed along the corridor in silence until the housekeeper paused to open a door. "Here we be, miss," she said.

Others might have noted the plush carpet, the velvet bed hangings, or the elegant furnishings. Erica's eyes went first to the tall, pieced windows framing rugged hills, closer and more imposing than she had imagined. To the left and right, she could just see the two wings of the house as Mrs. Dean had described, east and west. Or was it west and east?

"The rooms overlooking the park are prettier, to my mind," Mrs. Dean said, sounding apologetic, "but there isn't one to be had, I'm afraid. The Pilkingtons took the last."

"It's—" *Magnificent*, she had been about to say.

But she bit off the word just in time. She was the daughter of a Dublin solicitor, a well-respected gentleman in that town. Her mother was the daughter of an earl—albeit disowned by him for the unforgiveable sin of falling in love with an Irishman. Erica had grown up in a prosperous and genteel household. If she was rarely mistaken for an elegant lady, neither was she a bumpkin.

She refused to be awestruck by a mere room.

"It will do very nicely," she said to Mrs. Dean, who curtsied in acknowledgment. "Thank you."

Left alone, Erica set out to examine her surroundings more thoroughly. She would not be overwhelmed by a bedchamber twice the size of her family's drawing room.

Nor would she be impressed by the way things appeared in that chamber as if summoned by magic, conveyed by a bevy of servants before she could even think to ask for them: hot bathwater, hotter tea, even a pair of slippers that fitted her tolerably well.

Once bathed and dressed in a clean shift and clean stockings, she thrust her arms into the sleeves of an overlarge silk dressing gown and sat down before a mirror in an ornate frame. Her fingers traced the handle of a silver-backed brush.

No, she would not allow her opinion of the Duke of Raynham to be influenced in any way by these signs of his extraordinary wealth, for which she did not give a fig. Nor by the evidence of the authority he must wield, the very thought of which aroused her instinctual defiance. Since the moment they met, he'd been taking charge, giving orders, demanding deference.

Until a girl of perhaps twelve had dared to tease him, whereupon he had...smiled?

Prior to that moment, Erica had seen little sign that Tristan was ever anything other than a stick in the mud...with or without the mud. Lady Viviane, however, seemed to know another man entirely.

Had grief transformed him from whatever he had once been? She had watched it turn young people into old, stripping them of their vitality, just as a hard freeze sapped the life force from plants that had been green and blooming the day before. What had once been bright and full of promise became cold and brittle and black.

In the spring of the year, one made plans for the future. One did not think of death. This past spring, for instance, she had been planning her wedding to Henry Edgeworth. Then the frost had come, late and all the more cruel for being unexpected. Mostly to please her brother, Henry had joined the United Irishmen. Then he had been killed at the start of the rebellion, and she had grieved, both for his loss, and for her own.

Everything she had dared to imagine about her future had died with him. She was once more wholly dependent, trapped within the narrow cage society had constructed for unmarried young ladies.

Absently, her fingers tightened around the brush. Did she really imagine Tristan's situation bore any resemblance to her own?

He had known loss, yes, and she did not doubt it pained him greatly. But that loss had also brought him unimaginable gain. Death had made him a duke. A title, an estate, power...and with them, freedom. Even grief stricken, who would turn down such a bequest?

She, meanwhile, was stuck. Stuck at Hawesdale Chase until the rain stopped. And after that... Stuck at home, most likely. Unless she accepted her sister's offer to live with her and...do what? Become a maiden aunt to a passel of unruly lordlings?

The very thought sent the hairbrush skittering from her fingertips, across the marble top of the dressing table.

Henry had never minded her freckles. He had been willing to pluck and pot and press her botanical specimens. And once they were married, he had promised her, she'd have all the time in the world to fill the pages of her journal with notes and sketches and—

Her journal.

No. Not twice in two days.

Even she could not be that careless.

Well, yes...apparently she could.

She pushed to her feet, though she could not decide where to go. Tristan had put her journal in the saddlebag, probably with his own important papers. To the stable, then. Unless he'd brought it inside when they'd arrived? She squeezed her eyes shut and tried to remember the last she'd seen of the dark leather satchel. Had he been carrying it in his hand? Had he slung it easily over one broad shoulder?

Her mind's eye grazed over the memory of his form, lingering here and there for a moment longer than was strictly necessary.

When she opened her eyes, the mental image popped like a soap bubble. He was a duke. How ridiculous to imagine he did his own fetching and carrying. Likely, a servant had taken his bag to his chambers in the—

Finding herself on the threshold of her room, she paused. Mrs. Dean had said the family apartments were in the east wing, had she not? Was that to the right or to the left? Outdoors, growth patterns of plants or the position of the sun might have helped to guide her. In the windowless, candlelit corridor, she was all but lost.

Lifting her chin, Erica looked both directions, chose one, and set off in search of her journal.

While walking with Mrs. Dean, she had not noticed the inordinate number of doors leading off the corridor. Provided she found the east wing, how would she determine which was the correct door? Would the door to the duke's suite look particularly...ducal?

At the end of the corridor, past yet more stairs, stood a set of tall double doors, of the sort that a pair of liveried footman might have been expected to guard. But no one was guarding them, and so it did not immediately occur to her that if she opened them and went through, she would find herself anywhere other than in another corridor.

The room she entered was so large and stately she assumed she must have made a wrong turn and found herself in the state rooms of the west wing. The walls were covered in ivory silk with gold damask, the windows framed by crimson velvet drapery held back by thick, tasseled ropes of gold silk. On two sides, the room overlooked the slopes and hollows of the wooded valley. She understood why Mrs. Dean considered it the finer view, though for herself, she preferred the dramatic ruggedness of the hillside.

Though the day was damp and cool, no fire had been lit in the marble fireplace. It might have been insufficient to heat the room in any case, though the firebox was so large she could have stepped into it without ducking her head. On either side of the fireplace stood a suit of armor, and on the wall above hung a tapestry depicting the Knights of the Round Table. Below it, nearer the mantel, had been mounted an ancient-looking sword, meant to suggest Excalibur, she supposed. It could not have been the real one, could it?

Warily, she took two steps closer. Thick Turkish carpets muffled the sound. Around the room stood groupings of furniture: plushly upholstered chairs on spindly legs, sofas with curved backs, tables of gilt and mirrored glass. A drawing room? A...a sitting room? She hadn't the vocabulary for this sort of architecture. But who would sit here?

A duke, you dolt.

Erica flinched, though the voice spoke only inside her head.

All right, then. She was in the right place. But her journal could be... anywhere.

She forced herself to take a deep breath, hold it for a moment, and exhale slowly. Once, twice, thrice. Within four walls, she often felt panicky. Restless in small spaces. Overwhelmed in large ones. She tried to focus on the open sky beyond the windows, but dark clouds and lashing rain only increased her anxiety. Somewhere, her sister must be watching that same foreboding sky and fretting over what had become of her.

Forcing her gaze away from the storm, she swept her eyes once more over the rest of the room. Impossible to imagine her battered leather journal being allowed to mar any one of its gleaming surfaces. Ah, but behind her stood an antique secretary desk, placed near the door so a visitor would have to take no more than a few steps into the room to state their business to the one seated at it. She ran one hand over its polished edges. Just the sort of place a duke might keep his important papers...

"At the risk of repeating myself, Miss Burke, what in God's name are you doing?"

She gripped a little piece of scrollwork so hard she feared it would snap off in her fingers. "Your Grace." She closed her eyes, muttered a fierce, swift prayer, then jerked her chin a notch higher than its proper place to meet his gaze.

And promptly wished she hadn't.

Even before the rebellion, she had not been the sort of woman to be taken in by a man in a red coat. A military uniform was all trickery, the sartorial equivalent of smoke and mirrors. The gold epaulets were designed to make his shoulders appear broader. The cutaway of the coat, to make his legs look longer.

Yet she had the distinct impression that his tailor had found no need to embellish on what nature had given Tristan Laurens.

Worst of all were those tight white knee breeches, which drew the eye to places a proper lady's eye ought not to be drawn. And proved once and for all she was not a proper lady.

She squeezed her eyes shut once more. What was she thinking? He was a British soldier. That scarlet wool ought to make her think of nothing but the blood of thousands of her countrymen, shed in a futile bid for freedom.

"Miss Burke?"

She opened her eyes, lifting them only enough to focus on his high-shine black boots. "I beg your pardon. I—I was looking for... I'll just go—"

The boots took two deliberate steps toward her, one for each word. "Go where?"

Why on earth had she imagined she would find her journal in his private chambers? "To—to look elsewhere?" She hated that note of doubt in her own voice. The satchel had contained important papers, and a duke surely had a study or an office or some other room where the business of the estate was conducted. But she would just as surely get lost trying to find it. Who knew which wing it might be in?

"I think not."

Her chin jerked up again, seemingly of its own accord. "I beg your pardon?"

"I would not wish to impede your search, Miss Burke. Whatever it is you may be seeking." Something, not quite humor, glimmered in his eyes, though it did not displace their usual dark intensity. "But I fear you are in some distress." Now his gaze darted over her before coming to rest on some piece of furniture behind her. Was that a flush of color across his cheeks? "Hence, I presume, your...dishabille."

Oh, no. She'd been distracted. But she couldn't possibly have rushed from her room without...

As she clutched her arms instinctively across her chest, she felt the sides of the dressing gown gaping open. The braided silk cord designed to hold the garment closed had worked its way loose. She was standing in the private quarters of a gentleman with her shift on display. Briefly, she considered diving into one of the suits of armor to hide.

And never coming out.

Instead, he turned away, back toward the door through which he'd silently entered. "One moment, please." He was gone long enough for her to tighten the sash of her dressing gown, but not long enough for her to think of escaping. When he returned he held her journal in his hands. "Could this be what you're looking for? I intended to ask one of the servants to return it to your room."

She hardly heard him. Yesterday's encounter in the inn was replaying in her mind. Though Tristan readily extended the book to her, he maintained his grip for a moment longer than necessary, after her own fingers had clasped the cover. Her panic must have been visible on her face, for he said, a little defensively, "You may rest assured I am not in the habit of reading young ladies' secret diaries."

"It's not a—"

Well, it *was* a diary, if by diary one meant a book containing private thoughts not meant to be shared. More accurately, though, it was not *only* a diary. She'd begun it to keep a scientific record. On occasion, however, other things found their way into the journal, with the result that its pages were a cryptic jumble of lists, memoranda, notes, and illustrations. She'd been forced to create her own system—if *system* it could be called—to keep track of it all. If anyone ever did decide to look into the book, she took some solace in the idea that no one else would be able to make heads nor tails of it.

"It contains the botanical observations I've made over the last few months," she said, clutching the journal in one hand and the opening of the dressing gown with the other.

"Botany, eh?" There was surprise in his voice. It might have been matched in his expression, but she would never know. She could not bring herself to meet his eye. "Following in your father's footsteps?"

Papa was a dabbler, a dilettante. She was serious. A scientist. Still, she hesitated only a moment. "Yes."

"I'm sure he is gratified by your interest."

Gratified? Perhaps. She wanted to make him proud. Her given name might belong to a common shrub, but she intended someday to pin her surname on something extraordinary.

Of course, a botanical discovery was never easy to make. An unmarried young lady who wasn't even allowed to walk through a manicured park without a chaperone might find it impossible.

"Though I suspect he would advise you to take better care of your notes," he added.

She folded the journal against her breast like a shield. But the words had already found their mark. What must it be like to be so blessedly sure of one's self? "You're right, of course. I shall endeavor to do better." She curled her fingers tighter around the book's cover, feeling her fingernails dig into the soft leather. If it were not so precious to her, she might have lobbed it at his head. Instead, she turned toward the double doors, which still stood open behind her, intending to take her leave.

A youthfully pretty woman, clad all in black, stood on the threshold. Under ordinary circumstances, Erica might have taken her for Tristan's elder sister. But based on what he had revealed about his family, this elegant woman of not quite middle age must be his stepmother, the duchess.

Gathering her wits, her courage, and the trailing skirt of her dressing gown, Erica sank into a deep curtsy, from which she did not rise until the duchess said, "You must be Miss Burke."

If she did not speak, Tristan would speak for her. "Yes, Your Grace."

"Mrs. Dean told me of your arrival. How frightened you must have been to discover yourself stranded." The Duchess of Raynham was one of those rare women whose spark was not dimmed by the unrelieved black of mourning. Instead, the black crape set off her porcelain skin and fair hair. She studied Erica with lively blue eyes. "I've sent my maid to your room with some necessary items I hope will fit." There was amusement in her gaze, but no judgment, as she took in Erica's current state of undress. "I know you must be exhausted and terribly worried about your sister, but if you'll join us for dinner this evening, we shall try to supply a few hours' diversion, won't we?" Her eyes flashed to her stepson for confirmation.

Dinner? With the duke? Erica swallowed hard. Frankly, she'd rather have been left to starve in the cottage.

Nonetheless, she forced herself to answer in the affirmative. Because the duchess seemed to expect it. As she also seemed to understand that being alone might be worse. "Thank you, ma'am," she said, risking another, shallower, curtsy. "You are too kind." Despite her caution, the dressing gown slid off one shoulder, baring her shift to view.

Behind her, Tristan made a gruff noise in his throat. Disapproval, whether at the invitation or her acceptance of it, she was not sure.

Without waiting to be dismissed, without even begging the duchess' pardon, she hurried through the door, head bowed, as if charging back into the storm, praying she would be able to find the shelter of her room.

Chapter 5

Only vaguely aware of his movements, Tristan stepped forward, once more wondering which posed the greater danger: letting Erica walk away, or going after her.

His stepmother settled the question by taking his hands in her own. "Tris! Thank God you're home."

Her words and the gentle pressure of her fingers drew his attention to her face. People could be forgiven for wondering whether his father had married his second wife late in life solely because she was young and pretty. Others no doubt assumed that her inheritance, in both property and funds, had been the particular point of interest. But Tristan had always suspected her name.

He bowed over their clasped hands. "Guin."

The former Miss Guinevere Shepherd, now the Duchess of Raynham, turned her head obligingly to receive his kiss on her cheek. But even after he had straightened, she continued looking over her shoulder.

"Miss Burke seems rather a wild thing. Is it possible you stumbled upon a brownie?"

Tristan gave a small smile. Brownies were domestic spirits, helpers around hearth and home. The creature in this case seemed more likely to cause mischief and mayhem. "A will o' the wisp, I'd say. Or perhaps a leprechaun."

"Ah, yes. I thought I caught an Irish lilt."

"You did." He fought the impulse to free one hand to fidget with his collar. Had his uniform always been this uncomfortable? "I hope you did not think it was necessary to invite her to dine with us for my sake."

"For her own, rather. She cannot stay locked in her room, worrying herself into a shadow." She swiveled her gaze back to him. "Surely you don't mean to suggest that a stranded traveler is beneath a duchess' notice?" she asked, one eyebrow bent in a scold.

He knew better to suggest any such thing. Guin had never been one to pride herself on rank, contrary to the gossips' assumption that she had married a man twice her age solely for the elevation of status that had come with it.

As she studied Tristan, the flash of defensiveness in her eyes was quickly replaced by a flicker of curiosity. "She certainly seems to have caught yours…"

He pushed aside the memory of a vibrant curl caressing a curve of pale skin. No, no. It was her *journal* that had piqued his curiosity. *I am not in the habit of reading young ladies' secret diaries.* Not quite a lie, far easier to tell than the truth. And in fact he'd not succumbed to the temptation to read it, though it was impossible not to wonder what the leather-bound book contained. Something that had possessed her to go searching for it wearing…well, very little at all.

Rather than attempt to deny his interest, he led Guin to a chair. "You are well?"

The abrupt turn in the conversation seemed to draw attention rather than divert it. Eyes narrowed, Guin watched him for a long moment before answering. "Well enough."

Tristan sat facing her and crossed one booted leg over the other knee. "And my sister?"

"Vivi is…" Guin paused to arrange her inky skirts around her, her eyes following the restless movement of her own fingers. "Vivi."

"She hinted at some difficulty with her governess."

"I do not believe Viviane is the first child to sneak away from her lessons for an hour," his stepmother said with a shrug, though the gesture conveyed defeat more than indifference. "She's bored, Tris. I cannot find a governess whom the girl cannot outwit. Miss Chatham came with impeccable references, and yet…" Her shoulders rose and fell again. "I have thought of hiring a tutor…"

A young man teaching a girl, the two of them closeted alone together for hours? And not just any girl, but the daughter of a duke, who would one day be a wealthy young woman? No, not even for the sake of Viviane's bright mind would he countenance such a risk. "Next you'll be talking of sending her off to Harrow," he said, hoping the retort would pass for teasing. Truth be told, sometimes he feared that even the esteemed boys' school would be an insufficient challenge for his sister.

"Nonsense. The public schools exist for the sole purpose of beating the creativity out of children." If she also teased, the edge in her voice undercut the humor.

He dipped his head in acknowledgment. "Quite literally, I'm afraid. And in any case, you couldn't bear to be parted from your daughter."

"No," she confessed and smiled weakly. "You know me too well."

"I will speak to her," he said, leaning forward to pat his stepmother's hand.

"Thank you. She is not quite old enough for a formal dinner, so I did not ask for her to join us tonight." Perfectly proper, of course. He hid his disappointment with a nod of understanding. "But Vivi hopes to see you upstairs for breakfast, I know."

Guilt prickled along his spine, forcing him to sit up straighter. How could he have forgotten their schoolroom tête-à-têtes, mornings of toast and marmalade and giggling schoolgirl confidences? "Of course."

"The sight of your trunk had her in raptures—the fortnight between its arrival and yours was agony. I ordered the servants not to open it until you gave orders, but I learned later that she was so eager to imagine you here, she saw to its unpacking herself. Truth to tell, I could not fault her enthusiasm. Oh, it is good to have you back." With a sigh of relief, she looked him up and down, taking in every detail of his appearance, lingering over the showy trimmings of his uniform. "And home to stay."

The last words rose on a questioning note, but he made no answer to them. Though the matter of the trunk suggested she knew something of the secretive nature of his mission, as had his father, his stepmother could not be expected to understand his current dilemma. His disdain for the role that had been thrust upon him, as opposed to the one he'd chosen for himself. The irresolvable tension between society's expectation that an officer would of course resign his commission in favor of his obligations as a gentleman, and what Tristan had come to see as his greater duty.

The Duke of Raynham safeguarded the well-being of hundreds of tenants. Major Laurens, however, safeguarded the nation.

And from the moment he had set foot on Hawesdale lands, he had felt the difference like a weight. While his father had buried himself beneath weighty tomes of Arthurian legends, other men had managed Hawesdale Chase admirably. Doubtless they could continue to do so. To replace an intelligence officer's unique knowledge of the French army's movements and intentions would be considerably more difficult. Perhaps impossible. Considerably more was at stake than Tristan's family could ever know.

He had come home, yes. Duty—and his commanding officer—had demanded it.

But he could not promise to stay.

"I hope you are not angry with me?" she ventured.

"For what cause?"

Once more, she cast her eyes downward. "It is no longer my place to invite guests to this house."

"Into which house ought you to invite them, then?" he asked dismissively. "Hawesdale is your home, and Vivi's, for as long as you wish it to be."

"Your future bride may have her own ideas." She glanced up. Wondering, he supposed, whether he knew of Lord Easton's plan to marry him to his daughter. Worry clouded her bright eyes.

His first reaction to Vivi's announcement had been a huff of laughter. As a second son with a proclivity for finding himself in dangerous situations, he had adopted a philosophy of detachment where women were concerned. Lust was an inconvenience to be dealt with in the most efficient manner possible. Love—messy, unpredictable, unnecessary—was to be avoided. Marriage had never entered into his mind.

"Why do you suppose Percy never came to the point with Miss Pilkington?" he asked, skirting, but not entirely avoiding, the subject.

"Oh, you know Percy," she demurred, although truth be told, neither of them had known his brother especially well. Percy had always kept a rigidly respectful distance from his stepmother, refusing even her suggestion that he use her given name within the family. An attempt to punish their father for marrying a woman younger than his elder son, perhaps. But the shadow of pain that crossed Guin's expression as she spoke now made it clear she had also felt the slight. "He always was set in his ways."

A less charitable analysis would suggest that his brother had simply been too much like his father—focused on gratifying his own desires rather than fulfilling his responsibilities, despite the rapid approach of his fortieth year. But surely Percy had known that marriage would not require a duke's heir to give up the comforts of town life, his clubs, his mistress. "Perhaps he came into the country in the spring intending to propose," Tristan ventured.

The merest hint of skepticism played around her lips. "Perhaps."

"Did you ever hear him express any dissatisfaction with the match?"

"No, never. Anyone would say she is an ideal choice for a man in his position. She comes from ancient and impressive families on both her mother's and her father's side."

"And a substantial dowry, I suppose." Percy would have made sure of everything.

Guin nodded. "I believe so. She's also quite lovely," she added, not meeting his eye. Clearly, she did not relish the task of matchmaking, yet she plowed bravely on. "Both in temperament and, er, form."

He could not call Miss Pilkington's face to mind, nor anything else about her, but his brother had been nothing if not particular. He doubted Caroline would disappoint.

Upon reflection, he could really think of no rational objection to Lord Easton's scheme. Percy was gone; no need to wax sentimental upon that point. A woman of Caroline Pilkington's impeccable breeding and upbringing could prove a useful addition to the corps that managed Hawesdale. In practical terms, a duke needed a duchess. And an heir.

But if today had shown him nothing else, even he could not always be practical.

"Not if she dares to suggest that you and my sister belong anywhere other than Hawesdale."

Color burned into Guin's cheeks and disappeared as she rose and moved toward the door. "*She* had suggested nothing of the sort, and I daresay she would not. You will—you must judge for yourself." Almost over the threshold, she added, "You shall have ample opportunity to get to know one another—this infernal rain seems determined to hold us all prisoner here forever."

Though his stepmother had given him much food for thought, her mention of the weather sent his mind straying once again to Miss Burke. Years of gathering information on behalf of the Crown had taught him to be curious. Even, at times, suspicious. No doubt the secrets she kept were perfectly mundane. Nevertheless, he should tell Mr. Armitage, the butler, to post a footman at the entrance to his rooms. He wanted no future intrusions. No surprises.

No tantalizing glimpses of soft linen and softer skin beneath.

With a sharp tug, he straightened a perfectly straight sleeve. If he needed a woman—and obviously he did if he was foolish enough to feel a surge of arousal not just at the sight of Erica's bare shoulder but, earlier in the day, at even her muddy rump—perhaps he'd better focus his thoughts on Caroline Pilkington after all.

Half an hour later, he descended to dinner. Three steps from the bottom of the staircase, he heard a noise behind him and paused. A rustling sound, the irregular patter of hesitant footsteps, a quiet "oh, dear." Erica emerged into the sconce's light, looking over her shoulder as if fearful someone might be following her.

She was wearing a shimmering blue gown, something Guin must have put aside during her mourning. When compared to how Erica had looked in her mud-stained traveling dress, the transformation was extraordinary. And he'd been attracted enough—dangerously so—to the dirty, disheveled version.

He tried to shift out of her path, but too late. Another few steps and they collided.

"Oh. Your Grace. I'm dreadfully sorry. Sorry for bumping into you… Although…well, actually, I'm rather glad I bumped into *someone*." As she shifted slightly from side to side, her skirts swayed and caught the light. "I wonder if you could…or rather, if you *would*, for of course you must know the way to the dining room in your own house…"

He fought the urge to mutter an imprecation against Guin's generosity. Who was this woman in the garb of a duchess with titian curls tumbling down her back? Half lady, half…he hardly knew what. Siren, perhaps.

Erica caught him studying her. "Is everything all right, Your Grace?"

Perhaps he ought to be grateful for the opportunity to keep an eye on his unpredictable guest. "It would be my pleasure to escort you," he said, holding out an arm.

True to form, she did not take it. "I am sorry about this afternoon," she said as they walked along the first-floor corridor toward the west wing. "It must have seemed as if I were snooping. You have every right to be angry with me—"

"Nonsense," he said, a little more adamantly than he had intended. Many things in life were out of a man's control. All the more reason to keep a tight rein on those things that were well within it. Anger was a reckless emotion that could be easily exploited by one's enemies.

He *was*, however, frustrated. Frustrated with himself. He had laid out his life with the utmost care. He didn't need any diversions. Any distractions. If only he hadn't… Or she hadn't… *Damn this rain.*

"Because of your stepmother's invitation, then?" she prodded.

"Nonsense." A surprisingly useful response where Miss Burke—and his interest in her—were concerned. He would repeat it until he was convinced of its truth.

"I have no wish to intrude on a family party. If you'll make my excuse to the duchess, I'll gladly return to my room," she insisted. Panic flickered through her eyes as she cast a glance toward the footmen who stood ready to open the dining room doors. Despite the elegance of the gown, she looked like a wild creature caught in a trap.

Why subject her to the Lydgates' stares or the tight-lipped disapproval of the rector's wife? Why compare her side by side with Caroline just to remind himself of the sort of woman a man in his position ought to desire? It would be kinder just to let Erica go.

But he was a duke now. And if he'd learned anything at all from his father, he knew that dukes were rarely kind and sometimes—often—selfish.

"Nonsense," he told her, his voice softer now. Draping her hand over his arm, he led her across the threshold.

Chapter 6

After the earlier exchange with Mr. Davies, Erica had known better than to hope he would let her go. But she did not know what to do with the part of herself that had been hoping he wouldn't.

Partly, of course, because she might have wandered about the mansion aimlessly for hours—days—if he had. And partly because of the unexpected thrill of entering a grand, high-ceilinged room on the arm of a duke.

Some long dormant corner of her heart, steeped in foolish feminine fantasy, clattered into wakefulness and sent a rush of blood through her limbs.

Slowly she lifted her gaze from the intricately patterned marble floor to her hand, where it lay along Tristan's sleeve. Mama would scold her for forgetting her gloves. But at least she had scrubbed and pared her nails. No grime remained, though her skin was still rough and nearly as red as his coat. Not quite a fairy-tale princess, then. But as close as she would likely ever come, and anticipation squeezed through her tightly corseted ribcage.

When at last she worked up the courage to raise her eyes and survey the room, she found herself drawn instead to Tristan's profile, the Roman nose of an English aristocrat and the strong jaw of a man accustomed to getting his way. The meager glow from the stub of a tallow candle had already revealed those traits to her. But the brilliant light of the dining room's chandelier made it far more difficult to deny how attractive he was. She found herself wishing after all he were merely handsome. At least then her fascination might have been easier to understand, if not accept.

But no, she could find no more fitting word than *attractive* to describe him. In the sense of magnetic. Compelling. Undeniably so, though she did so want to deny it. Surprisingly dark brows and dark stubble—although surely he must have shaved not long ago?—shadowed a face carved by a sculptor who favored sternness, as she herself never had. His hair, which gleamed like polished bronze, more golden than brown, could do little to soften those granite-hewn features, tied as it was in a ruthlessly neat queue at the nape of his neck.

As if he felt her studying him, he dropped his gaze to hers, and at last the candles' glow revealed something she had not known. His eyes were not black nor even brown, but blue. Dark as sapphires and inscrutable as the night sky.

"Miss Burke." The Duchess of Raynham swept toward them, across a room even statelier than Erica had feared. Erica released Tristan's arm and curtsied, while the duchess surveyed her critically. "That color suits you better than it did me."

Generally, Erica chose her garments based on practical considerations, dresses and shoes and even stockings that could be worn out of doors and would withstand the strong soap and vigorous scrubbing her work sometimes made necessary. The last four months, in particular, had demanded the darkest, dullest colors she could find—not just because of the dirt, but because of Henry. Not widow's weeds, for her mother had forbidden it, as they had not been married. But as close to it as she could manage.

She had forgotten, or perhaps had never known, that dyed silk could compete with Nature's palette. How difficult it must have been to capture the precise blue-violet of the cornflower at its peak, the moment before the delicate blossom began to fade.

"Come," the duchess said. "Let me introduce you to my guests."

With a quick, shallow curtsy to Tristan, whose attention had been drawn by a pair of gentlemen standing nearby, Erica dutifully followed his stepmother to a loosely grouped trio of two women and a man.

"Lady Lydgate, may I introduce to you Miss Erica Burke? Mrs. Newsome, the vicar's wife. Lord Beresford." Someone else signaled to the duchess and she tipped her head to those standing before her. "If you will excuse me…"

When she had gone, Erica made another round of curtsies, conscious each time of the maid's promise that her bosom would not, in fact, overspill the top of the dress, though it threatened every moment to do so.

Lady Lydgate's quick, bright eyes took in every detail of her appearance. "So you're Raynham's waif."

Waif? She sucked in her breath in embarrassed surprise, forgetting for a moment how tightly the maid had insisted on lacing her corset. At home, she rarely wore one at all. "If you will have it so, ma'am. I would say rather, a stranded traveler. Like yourselves, I understand."

Lord Beresford's lips twitched at her pert reply. He was a man of middle age who might still pass for handsome, his dark hair only beginning to silver at the temples. Before he could speak, however, Mrs. Newsome broke in. "You were fortunate in his delay." The stress she laid on the first word made it clear that she did not consider herself similarly lucky. "A fortnight..." She shook her head sharply, lips twisted as if to prevent them from speaking words better left unsaid.

"Doubtless Raynham could not help it," Lord Beresford chimed in, one hand smoothing his embroidered waistcoat over the beginnings of a paunch. "We must all be grateful for the inscrutable workings of Providence, mustn't we, Mrs. Newsome? Certainly *He* must be held responsible for the rain, at least." The vicar's wife looked chagrined by his mocking rebuke. "And Miss Burke might have been troubled by vagrants, or worse, if Raynham had not happened by when he did."

His words echoed Mr. Davies's. Perhaps there were greater dangers in Westmorland than she had imagined. Or perhaps Tristan had taken care to circulate a version of events in which he had rescued her, rather than risk having others learn the truth: She had stumbled upon his hiding place.

A general move toward dinner began, and she found herself seated at table between Sir Thomas Lydgate and the vicar. Sir Thomas was a sportsman, busily bemoaning how the rain had curtailed his shooting. "Knew Raynham wouldn't begrudge me a few of his birds—a chap must do something to pass the time."

When Lord Beresford on his left claimed Sir Thomas's attention, she turned to Mr. Newsome. "Did I understand your wife to say you've all been at Hawesdale Chase for a fortnight?"

"The duchess kindly invited her neighbors to a modest celebration of Raynham's homecoming," he explained. "When he did not appear, Sir Thomas elected to wait for him. Of course, no one had any notion he would be delayed so long. As the Lydgates were kind enough to carry us with them from Summerfield, we were obliged to stay as well." Although he did not seem to share his wife's obvious displeasure at the protracted visit, nor did he seem to be entirely pleased by the situation. "One does not wish to take advantage of another's hospitality," he said, choosing his words with care. "I suppose the storms kept Raynham from leaving London when he intended."

"But it is not raining to the south," she corrected unthinkingly. Across the table, a fair-haired gentleman whom she had not yet met took in her reply with interest. Quickly, she amended her words. "That is to say, it was not raining in Shropshire the day before yesterday."

"Is that so?" Mr. Newsome said, absently. A half-smile lifted his lips. "Well, if the weather were more predictable, on what should we depend for conversation?"

For a homecoming celebration, the whole affair proceeded with unnatural solemnity and stiffness to Erica's mind, perhaps because the family was still in mourning. Or perhaps because she was accustomed to the boisterous dinners of home, enlivened by her little sisters' chatter and tales from her father's most interesting cases. Her mind rattled about, searching for the rules her mother had cautioned her to observe on more formal occasions; most, however, had disintegrated through disuse into a sort of mental dust.

She had not yet been introduced to half the party, most of whom sat too far away for conversation in any case. Across the table a young woman a few years Erica's elder drew her spoon back and forth through her soup, never lifting it to her mouth. She must be Miss P—something, and the other older couple, each seated in a place of honor beside their hosts, must be her parents. Lord—something, wasn't it? The one who meant for Tristan to fulfill some promise? She longed to be able to write all the names in her journal to help her remember. So the blond man must be—

"Captain Whitby." Lady Lydgate turned abruptly and spoke to him. "What was it you were saying about spies in the neighborhood?"

The muted clatter of conversation and silver fell silent as every ear strained to catch his answer. Captain Whitby laughed.

"Why, Lady Lydgate, I spoke in the strictest confidence." But his scold was delivered with a smile, and his pale blue eyes twinkled. Even on short acquaintance, Erica could guess that it would be unwise to trust Lady Lydgate with secrets. Captain Whitby clearly understood that too.

"Spies?" When Tristan repeated the word, it took on a more serious cast. The inevitable effect of his uniform, she decided, combined with his unsmiling demeanor. Tension crackled around the table like an electric spark.

"Actually, no." Captain Whitby laid aside his spoon and scanned the assembled company. "Poets."

A murmur of relieved laughter swelled and subsided. Though she still had not taken a bite of food, Miss P. blotted her lips with her napkin to mask her smile.

"The Home Office received reports of suspicious behavior. I was sent to investigate. A shrewd lady had recently observed two poorly dressed young men patrolling the countryside, speaking in code." A born storyteller, Captain Whitby paused to allow darting glances of speculation to pass among the guests. "As it turned out, the suspects were merely impoverished poets on a walking tour, spouting lines of verse to one another."

"O-ho," chuckled Sir Thomas. "Dangerous radicals, eh?"

"They might be both poets and radicals. Mightn't they?" The words slipped from Erica's lips before she could call them back. Captain Whitby resumed studying her, this time with a slight frown notched into his brow, and she felt it imperative to explain herself. "After all, both art and politics seek to rouse a person's deeper feelings, for good or ill."

"Very true, Miss—"

She did not wait for another to make the introduction. "Burke."

Lady Lydgate tilted her head toward Captain Whitby, and the ostrich plumes in her hair waved, giving her the appearance of a quizzical bird. "Trust the Irish to know something of rabble-rousing," she said, in a false whisper.

Heat flared in Erica's cheeks and spread right down to the plunging neckline of her borrowed gown.

"And poetry," Tristan declared from the head of the table without looking at her. Lady Lydgate deferred to his opinion, though grudgingly. Erica suspected he did not often have occasion to defend her country's artistry.

"Though one is certainly hard pressed to think of an example that joins the poetic and the political successfully," opined the gentleman she believed to be Miss P—something's father.

Miss P. at last looked up from her plate. "What about *The Wild Irish Rose?*"

Another hum rose from the table, punctuated with exclamations of "So thrilling!" and "What trash!"

Erica did not know where to look and as a result found herself imprisoned by Tristan's gaze. One dark brow lifted. She cleared her throat. "My sister is the author," she confessed quietly.

The murmur grew momentarily louder then stopped altogether, as it had when Lady Lydgate had spoken the word "spies." Astonishment, embarrassment, and amusement contorted the faces of the company as they recollected what had been said, or what they had heard, about the book. The captain once more regarded her with a look she could only describe as speculative. "Lady Ashborough writes feelingly of the plight of Ireland," he said. "Did your family know something of the rebellion firsthand?"

Warily, she nodded. Her elder brother had been a member of the United Irishmen, the group who had organized the uprising. Her younger brother had been gravely injured in it. And Henry—

"My betrothed was killed during the events of late May," she said after a moment, deliberately vague about whether he was a rebel, a soldier, or an innocent bystander.

Mumbled expressions of sympathy rippled around her. Inexplicably, a few also darted glances toward Miss P., whose father scraped back his chair, lifted his glass, and rose. "A toast," he proclaimed, "to the memory of those we have lost, and the fortune of those who have returned." He gestured with his wine toward Tristan, and other chairs screeched across the floor as the assembled company came to its feet to salute their host.

Beneath the clamor, Sir Thomas spoke into her ear. "You and Miss Pilkington have your sorrow in common, you know. She was engaged to marry Lord Hawes before he died. Raynham's elder brother," he added when she wrinkled her brow in confusion.

"Oh?" Erica darted her gaze across the table. Miss Pilkington had risen to her feet, she noted, but her glass remained on the table.

"Yes, indeed," said Sir Thomas, his eager whisper hinting that he had more to tell and, like his wife, would be only too happy to share what he knew. Erica tightened her hold on the stem of her glass. "Rumor has it Raynham intends to step into his brother's place in more ways than one."

He expects you to keep Percy's promise to their daughter. Suddenly the words made sense. She knew, of course, that great families generally regarded marriage as a means to solidify status or combine wealth. But she was chilled by the notion that a woman might be passed from one brother to the next, as if she were merely a soulless chattel, not a living, breathing being with feelings. As if she were marrying a title, rather than the man to whom it belonged. She could not bring herself to glance toward Tristan to see whether he looked pleased at the prospect of his impending nuptials.

What business had she with the wedded bliss—or misery—of strangers?

Uneasily, she moved away from Sir Thomas, only to discover that one leg of his chair now pinned the full skirts of her gown to the floor. A jerk of surprise and the next thing she knew, red wine was arcing from her glass into the air. It seemed to hover there for a moment, deciding where—or, pray God, *whether*—to fall. Her eyes snapped closed.

When she opened them again, it was not to discover that the wine had defied Mr. Newton's principle and stayed miraculously suspended in midair. Nevertheless, her first reaction was relief. She had managed, somehow, not to spill a drop on her borrowed gown. The linens, however…

Her gaze crept slowly, reluctantly across the table, following a murderous-looking trail that ended at Miss Pilkington. That young woman had sunk back into her chair, looking as if she were the victim of some heinous crime. Bloodred stains splashed across the pale yellow silk of her ruined gown.

Every eye, including Miss Pilkington's, was focused on the spreading stain. Every hand and pair of lips was frozen in shock. As a result, it was more than quiet enough to hear Erica's wine glass shatter as it slipped from her nerveless fingers onto the floor. Quiet enough to hear the fabric of the beautiful blue gown rip as she tugged it free of Sir Thomas's chair leg. And quiet enough that her footsteps echoed as she dashed across the threshold and fled down the corridor.

Chapter 7

Tristan watched David Whitby rise from a leather armchair and walk to the sideboard to refill his glass. "I would have thought you might balk at drinking French brandy, Captain. Given your current line of work."

Both second sons, he and Whitby had joined a cavalry unit together after school, where quickness, bravery, and an ability to be discreet had brought them to the notice of Colonel Zebadiah Scott. Though neither of them could recollect having ever seen the man before the day they were invited to his office, he had known them well.

They had left that meeting with new orders: to join an elite corps of officers whose task it was not to fight battles, but to ferret out and report the information that made it possible for others to win them. It was dangerous, delicate work, about which they could reveal next to nothing—not even, at times, to one another.

Then Whitby's identity had been exposed. One day, he was in Paris, playing the part of a disaffected artist with Jacobin sympathies. The next...gone. Weeks of uncertainty had followed, relieved only somewhat by a whispered report that he had been bundled back to London. Now, he was using his years of invaluable wartime experience helping the Home Office uncover domestic spies and smugglers—the sort of lawless men who made it possible for English gentlemen to enjoy a glass of contraband French brandy now and again.

Whitby laughed as he splashed a generous measure of Armagnac into his tumbler. "You don't suppose I smash every bottle we find, do you?"

Tris smiled into the cozy dimness of the study and lifted his own glass to his lips. "I'll pretend I didn't hear that."

The leather chair gave a soft sigh as Whitby returned to it and sat. For a long moment, neither spoke, reveling instead in the silence that can only exist between those who know one another's thoughts and do not require them to be spoken. Dark paneled walls, comfortable furniture, a crackling fire—everything about the space exuded ease. Tristan knew it was unreasonable to miss the cheap, rough quarters he'd grown used to in recent years.

"Will you do it? Will you marry Caroline Pilkington?"

Whitby's question caught him off guard, not least because he found himself calling his mind back from the memory of Erica running from the dining room and his mad impulse to go after her. He'd made do with sending a footman to make sure she found her way back to her room. Caroline had left too, calm and dignified, eschewing the offers of help from everyone, even her mother. Half an hour later she'd returned, wearing a simpler gown, though no less elegant, unwilling to hear any critique of Miss Burke.

If he'd staged a scene to amplify the contrast between the two women, he could have done no better.

"Can you think of any reason why I shouldn't?" he replied. "She'll make a suitable duchess."

"Indeed." Was it his imagination, or did Whitby's voice sound clipped? Tristan had never been disposed to let his imagination run wild.

"Only…" Whitby paused for a sip that left his glass half empty. "I am surprised to find you hurrying to marry. You have time, now, to look about and choose your bride. You will not lack for likely candidates."

"Simpering misses and their too-eager mamas? I haven't six weeks to waste in London looking over the wares on the marriage mart. I'd rather be done with the business." He recognized the word's crass, unpleasant connotations, but in the end, marriage among those of his class was rarely anything more than a business arrangement.

Most likely, settlements had already been drawn up between their families. All that remained was to obtain a Bishop's License and the deed could be done within the week. The less time he wasted at Hawesdale, the sooner he could return to the duties that mattered most.

Carefully, Whitby placed his glass on the table beside him, twisting it this way and that in the firelight and studying the patterns cast by the faceted crystal. "You're going back, aren't you?"

"I hadn't really—"

At last his friend lifted his gaze from the tumbler to his face. Demanding honesty.

Tristan shrugged.

"What about your responsibilities here? Hawesdale Chase? Lady Viviane?"

"My father never spared a thought for the management of Hawesdale. Yet it has been run efficiently and effectively all these years. I have no reason to doubt it will continue to be in my absence. My stepmother and sister are well provided for. Meanwhile…" He paused to finger the fringe of his scarlet sash where it draped onto the chair. "When I consider the greater need, the greater good, what other conclusion am I to reach?"

Whitby took in that information without a hint of surprise. "And how do you imagine your wife would feel about all this?"

"Relieved," he said, though he had no reason to think Caroline a reluctant bride. At Whitby's skeptical expression, he explained. "I cannot think it likely Miss Pilkington wanted to marry Percy particularly. She may feel no more enthusiasm at the prospect of marrying me. But I suspect she rather likes the idea of being the Duchess of Raynham. Once we're wed, she'll have everything her heart desires."

"It's not like you to speak of hearts, Tris," Whitby protested with a laugh.

Tristan conceded the point with a slight nod and an even slighter smile. "True enough. This brandy has me lapsing into the cant of poets and lovers," he said, studying his own, nearly untouched, glass. "But aren't most young ladies brought up with the expectation of becoming wives and mothers?" Certainly very few went about proclaiming their intention to become something else. A botanist, for instance.

He shook off the mental image of Erica's fierce expression as she clutched her journal. Tried and failed to replace it with a picture of Caroline. They'd just dined together. Why were her features still so indistinct in his mind? "My brother raised Miss Pilkington's expectations, and his death left her in an awkward situation. I can offer a remedy that will benefit us both. A wife will ensure the smooth running of my household in my absence. And with diligent application and a bit of luck, I'll leave her in anticipation of the birth of an heir."

"*Diligent application?* Good God, Tris. I think I preferred the talk of heart's desires. You make marriage—and the marriage bed—sound like a godawful chore."

"An obligation," Tristan corrected mildly. "One of several duties I'm now bound to fulfil."

Whitby swore, snatched up his drink, and finished it. "And how will you feel if it becomes something more in the nature of a permanent assignment?"

"Why do I get the feeling you aren't referring to the sacred vow to remain faithful to my wife 'until death do us part'?" Tristan eased forward, elbows braced on knees, glass dangling from his fingertips, imagining a lifetime of facing Caroline's complaisant smiles. "Charming story about the poet-spies, by the way."

"My hand to God, Tris, it happened just as I said."

"I know it did. Last year. In Somerset." Tristan fixed his friend with a stern eye. "So what really brought you to Westmorland?"

Whitby sighed. "Rumors." He rose but did not return to the sideboard. Instead he paused before the fire, his figure limned by its warm light, his face in shadow. "About you. Where you've been. What you've learned. Someone knows things you'd rather they didn't. And they've been leaking it out in drips and drops since you came into the title. Much more and Colonel Scott will be forced to reassign you to domestic duty too. With his regrets, of course."

With one fingertip, Tristan traced the rim of his glass. "Of course." Whitby knew something of regret. Restlessness. The loss of honor—though through no fault of his own. "So you were sent—or came—to Hawesdale to investigate."

"An agent intercepted a letter about a month ago, making mention of your return and the possibility that valuable information could be acquired at Hawesdale thereafter. Neither the sender nor the intended recipient have been identified. When I arrived in the country I hoped to be able to nose around without rousing suspicions, talk with your servants, anyone who might have access to your papers or other possessions. Instead I found a houseful of guests, all invited by the duchess to welcome you home, it seems. And all with a little something to hide."

In his mind's eye, Tristan scanned the length of the dining room table, reviewing the assembled guests. "Surely neither the Lydgates nor the Newsomes can be serious subjects of investigation."

It was Whitby's turn to shrug. "Did you know that Mr. Newsome's youngest brother was a naval officer aboard a ship that went down? Rumor has it there are survivors being held in a French prison."

And probably wishing they had drowned, Tristan thought, as he glanced toward the window and watched rain streak down the glass. But he could not deny that the vicar might have come to Hawesdale hoping to uncover information about his brother's whereabouts.

"And Beresford?" Though it would be a stretch to describe the man as an enemy, Tristan found himself hoping his stepmother had not been taken in by the youngish widower's oily charm. A lecher, almost certainly. But a spy?

"Been muttering about bad investments and dashing off notes of hand for his losses at the billiards table," Whitby told him.

Tristan nodded. A man desperate for money might do anything to save himself, even commit treason. "What about the Pilkingtons?" He had too much experience to dismiss them out of hand. Did Whitby's suspicions lie behind Guin's halfhearted endorsement of the proposed match between him and Caroline?

Whitby laughed. "Nothing beyond the fact that the young lady prefers her gowns in the Directoire style, which Mrs. Newsome has hinted may mean she is a republican of easy virtue."

Tristan mustered a smile and lifted his glass to his lips. "Have you learned anything else?"

Whitby shook his head, but only after the slightest hesitation. Someone unaccustomed to reading behavior or looking for clues would never have noted it.

"Captain..." The warning note in Tristan's voice was unmistakable.

Still, Whitby weighed his words before continuing. "I wonder how much you know about that firebrand you rescued."

"Miss Burke? But how could she be involved? She arrived in Westmorland only today."

"Are you certain?"

The simple, quiet question struck him with the force of a blow. Despite his experience in the field, he'd committed two grave errors in the space of a day. He'd let down his guard. And he'd trusted another person to tell the truth.

With exaggerated care, he returned his glass to the table. "So she was not accompanying her sister the novelist on her wedding trip to the Lakes."

"She might very well be. But it's not a connection to ease suspicions. Her sister's work has undeniably seditious implications."

"Published before the rebellion?"

"After. But written earlier, as her publisher confirms. And the man she married—"

"Ashborough?" He'd persuaded himself the name and title were a fabrication, and his mind was unusually sluggish to grasp the facts of the case.

"Marquess of. But you might better know him as 'Lord Ash.'" Tristan scoured his memory for the name but came up empty. "Notorious gambler and ne'er-do-well. Earlier this year he came very near to facing his peers over a little matter of treason," Whitby continued. "And his uncle still insists Ashborough was in Dublin at the start of the rebellion, aiding and abetting the men who have since become his brothers."

"His wife's brothers, you mean."

"Which is to say, your Miss Burke's brothers. Suspected of involvement in the Society of United Irishmen."

Along with the man she had planned to marry? Tristan's lowered gaze caught the gleam of firelight across the brass buttons and gold trim of his uniform, and he recalled Erica's expression as she'd spoken of the man. Had he been killed by British soldiers? Vengeance could be a powerful motivation for many things.

"But the uprising has been put down," he insisted.

"Are we certain? The rebels have proved remarkably persistent. And twice now French forces have come to Ireland's aid. Could a third effort be in the works?"

Tristan laughed dismissively. "I think I would know."

"Exactly." Whitby folded his arms across his chest. "But what might change if one of Britain's best agents in France were suddenly discredited? Exposed? Removed from his post?"

Several of the foulest curses Tristan knew, in a variety of languages, sprang to his tongue. But he found himself reaching for the one whose pronunciation still eluded him. *It's blasphemous, you know.* Those cognac-colored eyes, wide with concern for his very soul. Pretended concern?

He contented himself with muttering, "Preposterous."

"She's done nothing, then, to arouse your suspicions?" Whitby prodded.

Quickly, he shook his head. Too quickly. Despite the dimness, he thought he could see Whitby's skeptical expression.

His mind seemed determined to shy away from the evidence before him. He forced it to the fore. An apparently chance encounter in the abandoned cottage. A guest caught wandering in a part of the house in which she had no business. Her spectacular departure from dinner, which, if she'd succeeded in getting away alone, would have provided the perfect opportunity for her to explore while every other guest was occupied for hours. And then, of course, there was her journal...

Her journal. Of course. He could almost feel its worn cover in his hand. Why in God's name hadn't he looked into it when he had the chance?

A servant's muted tap at the door interrupted his mental checklist. "Come," he barked, uncertain when he had got to his feet.

Armitage, the butler, stepped into the room with a tray extended. "A letter for you, Your Grace. From Mr. Davies. He did not wait for a reply."

Tristan's fingers closed around the cold, damp rectangle of folded paper. Armitage nodded sharply, tucked the tray beneath his arm, and left. Without waiting to be asked, Whitby rummaged for a spill and set about touching it first to the fire, then to the candles along the mantel and atop the desk. Soon the room blazed with light from which no print, even the most crabbed, could hide.

Still, Tristan held the letter perilously close to a flame, close enough that a little hiss of steam went up from the paper. What did he hope to find within? Some plausible explanation for Miss Burke's behavior? An excuse to send her away?

> *My Lord Duke,*
> *With deepest apologies for the delay, I write to tell you that Kevin has returned from what was, in the end, quite a perilous journey. The River Kent has overflowed its banks, sending water along every stream, crevice, and path it can find. The bridge at Kendal is washed away, but the old toll-keeper informed him that not long before its collapse, a crested carriage accompanied by a baggage coach made it to the other side safe and sound. The two conveyances must have belonged to Miss Burke's family, as they can by no means be found on this side of the river. However, the destruction of the bridge means they will remain quite out of reach for some days and regrettably must continue without knowledge of her safety. As you requested, word was left at Endmoor against their return.*
> *Your obedient servant,*
> *W. Davies*

"What news?" Whitby stood too far away—deliberately so, Tristan understood—to glean the letter's contents.

With a twitch of his fingers, Tristan touched the paper to the flame. Despite the damp, it caught. When smoke began to curl into the air, he tossed the letter into the fireplace, where it soon disappeared into ash. "It seems my guests—all of them—must resign themselves to the hospitality of Hawesdale for the foreseeable future."

However long it took for him to unmask a spy.

Chapter 8

When the thunder began to rumble once more, Tristan rose and walked to the window of his bedchamber, though the sky was still too dark for him to watch yet another storm roll in. No gleam of light caught his eye. All of Hawesdale was asleep—even the villain who meant to expose his secrets, endanger countless British troops, and rip from him the only meaningful work he had ever done.

Once the sky had lightened to an ominous gray—he could not bring himself to call it dawn—he rang for hot water and thumbed through his clothes, rejecting three coats before selecting one of such dark blue it might have been black. The perfect accompaniment both to the weather and his mood.

As he ascended the stairs to breakfast with his sister, he ticked off each guest, once more weighing his suspicions. Almost to the schoolroom door, he came to the final set of facts Whitby had laid before him, and the most damning: Erica had close ties to known traitors with French allies, and her excuse for wandering in the vicinity of Hawesdale could be neither proved nor disproved while the rain continued.

Unless her journal held a clue…

"Thank you, Miss Chatham. I'm most obliged."

The last voice he had expected to hear this morning was Miss Burke's. He knew, of course, how much could be gleaned from an overheard conversation. But it would mean behaving like a spy in his own home, and he had always made it a point never to think of himself as a *spy*.

Silently, he rocked back onto his heels, out of the swath of light from the partly opened door, into the shadowy corridor.

"For such a small service, gratitude is hardly necessary." He had imagined the governess to be a young woman, but the voice belonged to someone well beyond the middle years of life.

A moment's quiet. For whatever reason, Miss Burke did not seem eager to leave the schoolroom. "I hope you find yourself fortunate in your pupil, Miss Chatham. Lady Viviane seems a clever girl."

"Too clever, sometimes, for her own good."

The governess' reply drove all thought of catching an informant from his mind. Miss Chatham's words were creased with the sort of prim disapproval that would crush Vivi's spirit. Tristan drew a deep, quiet breath.

Miss Burke laughed. The sound was strange, however. Sharp. Almost humorless. "Oh, dear. I'm afraid I was sometimes such a pupil myself, Miss Chatham. Why, on occasion, I surely spent more time concocting schemes to avoid a lesson than I would have spent completing it."

Miss Chatham found nothing amusing in the younger woman's response. "You defied your governess?"

"I never had a governess." *That explains a great deal.* "My papa was my only teacher."

"A man is hardly capable of offering an appropriately feminine education." Censure rang in her voice. He half expected the woman to retract whatever favor she had earlier granted.

"Indeed not," Erica agreed, apparently unperturbed.

"Lady Viviane Laurens is an accomplished young woman." Miss Chatham stressed certain words to offer a clear rebuke of Erica's lopsided instruction. "I did have some hope she would share her father's fondness for history," the governess added after a moment. "But she refuses to settle her mind to it."

Tristan heard the sound of a something being slid across a table. Evidently a book. "Thucydides," said Erica in a voice of mild surprise. "But not in Greek?"

"No. I generally have found that young ladies' minds are not well suited to the study of ancient languages." Tristan forced another calming breath into his lungs. His sister was not just any young lady. "I have limited my instruction to the modern tongues. French, of course, though one does have reservations about it at the present hour. And a smattering of German."

"I myself never enjoyed reading history. In any language." A rustle of fabric followed those words. He pictured Erica pacing the schoolroom and wondered, against his better judgment, what she wore today. "Why, there are hardly any women in it. And all those invented speeches." He could almost hear her eyes roll. "Stirring, yes. But did no one ever wonder what the general's wife, left at home with a half-dozen children and a household to manage, might have said in his place?"

Tristan bit back a smile, but the governess clearly lacked such power of imagination. "I—I beg your pardon?"

The book thumped onto the table once more. "Perhaps studying war distresses Lady Viviane. Perhaps it turns her thoughts to current events. Her brother is, after all, a soldier."

Erica's words, wiser than he wished, settled over him, as chilling as yesterday's rain. Of course his poor sister did not want to read of battles and generals. The great military conflicts of history would easily turn her mind to the dangers he faced in the present.

"Children cannot be educated according to the dictates of sentiment, Miss Burke."

Tristan breathed deep one last time, but the influx of air fanned rather than doused the fury that was smoldering in his chest. One hand lifted to rap on the doorframe to announce his presence. He meant to begin with, "Miss Chatham, your services are no longer required…" and go on from there.

"Tris?"

Vivi's quiet voice behind him almost made him stumble. He dropped his arm and tugged his coat into place, suddenly wishing he had opted to don his uniform. By custom, an officer caught in the act of espionage while wearing it was granted some leniency. A moment too late, he plastered a strained smile of greeting on his face.

Instead of throwing herself into his arms as she had the day before, she hesitated in the corridor's shadows, head tilted, studying him. "Why are you standing out here?"

"I—"

In the schoolroom, he heard the scuffle of footsteps across the board floor as Miss Chatham came toward the door. "You're late, Lady Viviane." The governess stepped into the doorway and fixed her charge with a frown. Though her proportions were ample, nothing about her suggested softness, and her brown hair was liberally frosted with gray. "Oh, Your Grace. I did not see you there."

Her creaky curtsy revealed Erica standing behind her, framed by the schoolroom's large windows. Today's gown might have been borrowed from the governess' wardrobe rather than Guin's, so plain was its style. But its claret color, combined with her red hair, rendered her a pillar of fiery warmth against the gray morning sky. At the moment, her narrow-eyed gaze was focused squarely on Miss Chatham's back. Her obvious dislike of the governess put him in charity with her. So much so that he was in danger of forgetting last night's vow entirely.

Until he saw a leather-bound volume lying on the table beside Thucydides's account of the Peloponnesian War.

Erica's journal.

He kept it in his focus a moment too long. She must have followed his gaze, for she turned quickly and gathered it into her arms. The movement restored him to his present purpose. "Miss Chatham, I regret to—"

"I am sorry I'm late." Vivi brushed past them both, into the room. "I went all the way to the kitchens to remind Cook to send breakfast up here, now that my brother is home." She sent a smile over her shoulder at him, as if nothing had happened that might alter their old habit. As if dukes regularly ate with children in the schoolroom.

Miss Chatham, however, looked scandalized by the notion. Fine lines deepened into grooves as she pursed her lips. "I'm quite sure, Lady Viviane, that His Grace would—"

"Be delighted?" His voice made the sturdy governess quaver like a sapling in a strong breeze. She made no attempt to meet his eye.

"Why else would he be here?" Vivi said brightly. He ought to have known better than to think Miss Chatham had quashed her spirit.

"Indeed, Your Grace." Miss Chatham deflated a little and tried to pass it off as another curtsy. "I have a letter to my sister to finish in my room. With your permission."

With a magnanimous dip of his head, he dismissed her. A more permanent dismissal could wait for a later hour.

Erica hurried after the governess. "I'll just—"

"Oh, Miss Burke, won't you join us for breakfast?" Vivi's offer surprised each of them in turn, though for different reasons, he suspected. Almost to the threshold, Miss Chatham looked as if she had swallowed something bitter-tasting. Erica once more wore a hunted expression. And he…well, he found himself strangely hopeful she would nonetheless accept Vivi's invitation.

Apparently assuming such a request could not be refused, the slighted governess stiffened her spine and strode from the schoolroom. After making a careful study of the wide-plank floorboards, Erica returned to the table. Vivi tangled his fingers with hers and dragged him to sit between them.

In another moment, a maid appeared with a heavily laden tray and his sister busied herself pouring chocolate and distributing triangles of toast. "I think you must be the only guest in this house who's awake at this hour, Miss Burke."

"I have always been an early riser, Lady Viviane. And I"—the topaz gleam of her eyes flashed his way, then back to the plate Vivi had placed before her—"did not stay late at dinner."

In the nick of time, he disguised the twitch of his lips as an attempt to cool the steaming cup his sister handed him.

"But whatever could have brought you to the schoolroom?"

Erica's expression looked vaguely apologetic. She must know that houseguests did not typically wander hither and yon and turn up in inappropriate places. Her plot to escape the company last night had proved only partially successful. Had she hoped to make up for lost time this morning, to explore the house before anyone but the servants was awake?

Slowly, she eased her journal away from her chest and returned it to the table, followed by several other items he had not realized she was holding: a small corked bottle of black liquid, pencils, and a couple of rather bedraggled looking quills. "I needed pen and ink, and it seemed a likely place to find them..."

"You might have rung, Miss Burke," he told her. "The servants will procure whatever you need."

Her chin rose a notch higher. "I'm used to doing things for myself."

"You are our guest," Vivi declared with an airy wave of her marmalade-smeared toast. "You must let us do what we can for your comfort."

"I hope I shall not be an inconvenience to you for long, Lady Viviane." She sent another quick, questioning glance his way. "Your Grace."

Belatedly, he realized he was still holding his cup to his mouth. He choked down a sip of the grainy chocolate, wishing all the while it were coffee.

"I suppose they serve better in France?" Vivi asked, catching his grimace.

France? How did Vivi know where he'd been stationed? Had her father let it slip? Or Guin? Careful not to let his consternation show on his face, he returned his cup to its saucer. "How should I know, Viv?" Turning to Miss Burke, trying to gauge her reaction to his sister's revelation, he said, "I'm sorry to report that Mr. Davies sent a less-than-encouraging message late last evening." Erica's jerk of alarm at the news made all the china on the table rattle. "It would appear that sometime after Lord and Lady Ashborough's coach crossed the Kent, the nearest bridge was washed away, cutting off all communication between here and the Lakes."

"You are—you are certain she was not—" Erica's freckles stood out dark against alarmingly pale skin. Even Vivi's eyes were wide with worry.

"There was no report of any injuries or accidents," he reassured them. "But it will be some days before we can expect to reunite you with your sister."

"Oh. I—" Erica's fingers played restlessly over the silver, the pens, the cork of the ink bottle before settling on the cover of her journal. "Of course." With a frown of concentration, she picked up a pencil, opened her journal, and began to scratch something onto its weathered pages.

It was agony to be so near to the prize he sought, yet unable simply to snatch it up and discover the truth. But he knew from long experience that recklessness was not his friend in such an endeavor. He pretended to busy himself with his breakfast, all the while mulling over a plausible excuse to get close enough to see what she wrote.

"What's that you're doing, Miss Burke?" Vivi, suffering from no such compunction, stretched out her neck to peer across the table.

At first, Erica did not seem to hear the question. The pencil continued its rapid movements across the page. Only when its *scritch-scritch* fell silent did she seem to realize anyone had spoken. She glanced rapidly between the two of them, a wary blankness in her expression. "Did you—? Oh. I—" The pencil listed, nearly slipping from her fingers. "I'm dreadfully sorry. My—my thoughts have a tendency to scatter. It helps if I write down what I..." Her gaze dropped to the page, then she turned the book toward them, though with obvious reluctance. Tristan held his breath. No spy would offer up her secrets so readily.

Unless by doing so, she hoped to persuade them she had nothing to hide.

"Why, it's a picture of Hawesdale," Vivi exclaimed, drawing the book closer to her. "Look, Tris. However did you manage to make it so quickly?"

With every ounce of apparent indifference he could muster, he scanned the spread of pages held up to his gaze. Hastily done, yes, but unquestionably his home. Here and there, illegible squiggles suggested a system of signs he did not immediately recognize.

"Please forgive me." Erica's cheeks were still pale. "I suddenly realized that if I am to stay for several days, I really ought to have some notion of how to get around."

"Oh, it's a map! How clever. But Miss Burke—you've mislabeled. *This* is the east wing." Vivi pointed at the right side of the drawing, and he realized the illegible marks were simply sloppily written letters intended to denote the cardinal directions. "You'd be lost in no time if you followed that. The schoolroom is just here," she explained, tracing her fingertip across the paper as she spoke, "and your room somewhere along here, I suppose."

As quick as that, she'd gained an insider's knowledge of her target's environment. *Brilliant.*

"Thank you, Lady Viviane." Erica closed the journal around the pencil after making the suggested corrections. "I hope you can forgive my rudeness. I can be rather...shatterbrained, as my mama is fond of saying."

"As can I," Vivi confessed eagerly. "At least, according to my governess. We must think of something amusing, Tris," she added in a whisper, leaning closer to him, her mother's kindness gleaming in her eyes, though Viviane's were darkest brown. "A real distraction. The library?"

The library had been his father's preserve, the last room in the house in which he would want to be trapped. Still, the walls of bookshelves would keep Erica occupied for the better part of the day, if she did not throw up her hands and flit back to her chamber or wander off in another direction. The longer he kept her in his sight and in his company, the better chance he stood of determining who she was and what she really wanted.

"An excellent idea, Vivi—if Miss Burke is amenable, that is." Erica gave a wary nod. "And I suspect our guest is not the only one who would welcome a diversion," he continued, turning back toward his sister. "What would you say to a break from your regular lessons for as long as the storm lasts?"

Vivi loosed a most improper squeal. Then her shoulders sagged. "Miss Chatham will never allow it."

"Leave me to deal with her." He would undertake the task only too gladly. "Come," he said, after lifting the cup of now-cold chocolate to his lips and swallowing its contents with unanticipated relish. "Finish your breakfast and I'll take you both down myself."

* * * *

Inside the library, Tristan's eyes went first to the massive mahogany desk, half expecting to find it still buried beneath sliding, sloppy piles of his father's books and papers. But the desktop was empty save for a neat stack of baize-covered volumes: account books, presumably left for his review. No doubt they contained ample proof that Hawesdale got on very well without him.

Just now, however, the thought provided little comfort. What if his mysterious adversary succeeded in exposing him and he were forced to abandon necessary work for...this? He looked around the library, at the comfortable furnishings, the artwork, the walls lined with books. A very pleasant sort of prison, but a prison, nonetheless.

Vivi snatched a volume from a nearby shelf and threw herself into an oversized, high-backed chair near the fireplace. "What suits you,

Miss Burke?" he asked, turning toward his guest. "A tale of romance or adventure? Something to dispel the clouds?"

Her eyes wandered to the window and she watched the rain fall for a moment. "Will it work, do you suppose?"

Years of training and the exigencies of war had taught him how to cordon off his emotions, his fears, when necessary. He had almost forgotten the strength of their teeth and claws, their ability to drag a person down. Erica was worried. If he asked, she would likely confess to worrying for her sister. Was she in fact afraid for herself?

Afraid of being caught?

She still carried her journal, along with the pencils, the pens, and the ink she had acquired. When he held out his hand, she carefully extracted the writing implements and gave them to him one by one. Everything but the journal, which she kept clutched to her chest.

Relieved of most of her burden, she turned toward the nearest bookcase. After studying the shelves for a moment, she said, "It would appear that your father stocked his library on somewhat different principles from my own."

"You may find little other than history books and Arthurian legends lining the shelves," he warned. Almost certainly, unless Davies or someone else had been charged with ensuring the collection contained the essential works of the age.

"I am the last person to fault a gentleman for having a hobbyhorse." Her eyes continued to scan the titles. "If my own father had not been somewhat single-minded, where would I be?"

Not here.

Such an outcome would have been infinitely preferable to the current state of affairs, of course. Still, he found himself oddly glad that some Irishman had chosen to pass down his peculiarities to his daughter and inspired her interest in the flora of the British Isles. Unless it was her brothers' radical politics that had brought her here, instead...

He allowed himself a moment to watch her. Her gaze traveled without apparent rhyme or reason from one shelf to another, and he wondered whether it was her mind or the bookcase that was haphazardly organized. For a spy, she was remarkably open about her foibles. The only thing she seemed to guard was that damn journal.

Or was her behavior a ruse, an attempt to exploit his sympathies, to lure him into a trap and steal *his* secrets? But surely if that were the case, she would have been given information about him, his preferences, his... weaknesses. Even the best agents had them. Who, knowing his love of order and precision, his reputation for cool detachment, would have sent this fire-haired woman into his life and given her orders to make messes, speak wildly, act erratically?

Except…it had worked, hadn't it? She had caught his notice, all right, just as Guin had said. Even now, in his memory, he could see the spark of determination and defiance in her eyes. He could also see her dressing gown slip from her shoulder and the temptations it had revealed. He crossed to the window and leaned his forehead against the pane under the pretense of surveying the park, hoping the chill of the glass would drive away his fever. Never before in his career had he let desire cloud his judgment. If it had been just physical desire, he could have managed to ease it. But this was something deeper. Something more. Everything she said or did was unexpected. Unpredictable.

And for the first time in years, he found himself drawn to the element of surprise.

Behind him, he heard the unmistakable sound of a book being pulled from the shelf. He turned back and saw Erica carrying a heavy volume toward the sofa near where Vivi sat. Telling himself this was just the sort of opportunity he had sought, he followed her there.

"Have you found something to your liking, Miss Burke?"

For answer, she showed him the cover of the book, where *Introduction to Botany* was stamped in fading, leaf-twined letters, the gilt long since worn away. "It's an older text. From 1760 or so. Still, it suggests someone at Hawesdale must have had an interest in plants."

He held his breath until he could be certain it would be under his control when at last he released it. "My mother loved a garden."

And a gardener.

That damning voice inside his head spoke in the broad Yorkshire accent of Hawesdale's late cook. Good God, he had no proof that the accusation was even true, yet he'd been repeating it to himself for twenty years.

Or was the diffidence and insolence with which the servants of Hawesdale treated him now a kind of proof?

"Botany?" Vivi's face appeared around the wing of her chair, glowing with curiosity. "Miss Chatham says that's not a proper subject for young ladies."

"Viv," he said warningly. "Miss Burke is a botanist."

"Oh." Vivi considered this revelation. "Will you teach me?" Her governess' disapproval was evidently a greater lure than a ringing endorsement would have been.

"But your brother promised you a reprieve from your lessons, Lady Viviane." Erica rose, book in hand, clearly poised to put an end to the discussion.

Tristan stood too. Vivi had provided the perfect excuse for him to get even closer to Erica. "I did. But Viviane has always been an eager learner. And I had not considered the unique opportunity of which I might be depriving her."

Vivi weighed her choices. "I *should* like to finish my book. Miss Chatham disapproves of novel reading too, you see. But..." She closed her book, keeping one finger between the pages to mark her place. "I should also be very glad to understand something of the sciences."

For the first time that morning, Erica smiled, albeit in the manner of one accustomed to humoring children. But the gentle expression was quickly erased by a flicker of worry. She glanced over her shoulder at the bookcase where her journal had been laid aside, shifting *Introduction to Botany* in her arms like a burden she was eager to return to the shelf. "If I might have a word in private, Your Grace?"

Vivi's dark brows shot up her forehead as she looked at her brother. With the slightest lift of his shoulders and a wave of his hand, he motioned her back into her hiding place. She slid obligingly out of sight, back into the depths of the chair. He nodded toward Erica and the bookcase, indicating she should step to the other side of the room. He followed. Neither of them spoke, however, until they heard the reassuring flick of pages from Vivi's corner of the room.

"I am perfectly willing to teach your sister the rudiments of botany if both you and she wish it, Your Grace," Erica said, her voice low. She was still holding *Introduction to Botany* in one arm, her journal now stacked on top of it, and as she spoke, she laid one palm on both books in the posture of one taking an oath. "But I would not wish to proceed without making sure you understand that there are many who agree with your sister's governess. There is vigorous debate over the appropriateness of the subject for ladies."

By her expression he could guess his face revealed his bafflement. "Who could see harm in a lady's careful study of flowers?"

Her lips quirked with something that was not quite humor. "Anyone, forgive me, who knows much about plants." Carefully, she opened her journal to a pencil sketch of a flower, exquisitely done, every suggestive curve and hollow labeled in Latin terms that needed no translation. "There are those who believe that botany can never be suitable for ladies, because the fair sex must be thoroughly protected from knowledge of, well..."

She had been watching his face study the picture; now her gaze flickered away and back. "Sex."

Suddenly, the library felt much too warm. But the source of the heat was internal, a bright flame burning at his core, casting its glow into every dark corner of his being, and making him weigh the necessity of taking refuge behind the desk to hide his arousal.

Though she had kept her voice low, the last word seemed to reverberate around the room. He shot a glance over his shoulder, but Vivi remained fully absorbed in her book. "I—I see," he muttered as he turned back to face her, thunderstruck by the direction the conversation had taken and once more craving the cooling touch of the glass. "And your father did not object?"

"He did not. He is fond of saying that those who truly value a woman's innocence would do better not to promote her ignorance."

"A sound judgment." And a comfortable way to rationalize allowing Vivi to get closer to Erica. Never before had he used a child to gain an informant's trust. Would he be putting his sister in danger—of either the moral or the mortal variety—to do so now? "But my sister is not yet thirteen..."

"And possessed of an admirably curious mind. She will find ways to learn what she wishes to know, Your Grace, both about botany and...other matters." A pause. "Servants' gossip can be a dangerous teacher."

The words struck him like barbs, though of course she could have no way of knowing how pointed they were. "Indeed."

As if suddenly aware of his discomfort, she closed her journal and her voice took on a curiously formal, distant tone. "You may rest assured that Mr. Lee's work does not contain anything too scandalous. He does an admirable job of translating Linnaeus's ideas into more familiar language. Metaphors, if you will. Courtship, marriage, and the like." As she spoke, she returned the heavy volume to its place on the shelf, sliding it between two similarly dusty tomes. "Of course, the truth of the matter is that many plant, er, *relationships* are neither especially modest nor monogamous. Those showy blooms are not for naught, you see—not unlike how a lady's gown, if well fashioned, may catch the eyes of several different gentlemen at a ball."

Would he ever look at a lady's dress—at Erica—the same way? Or would he forever imagine her skirts as the curved petals of a flower hiding something extraordinary at their center? He swallowed hard. "Is there no other way to explain—?"

Disappointment flickered in the depths of her amber eyes. He could see she was mentally classing him with Miss Chatham. "I can think of one botanist who instead organizes the plant world into armies engaging in battles. Perhaps, as a soldier, you find that metaphor more suitable?"

From what he had overheard in the schoolroom, he could guess how Vivi would react to further talk of war. He shook his head and folded his arms over his chest. "Between combat and coquetry, regrettably, there is not much to choose."

Erica mirrored his posture and he was struck, not for the first time, by the notion that she would have made a formidable ally—or adversary—on the battlefield, for all that she was a head shorter than he. "Take heart, Your Grace. I have a theory that the study of botany is in fact the finest means of preparation for a young woman's entry into the marriage mart. One day, in the not too distant future, Lady Viviane will be paraded about in the finest gowns to catch the eye of the fattest purse with the loftiest title—in short"—her eyes flashed—"like every other delicate blossom, she'll be engaged in a battle for survival and wary every moment of being crushed."

Her words made him recall, as he would rather not, his dilemma with Caroline and her family's expectations, and he responded to Erica's unanticipated rancor with sharp words of his own. Words that he did not trouble to whisper. Words he regretted as soon as they passed his lips.

"And I suppose your own engagement was a love match?"

As soon as he spoke, he knew he had damaged his hopes of earning her trust, and with it, his plan to gain easy access to her journal. Worse, he was dangerously close to having to admit to himself that her journal was no longer his primary point of interest. Worst of all, he could offer no rational explanation for his callous words—for surely the flicker of jealousy he felt whenever he imagined her dearly departed paramour could not be called *rational*.

He waited for her to blush with either embarrassment or, more likely, fury. Instead she grew pale—so pale, he feared she might faint. With trembling hands, she snatched up her journal and tucked it against her breast, then swept from the room without speaking a word, without even indulging in the cold comfort of slamming the door behind her. Silence reigned over the room, except for the occasional rustle of paper as Vivi turned a page in her book.

After perhaps two minutes had passed, two minutes that felt like an hour, she closed her volume and unfolded herself from the chair. "Miss Burke has spirit," she declared. "I like her."

Tristan nodded. In spite of Erica's occasional outrageousness, in spite of Whitby's words of warning—hell, in spite of himself—he liked her too. And what a fine job he had done of showing her how much.

"If you are thinking of a way to apologize, you might offer to show her the conservatory," Vivi said, stepping closer, and he was struck afresh by the realization his sister was no longer a little girl. She had a knowing looking in her eye, and he suspected she had overheard every bit of his and Erica's conversation, even the parts that had gone unspoken. "It would be an excellent place for a botany lesson."

With a grateful smile, he settled an arm around Vivi's shoulders and gave them a squeeze. "It would," he said, and led her from the room.

Chapter 9

Erica set off with only the vaguest sense of her intended destination. Not because she was lost, but because she needed to walk, to work off the energy that coursed through her blood and animated her limbs. If she had not left the library, she would have spoken—or worse, acted—most unwisely. Something about the Duke of Raynham not knowing a love match if one slapped him across the face…followed by actions suited to her words.

All her life, she'd been impulsive. But rarely had she been so intemperate, so angry. Since the spring, however, her emotions had lingered close to the surface. Everything about Henry, including his proposal, was a reminder of what she'd never have. Because Tristan was right, the insufferable prig. It had *not* been a love match.

She'd known him from childhood, her elder brother's best friend. He had accepted her for who she was, just as she'd accepted him, and she had told herself it would be enough. More than enough. Her heart still ached, would perhaps always ache, whenever she thought of Henry, the sacrifices he'd been willing to make.

How dare that same heart hammer like raindrops on the roof whenever Tristan looked her way?

Henry had been gentle and laughing and, most of all, kind—in other words, everything the Duke of Raynham was not. Over the years, however, she'd also caught glimpses into the shadowy place that hid behind Henry's smiles. She had known what he wanted, what he feared. Whereas Tristan…

Well, perhaps that was part of the difficulty. Perhaps the two men were not so different after all. For despite Tristan's show of sternness and strength, she could not shake the feeling that he too had a secret. Some soft spot that had made necessary his hard, protective shell. The thorns that guarded the tender shoot beneath.

As did she, of course. As did probably every living being. Even a duke. How foolish to want to discover his.

A confrontation with a closed door put a stop to her peripatetic musings. Unbelievably, her wayward feet had taken her back to her chamber. If she'd tried, she couldn't have found a more direct route. With a sigh, she let herself in. Such a lovely, elegant room. And stuck in it, she felt as out of place as a weed in a crystal vase.

Through the large windows she watched gray clouds shed raindrops that coursed down the glass like tears. No matter how large, the room felt like a cell and the weather was her jailer. She didn't belong at Hawesdale Chase, and she didn't know what to do with herself. *The devil finds mischief for idle hands*, Mama was fond of saying. But the trouble wasn't really idleness. She glanced down at rough, stained fingers that had ruined a small fortune in embroidery silks before her mother had conceded defeat. The trouble was that her hands were no more proper than the rest of her.

The notion of teaching Lady Viviane had been a momentary bright spot. She'd never had the opportunity to share her knowledge. Not one of her younger siblings had ever expressed any interest in plants. But she'd put an end to that potential diversion with her talk of...

The blush that she'd managed to keep at bay in the library burst into flame on her cheeks at the memory. Not the memory of what she'd *said*, for that was simply science. Or nature, if one preferred.

But, oh, the memory of his face as she'd said it, the flare of shock in his face...and more than shock too. Something that had made his dark eyes darker still.

She had needed him to understand the controversy surrounding ladies and the study of botany. She would not have wanted to teach his sister without his knowledge and at least a modicum of support. But she would have lived much more comfortably without ever knowing what his face looked like when he set aside the mask he wore so habitually—that of the overbearing officer, the starchy duke—and showed himself to be a man with all-too-human and quite ungentlemanly desires.

Good heavens. Another moment and she'd be proving right all the naysayers who insisted that ladies ought to know as little as possible about...about...

"Sex."

She forced herself to say the word aloud, to break the spell her imagination seemed determined to cast. Curling her fingers into the soft leather cover of her journal, she made her way to the vanity table, for there was no desk in the room. The weather might have curtailed her research, but she could still work. She had drawings to refine and notes to organize. She would spend her day sitting right here, writing...

She had left the pens and ink in the library.

With a sigh, she flipped through the journal. Its pages crinkled crisply since they'd been wetted by the rain. Drawings, descriptions, observations, lists flickered past beneath her thumb. At her roughly sketched map of the house, she stopped, her progress impeded by the stub of a dull pencil still marking her place. It would have to serve.

No sooner had she settled to the task of translating her shorthand notes about the varieties of moss to be found in Shropshire than she heard a knock. A servant, perhaps, though she had not rung. Tucking the pencil between two pages, she rose and went to the door.

Tristan was the last person she expected to find on its other side.

"Miss Burke," he said, and dipped his head. "I had neither cause nor license to make such a remark. I've come to make amends for my behavior." He spoke stiffly, as might be expected from one without a great deal of experience in offering apologies. Though to be fair, his expression was sincere.

When he bowed, she could see that his sister stood behind him, arms folded, and Erica found the scene so familiar, she had to stifle a laugh. How many times had one of her elder siblings marched her before an authority to exact a confession of wrongdoing and to witness the gratifying spectacle of her punishment?

In this case, however, she gathered that Lady Viviane would gain no benefit from seeing someone slam a door in her brother's face.

"What sort of amends?" Erica asked instead, wary.

"We wish to show you the glasshouse," Viviane said.

"Hawesdale's conservatory houses more than a hundred varieties of plants, many of them tropical species," he explained. "And it has the added appeal of being always temperate, no matter the weather." As if on cue, a blast of rain and wind rattled the windows behind her. "You might study or sketch there to your heart's content."

His words—an echo of Henry's promise to give her time to fill every page in her journal—pierced to her very heart, far sharper than his jab at the notion of a love match, though of course he could have no way of knowing how the offer would affect her. In looking for somewhere safe, somewhere other than his face, to rest her eyes, she discovered he was carrying Lee's *Introduction to Botany*, along with the pens and ink she had abandoned.

"And we can begin our first lesson," added his sister.

Tristan sent a warning glance over one shoulder. "Now, Viv. Miss Burke has not agreed..."

Disappointment streaked across Viviane's thin face.

"A teacher ought never to deny a willing pupil, Your Grace," Erica said quickly. "And I'm sure the glasshouse is a lovely place."

His reply, when it came, seemed to require an unexpected degree of fortitude. "I'm told it was one of my mother's favorite haunts."

She nodded. "Let me get my journal."

* * * *

Inside the conservatory, the air steamed and the scent of peat filled Erica's nose. Her attention darted from one pot to the next. Plants she had known only through careful pen and ink drawings and pale watercolors burst into life around her: thick vines, delicate blossoms, sharp thorns.

Despite the dreary skies beyond, the glass-walled room was almost painfully bright, as well as deafeningly loud. Raindrops pounded against the roof and chased one another in erratic races down leaded window panes. She cowered against the assault on her senses, fighting the impulse to cover her ears, narrowing her gaze against the light and discovering as she did so that there were tears in her eyes.

At that very moment, Tristan turned to say something to his sister and glimpsed what she would have given anything to hide. "Are you all right, Miss Burke?"

"Yes, yes." She lifted one hand to dash away the evidence of her foolishness.

The movement drew Lady Viviane's attention. "You are disappointed by the conservatory?" she asked, her own expression less skeptical, more pained.

Disappointed? What a pallid word to describe the inconvenient emotions welling to the surface at this moment.

Erica looked from one to the other, and a hiccup of panic rose in her chest. What right had she to feel disappointment? Her lifelong dream was about to be realized. What did it matter that she stood in a greenhouse in Westmorland, where all had been arranged for easy perusal, like creatures in a menagerie: clipped, cataloged, and tamed?

And how ridiculous of her to feel grief—or was it guilt?—at the notion that Henry's fond promise was about to be fulfilled by the Duke of Raynham. Erica shook her head and blinked away the last persistent tears. "Not disappointed—never that." As she drew in deep lungfuls of the humid air, a sort of peace dripped into her veins, keeping time with the drumming rain. This was her element—or as close to it as she would likely ever get. "I am grateful. Your brother has been..." *Some other word. Any other word.* "Kind."

Tristan still watched her with furrowed brow, as if he suspected her of being not entirely truthful. But before he could speak, they were interrupted by the approach of a man wearing a heavy apron. His face was weathered, his head bald but for a fringe of white above his ears. "Miss Burke, allow me to introduce Mr. Sturgess, the head gardener. Miss Burke is something of an expert on plants."

Mr. Sturgess's frown rivaled his employer's. "That so?" His eyes flickered over the journal she clutched in her arms. "Suppose you want to make a few pretty pictures of flowers 'n the like?"

"We will not interfere with your work, sir," she promised, with a tip of her chin to include Lady Viviane.

The word *we* visibly increased the man's discomfort with the plan. Clearly, he had not anticipated the double threat of having his greenhouse invaded by two women. Still, he conceded with a nod, and she laid her notebook on the empty corner of a nearby table. Beside it, Tristan made a neat stack of the textbook, the pens, and the ink bottle. The knuckles of one long-fingered hand brushed the spine of her journal, and for some reason, she had to quell a shiver.

"Thank you, Your Grace."

"Will I show you around?" Mr. Sturgess's posture was a curious mixture of resentment and pride as he gestured with one arm toward a long row of potted plants and watched warily as Erica preceded him.

In the center of the rectangular room, under the very peak of the glass roof, stood a stone circle filled with orange trees and ringed by wrought-iron benches. She and the gardener walked toward it between two rows of waist-high tables, past the bright colors and heady scents of gardenias and orchids, while Tristan and Viviane passed between two more sets of tables covered by ferns and even a few cacti. Beyond the miniature orange grove, four more rows of tables formed three paths to another door. "To the kitchen," Mr. Sturgess explained, as she noted the various vegetables, herbs, and medicinal plants nearest the exit.

Heedless of her gown, Erica knelt and touched her fingertips to the stone floor. "How is it kept warm?"

"Well, now, that's down to a fancy bit o' Roman engineering. A fire's kept burnin' at that end"—Mr. Sturgess nodded toward the door through which they'd entered—"and the heat passes through channels underground. Comes up through vents in the floor." He pointed to small, periodic openings beneath the tables. "We keep the plants that like it hottest nearest the fire."

Her mind reeled at any attempt to calculate the window tax on a room made entirely of glass, or the price of the coal required to keep it temperate. Tristan was watching her, his gaze hooded. Perhaps he was performing similar arithmetic. She half expected him to decry the extravagance.

But of course, some one of his ancestors must have ordered the conservatory built, and his father must have seen to it that it was stocked and maintained, perhaps to please his mother. And with more than half its space taken up by plants that benefitted the estate in some manner, either as food or medicine, no one could call it an entirely useless expenditure.

"Ingenious." She stood and dusted off her hands.

Tristan turned to his sister. "I should go. But I leave you in Miss Burke's capable hands," he told her, "and you"—his gaze lifted to Erica—"under the watchful gaze of Mr. Sturgess."

Erica's knee bent in a curtsy. "And who will keep an eye on you, Your Grace?" She hardly knew from whence the teasing words had come.

Tristan's expression tightened. What had been open became opaque, and despite the room's heat, a chill tickled along her spine. Mr. Sturgess looked away, uncertain what to make of Erica's presumption. Viviane, however, laughed. "Miss Pilkington, I daresay," she teased.

Something like a smile twisted across Tristan's lips. But he said nothing, merely bowed to them both and gestured for the gardener to accompany him to the door, speaking low as they walked away. In another moment, he was gone.

Viviane asked, "Where shall we begin our study, Miss Burke?"

"At the warmest end of the room," Erica said as soon as Tristan's broad shoulders disappeared through the doorway. "We shall imagine ourselves as far away from this cold, wet day as we can. Somewhere on the banks of the Amazon should do it, I think."

One arm upraised, the girl forged her way across the conservatory, a dauntless explorer. As she followed, Erica sent an apologetic glance at Mr. Sturgess. She expected him to ignore them and resume his duties now that the duke was gone. But he approached them with shuffling steps. "In case you have questions," he said.

He was relishing this moment in the spotlight, she realized. Had Tristan known he would? "I did hope you might tell us the history of a few of these more unusual specimens, Mr. Sturgess."

"'Spose I've got the time," he replied with a weary-sounding sigh.

Trying to hide her smile, she collected her journal and busied herself with finding a blank page, as the gardener began to explain how plants from South America and the Far East had come to be under his care. Afterward, she gave Viviane a brief lesson, as bland as she could make it, in the parts of a flower and their various functions, then set her to work sketching the pinnate leaf of a fern suitable for a beginner's talents.

Once Viviane was occupied, Erica turned her attention to a wild vine that wound its way up and around a trellis surrounding the doorway: a *Passiflora caerulea* that had survived the journey from Brazil. Certainly nothing she had expected to find on a journey to the Lakes.

"A gift to the late duchess, I'm told." Sturgess spoke behind her.

"The present duke's mother?" He nodded. "I understand she loved plants."

The gardener lifted one shoulder in a shrug. "Mebee. Before my time, miss."

Erica glanced toward Viviane, who was still bent over the fern leaf. Though she suspected the girl had overheard more of the conversation in the library than was wise, she seemed perfectly indifferent or perhaps oblivious to the current one. The noise of the rain against the glass was terrific, and their voices were low. Still, Erica dropped hers almost to a whisper when she asked, "Does the duke make frequent visits to the conservatory?"

"Never, in my experience," Sturgess said with a shake of his bald head. "You could have knocked me over with a feather when I saw him walk through the door."

"I wonder why he stays away." She let her gaze drift over the beauty that surrounded them.

"Couldn't say, miss." He fished a small pair of clippers from a pocket on his apron and fingered them absently as he spoke. "But folks do say he likes things orderly—always has, even when he was lad. Bit too dirty and wild in here for his taste, p'rhaps." He snapped the clippers shut, as if pruning a useless branch. "Well, I'd best get back to my work and not keep you from yours."

With a nod, the gardener returned to the kitchen end of the conservatory. She watched him until he began watering a row of seedlings, then opened her journal and prepared to begin a thorough study of one of the *Passiflora*'s palm-sized blooms, a corona of pale petals starred with purple filaments.

Any attempt to capture the complex flower would require complete concentration.

Instead, her mind still flitted to and fro like a butterfly at midsummer. Did the butterflies and bees relish the exotic delicacies of the Hawesdale conservatory? Or did they politely decline and declare to one another that the fare was simply too rich or too strange? Like gaudily dressed rustics at a town ball, suspiciously eyeing the epicurean delights of the supper table...

She caught herself tapping the end of her pencil against her journal, mimicking the erratic rhythm of the raindrops. With a shake of her head, she set herself once more to her task.

On the sixth such starting over, she thumped her journal down on the nearest table, not thinking how such a display of temper might look. Frowning over her leaf, Viviane did not appear to notice. Mr. Sturgess, however, cast her an assessing look, then left the conservatory through the door nearest the kitchen. Briefly, she wondered if he had gone to ask for assistance in removing her for making a disturbance.

After a few moments, however, he returned, something clutched in either hand. When he was within a yard from her, he held out a plain holland apron in the pinafore style, intended to protect her dress—or rather, the dress that the Duchess of Raynham had loaned to her. With a smile of gratitude, she slipped the apron on. Then he opened the fingers of his other hand. On his palm lay two bits of creamy white fluff.

"Cotton wool," he explained in a louder than usual voice. "For your ears. Hard to concentrate with all that racket." With his free hand, he pointed up to the rain-battered roof, and as he turned his head, she could see he had stuffed his own ears with the batting.

With an uncertain smile, she accepted the gift. When he walked away again, she furtively tucked a tuft in each ear. The sound of the rain still came to her, but was muffled now by the thrum of blood in her veins.

How odd she must look. If Tristan could see her now, would his dark eyes dance with suppressed laughter? Or would they turn cold instead?

He likes things orderly, Mr. Sturgess had said. No one would ever apply that word to Erica. But perhaps it explained his willingness to marry his late brother's fiancée. Their wedding would certainly tie up any loose ends.

Did perfect ladies, like Miss Caroline Pilkington, ever think odd thoughts or say odd things?

Erica squeezed her eyelids shut, drew three deep breaths. Her mind might be distractible, but her heart was steady.

Steady.

Steady.

* * * *

Guin raised the fan of playing cards, but not high enough to hide the sudden lift of two delicate eyebrows. To Tristan's left, Miss Pilkington gave a small cough. Her partner, Sir Thomas, was less circumspect.

"Oh, ho, Raynham," the baronet chortled. "If I didn't know better, I'd suspect you of trying to lose."

Tristan looked down at the small pile of cards lying face up in the center of the table, his own uppermost. Trumps, when he ought to have thrown off and let his partner take the trick. Guin's blue eyes sparkled above her cards, darting quickly to Caroline and back to Tristan.

"My apologies, ma'am," he said, dipping his head to Guin as he snapped his remaining cards face-up onto the table, conceding the hand. "I will confess to being distracted just now."

If Caroline suspected herself the cause of his distraction, she gave no sign of it as she gathered the cards to herself and prepared to shuffle. Her hands were pale and smooth, her movements deliberate. Though both her hair and eyes were ordinary shades of brown, no one would hesitate to describe her as pretty. He could complain of nothing in her behavior: She was neither shrinking nor forward, but assured and confident in her manner. She talked knowledgeably but not pedantically about every subject he had introduced at dinner, from the paintings in the Long Gallery where they'd strolled earlier, to the negative repercussions of the Poor Laws. If she did not precisely grieve for his brother, she made clear her regret at his untimely death, and not simply for its effect on her own prospects. She was pragmatic, polished—in short, the perfect bride for a man his position, just as Guin had said.

Lydgate laughed, silently this time, though his red face and jiggling belly made no secret of his amusement. "Distracted *just now?*" he echoed in a breathless mutter, wiping a tear from his eye. "Say rather, all day." Tristan made no attempt at denial.

But Miss Pilkington bore no blame—or credit—for his current state.

Thanks to Whitby's words the night before, he'd spent most of the day observing his guests with the practiced eye of an intelligence officer. His efforts had indeed uncovered several bits of new information: Sir Thomas sighted along a billiard cue no better than he sighted along a hunting rifle; Beresford and Lady Lydgate were indulging in a flirtation; and Lady Easton Pilkington suffered from the megrims when it rained.

Whitby had been similarly occupied. After dinner, rather than take port with the gentlemen, David had taken tea with the ladies. For his sacrifice, he had learned that the five shades of green embroidery thread in Mrs. Newsome's sewing box were not to be intermingled, even in an effort to help detangle them, and that Lord Easton Pilkington snored, which surely contributed to his wife's headaches.

With a nod to his partner and his opponents, Tristan pushed away from the card table. "You will excuse me, I hope." Caroline looked up at him with perfect equanimity and smiled. If she minded his attention, or lack thereof, he would never know it.

He did not think he had ever been less curious about a matter in his life.

His place at the card table was quickly taken up by Beresford, who seemed to understand the wisdom of putting some distance between himself and the baronet's wife. Nevertheless, Lady Lydgate followed and stood behind him, inches from her oblivious husband, commenting on Beresford's play with very little subtly and running her fingertips along the top rail of his chair with even less.

How insipid it all was, especially to one who had known real intrigue. Real adventure. Real danger. Cards, billiards, flirtations—oh, he'd known agents to indulge in such diversions. Sometimes to encourage a subject of interest to reveal more than he, or she, ought. And sometimes because espionage was a waiting game and boredom must be countered.

But this…? Well, he very much feared that this was simply life at Hawesdale. The life to which he must look forward if he could not return to the field.

Mustering a pretense of aimlessness, he made his way to the windows facing the courtyard at the back of the house. The rainy night sky absorbed the light. He could see nothing but his own reflection. Leaning closer to the glass, he searched for some sign of life beyond this room and caught the distant gleam of the conservatory, where a lantern still burned, turning the glasshouse into a rough-cut diamond.

Sturgess had promised to send word when Erica left the conservatory. Before dinner, Viviane had reported in notes ringing with amazement that she had left Miss Burke still bent over her journal, sketching, "and likely to get a crick in her neck." Tristan had assumed that further lack of news from that front indicated that Miss Burke's behavior had done nothing to arouse Sturgess's suspicions. She'd not joined the rest of the party for the meal, but at the time, Tristan had attributed her absence to yesterday's debacle.

But what if she had simply never left the conservatory? He glanced back at the mantel clock. Surely no one as restless as she could bear to be confined in a single room for some fourteen hours?

Turning away from the window, he surveyed his guests. Behind him, the card game went on, his absence no doubt having improved play immeasurably. Near the fire, Mrs. Newsome stabbed at her embroidery. Whitby sat beside her, holding her sewing box but not daring to touch its contents. Lord Easton and the vicar faced one another over the chessboard, though neither appeared to be engaged in the game: Mr. Newsome rattled on about something while Lord Easton looked on the verge of sleep.

Without drawing attention to his movements, Tristan crossed the floor and slipped out the door, startling the footman who waited on its other side. He shook his head sharply, putting an end to the servant's fumbling attempt to make himself useful. In a matter of moments, he found himself standing before the door to the conservatory. He peered through the small, square window in the top and saw Erica perched on a high stool, bent over her journal, which lay open on the table before her, in precisely the posture his sister had described.

Had she been sitting there all this time? Not exactly the sort of behavior he would expect from someone eager to explore the house. But still suspicious. Yesterday, Erica hadn't been able to sit still for three minutes together—pacing, fidgeting, spilling her wine.

Had all that been an act?

Gathering his resolve, Tristan grasped the door handle and turned it. He made no particular effort to be quiet—the hinges were prone to rust and squeaked, his boot heels rang on the flagstone floor—but Erica did not lift her head from her work or give any sign of noting his approach. Even when he cleared his throat, her journal continued to absorb her entire attention, until he stepped close enough that his shadow must have fallen across its pages and she jumped.

This time, dirt rather than wine arced into the air, the contents of an otherwise empty flowerpot that went spinning across the table when her arm swung out in surprise. Her pencil too skittered away, and the journal slid onto the floor and fell facedown and open at his feet.

No Gaelic blasphemies this time. No plain English curses either.

Just wide-eyed surprise. A sharp breath drawn in through flared nostrils, lifting her breasts. And trembling hands as she fumbled to collect her journal.

Swiftly, he knelt and reached it a moment before she did, his fingertips skimming over its leather spine to grasp the thick paper of its pages. The temptation to pick it up and leaf through its contents made his fingers twitch against its cover.

Then her outstretched hand touched his. Wobbling slightly in her crouched position, she steadied herself rather than immediately withdrawing her fingers. Reluctantly, he lifted his eyes and met hers, warm and golden brown and wide. A day spent in the damp heat of the conservatory had pinked her cheeks and left her skin dewy. A halo of fine red curls framed her face, and her lower lip curved invitingly, rosy and slightly swollen, as if she'd been worrying it between her teeth while she worked.

Exactly how she would look if she'd been thoroughly kissed.

He closed his hand around the book and snapped it shut as he stood. With an impatient flick of one wrist, he slapped its leather cover against his open palm, hoping the sting would restore some fragment of his good sense. How many chances to examine the journal did he expect to get? But he would not learn anything of value from a quick glance. He needed time to study its pages thoroughly.

She rose a beat behind, and before she could extend her palm to demand the journal's return, he held it out to her. Almost warily, she took it from him.

"I apologize for startling you," he said as she brushed dirt from the book's worn cover and turned it over in her hands, inspecting it for damage.

"Hm? Oh." With one hand she tucked the journal against her chest, while with the other she reached toward the side of her head, the movement furtive, a little embarrassed. Quickly, as if she hoped he would not notice, she plucked a bit of cotton wool from each ear. "Mr. Sturgess recommended it, to muffle the noise of the rain," she explained. "So I—oh." Her voice, which had been slightly louder than necessary, dropped almost to a whisper. "Has the rain stopped?"

He made no attempt to hide the smile that had sprung to his lips. "Almost. The locals would tell you it's mizzlin'."

She looked as if she were emerging from a trance. Her eyes flickered to the darkness beyond the windows. "Is it—very late?"

"Rather." As he took a step closer, he glanced around the room, which had always before struck him as an odd, artificial space. Now he saw its strange beauty: the warmth, the windows misted with steam, the profusion of plants creating the sort of lush bower in which mankind's First Parents had been tempted to sin. "I'm glad the conservatory could furnish some distraction from the weather. I take it you found something worthy of your attention?"

"Oh, yes." She nodded, breathless with excitement. "Passion."

The temperature in the room seemed to rise a few degrees more. "I beg your pardon?"

"*Passiflora caerulea*. Blue passionflower." She nearly brushed against him as she walked past, her eyes fixed on the plant behind him. "I had seen pictures, of course, but never thought to see it in bloom."

Though he found the glow on her face far more compelling than any plant, he forced himself to turn and look in the direction she had indicated. Some sort of tropical vine had been trained to climb the wall surrounding the doorway. As he glanced over its profusion of green leaves, he did not immediately see the flower to which she referred.

"An extraordinary blossom." With a delicate touch, she drew her finger along the pale, puckered cluster of petals that drooped from one branch. "And it lasts only a day. I knew I might never have such a chance again."

Tristan could both understand and appreciate single-mindedness, though at present he was having difficulty concentrating on the flower. His eye persisted in wandering to the woman beside it. Worse, his mind—and a few other organs besides—seemed content to ignore the real possibility that she was a spy determined to ruin him. He needed to regain control, to shift the conversation onto safer ground.

"My sister did not share your enthusiasm, I take it?"

She drew to her full height. He recognized a defensive posture when he saw one. "I would not expect it of her—of anyone," she said, a little sharply. "But in fact she was a most eager pupil. When Mrs. Dean came to announce dinner, I urged her to leave. I did not want her fervor to fall victim to fatigue."

He noted Erica's pallor, the stiffness of her movement. "And what of you, Miss Burke? Surely you must be tired. And hungry. Have you eaten nothing all day?"

"Mrs. Dean was kind enough to bring me a tray." With one hand, she gestured toward it, still sitting on the table, mostly untouched. The fingers of her other hand played nervously over the cover of her journal. "After Lady Viviane left."

"So long ago as that?"

"I knew I had but a few hours with the *Passiflora*, Your Grace. You see..." Fumbling with her journal, she found a page and extended it to him. With a hand he willed not to tremble with eagerness, he reached out for the book. But she did not release it. So together, they held it while he studied the sketches she had made, different views of a spectacular bloom that made him wonder what it would be like to be the whole focus of her attention. "In light of that, how could I concern myself with such mundane matters as dinner?" She swayed slightly, not quite steady on her feet.

He released the book. "Then you must concern yourself with them now." Daring to step closer, he set his palm at the small of her back, urging her toward the far door and the kitchen beyond. "Come."

Chapter 10

The drop in temperature from the conservatory to the kitchen sent a shiver down Erica's spine. Tristan must have felt it pass through her. She told herself not to ascribe any meaning to his touch—or to its absence, for his hand dropped away as soon as the door swung closed behind them, making her shiver again. He stepped to the enormous hearth, where the fire had been carefully banked, and stoked it into life once more. Almost involuntarily, she glided closer to its warmth. Closer to him.

In the firelight's glow, the outlines of tomorrow's breakfast, already laid out by the kitchen staff—loaves of bread under a cloth, a basket of eggs waiting to be broken and coddled, a flitch of bacon—grew distinct. Her stomach gave a low rumble.

"Sit."

His voice of command was softened by the unexpected coziness of the kitchen. Or perhaps her usual resistance was weakened by hunger. Either way, she sank onto the bench beside a scarred worktable, still facing the fire, and watched him as he moved efficiently around the room, collecting the remains of dinner and liberating a fresh, crusty loaf from its flimsy linen fortress.

"I would not have guessed a duke would know his way around a kitchen." As she spoke, she turned partly toward the table, allowing the heat from the fireplace to soak into the weary muscles of her back. How many hours had she spent bent over her sketches?

"I have not always been a duke," he pointed out.

She tried to imagine him as a small boy, sneaking down to the kitchen for a treat. The behavior seemed out of character, but even if he had done it, the staff would never have dared to scold him. "Always the son of one, though." He stilled. Just for a moment, but long enough for her to realize her misstep. "I'm sorry. That was thoughtless of me. You must miss your father a great deal. I did not mean to—"

With one hand, he brushed aside her fumbling apology. "Regrettably, loss is common—as you yourself know." In the semi-darkness, his eyes glittered and held her gaze. She recalled his words in the library that morning and, once again at the reference to Henry, part of her longed to make some escape. This time, however, Tristan was the first to move, striding toward the opposite side of the room. "We must learn to bear up under our grief."

Had she borne up under hers? Or had she tried to shrug off the burden? Begging her father for her dowry, pleading with her sister to leave Dublin, hoping to put the past behind her...

Whereas Tristan had been required to confront his past, to return to his childhood home, to assume a role he likely had never expected to assume. She'd seen evidence of his reluctance to come back, but he had done it nonetheless. *Folks do say he likes things orderly—always has, even when he was lad.* Military life must have suited him well.

"Were you stationed in Paris?"

Dishes rattled against one another as if something had been dropped on them, and Tristan's head emerged from the depths of a cupboard. "I beg your pardon?"

She managed a feeble smile. "You are not yet accustomed to non sequitur in my conversation, Your Grace? I had been thinking this must have been a difficult homecoming for you. And I remembered that your sister mentioned you had been in France. Which naturally made me think of Paris... I hear it's lovely. Or rather, *was.*"

His answering smile was strained. "Regrettably, Miss Burke, I am not at liberty to satisfy you as to the particulars."

"Oh." Despite the ache in her back, she sat up a little straighter. "Of course."

He came toward the table, bearing stoneware plates and plain flatware—presumably the china and silver used by the family were kept elsewhere, under lock and key. "But you do well to remember that I am a soldier." After setting down his burden, he gestured with that same arm toward the makeshift banquet now crowding the table. "A resourceful one."

Did he expect her to believe he spent his days cooking and serving? She took up a cold leg of chicken and pointed it at him. "An *officer.*"

"It is not the life of ease you imagine it to be," he said, joining her on the sturdy bench.

A sudden memory of touching him yesterday morning, his solidly muscled chest disguised beneath layers of wool and silk and linen, made her fingertips tingle. Reflexively she reached for her journal with her other hand, finding it on the bench between them and moving it to her lap. "No. No, I haven't been imagining any such thing."

"It bothers you." His voice was matter of fact as he began to pile food on a plate. "That I'm a soldier."

Did it? She rather suspected it ought to bother her more.

What right-thinking Irishwoman would admit her fascination with an English duke and a British soldier? Surely this was a betrayal of Henry's memory and the cause for which he had given his life.

But even as she thought it, she knew Henry would have been the very last person to fault her. The person she seemed to be most in danger of betraying here was herself.

"You *were* a soldier," she corrected, daring once more to contradict him. "Now you're a duke."

"May not a man be both?" He set the full plate before her.

Ignoring it, she took a bite of chicken instead, chewed thoughtfully, swallowed. "I daresay a man may be most anything he chooses. Men are fortunate in their freedoms, and wealthy noblemen most of all."

"Am I harboring a radical, Miss Burke? A leveler?" His voice teased, but his tight jaw and narrowed eyes told another story. Her elder brother was a barrister, and she had once seen that very expression on his face in the courtroom as he interrogated a criminal. The tension only heightened when Tristan added, in a wary voice, "Perhaps a Jacobin?"

Laying aside the chicken, she picked up her fork and stabbed a shade too violently at the contents of her plate. Something that might have been aspic jiggled. "Two days ago, I was accused of being an Irish rebel. I had no idea a botanist touring the countryside to examine the local flora was assumed to be a dangerous creature. Perhaps I ought to study the moral of Captain Whitby's story about the poets more carefully."

His lips curved into a smile. But only after his eyes had scoured her face, leaving her certain he had ways of reading whatever secrets were written on her soul. Her fingertips tightened automatically around the spine of her journal. When he spoke, his soft voice curled around her like the heat of the fire, sending off sparks of—alarm? *Oh, let it be alarm.*

"Wandering women are the most dangerous kind," he said, looking for all the world like the kind of man who thrived on danger.

She swallowed hard, though she had not taken another bite of food. "Must everything—every*one* follow the same straight line, the same narrow path?" she asked once she trusted her voice. "In nature, one sees little respect for such artificial boundaries. Even the tamest farm animals break down fences, and plants' roots tunnel under walls. Only in humans do we seem to expect domestication as the natural state." She prodded at the abandoned chicken leg. "Perhaps some people—some women—are simply not meant to stay at home."

He gave her words a thorough weighing before he spoke. "And you are such a woman."

Not a question, steeped in curiosity and judgment. A simple statement of fact. Of understanding, too? But not even her family really understood. The prickle of awareness along her spine intensified until it took every ounce of willpower she possessed to keep from leaping to her feet. As if she could shake free of the sensation of his touch. As if she could outrun her longing for it.

Instead she drew a shaky breath and dug her fork into a piece of apple pie, fully expecting Tristan to chide her for eating dessert before she had finished her meal. But if he were tempted to do so, he held his tongue. Her second breath rattled a little less, and the third felt almost normal.

The spicy-sweet tang of the first bite of pie made her give an involuntary hum of pleasure, but it caught in her throat when he said, "Which, I confess, makes me curious about the fact that you spent the whole day, and evening, sitting in one place." He walked his fingers around the edge of his still-empty plate as he spoke.

She coughed and said, "I've told you—"

His fingers left the plate to brush aside her words. "The flower, yes." He did not, however, raise his eyes to hers.

Clearly, he found her interest in the rare, short-lived bloom an inadequate explanation. And when she thought back over their previous encounters, she believed she understood why. He imagined her restlessness a mere physical behavior, not a manifestation of her deeper...*peculiarity*.

"When I told you I am not always ladylike, I did not refer exclusively to an excess of *bodily* energy—"

The corner of one dark brow lifted; she did not need to see more to imagine its sardonic arc.

Oh, she ought not to be discussing *bodies* at all. Certainly not with a man. Not when they were alone. Alone in a room so dimly lit they had to sit close enough to touch just to see one another's faces. No, she would *not* blush. She absolutely would not blush.

She blushed.

"My—m-my mind—" Could he feel the flame spreading across her cheeks? Certainly, if he lifted his fingers to her cheeks, or brushed his lips across...

"Your mind is prone to wandering, too?" He spoke in the sort of soft, soothing, coaxing voice she imagined a physician might use when examining a patient bound for Bedlam.

"No. I mean—well, yes. It does. Terribly sometimes. Or rather—" She sucked in another breath. From the sudden frown on his face, visible even in profile, she guessed that this time she wouldn't be at leisure to take three. "I would not say it wanders, exactly. Wandering implies aimlessness, a leisurely drift from place to place, or subject to subject. My thoughts seem to bounce along, rather like a trotting horse."

Those words captured his full attention. He was still leaning forward, bent toward his plate, but his head turned enough that he could fix her with one eye. The firelight caught the hard turn of his jaw, gleaming along the growth of a day's beard. It must indeed be late. Would the stubble feel rough to touch? Or smooth yet sharp, like the edge of a knife...?

Her fork clattered onto her plate as she reached down to clamp one hand tightly around the other, both around her journal, determined to keep herself from indulging her curiosity.

She saw his gaze dart to the movement of her hands, then back to her face. "It would seem botanists enjoy employing metaphor," he said, rather wryly. "Very well. A trot is steady, efficient..."

"For an experienced rider, yes." She nodded, pressing her hands so firmly into her lap that she had to sit up straighter. "But the novice is likely to be jolted and jarred, fearful of being thrown, exhausted after a quarter of an hour—to say nothing of a day." His silence left a void that her words rushed to fill. "Regrettably, despite a lifetime of experience, I have not entirely mastered the pace and sometimes find myself in danger of being unseated."

He was watching her warily, and why not? She sounded like a madwoman. *Oh, God.* Why had she ventured to explain to him what no one had ever understood?

"But when I'm focused on certain tasks," she continued, forcing herself to look away from him, "on plants, particularly—the intricacies of a flower, the pattern of a leaf—the pace changes."

"To a walk?"

Did he ask out of genuine curiosity? Or was his question mocking? She dared not look at him to determine which. "No. More like a...a canter, I'd say," she said, plowing ahead with the analogy. "Deceptively smooth.

Dangerously fast. Too easy to find yourself miles from where you started and totally lost."

"Hence a dozen hours spent in the conservatory without realizing how much time had gone by," he said after a moment. She let her chin wobble and hoped it would pass for a nod. After another long silence, he spoke again. "You should eat." Not, for once, a command. But even if it had been, she would have complied, for it was abundantly clear she needed something to occupy both her mouth and her hands.

To the sound of little more than the chink of utensils against stoneware, she finished the pie, returned to the plateful of chicken, herb pudding, and creamed turnips, even sampled the aspic. Despite her current unease, after passing the better part of the day without food, her appetite was voracious.

Though she tried to pay no attention to Tristan, she knew when he cut a piece of pie for himself, knew too that he prodded it with his fork, never raising a bite to his lips.

"Sometimes I fear..." he began after a long silence. "That is, I wonder... Did you see any evidence that my sister suffers from a similar...disorder in her thinking?"

If she had not already been sitting stiffly, his words would have drawn her upright. "I do not *suffer*, Your Grace, except under the judgments of others. And if your sister—"

"Forgive me. I chose my words poorly." Pushing aside his plate, he turned toward her, and his expression was grave, filled with something she had never expected to see written on his face. *Uncertainty.* A weak smile lifted one corner of his mouth. "As I seem prone to do of late. I only meant—"

She set down her fork but kept her fingers on its handle, rather than laying them on his arm as she was sorely tempted to do. "I understand. The truth of the matter is, Your Grace, I do not know Lady Viviane well enough to answer. She gives every indication of being a clever girl, an eager pupil—"

"Too clever for her own good, according to some."

The very words Miss Chatham had spoken. In her mind's eye, Erica could see the woman's disapproving posture. Did he know? "Too clever for her governess, at any rate," she agreed. "Perhaps another—?" But the words were hardly out of her mouth before his broad shoulders drooped in defeat, and she understood then that Miss Chatham was only the latest in a long line of failed teachers. "You must not give up hope," she tried to reassure him. "The right person is out there. You must find someone who understands—"

"What it's like to have one's mind always flitting from one subject to the next?" There was a note of skepticism in his voice, as if he struggled to imagine anything so thoroughly out of his control.

"I daresay we're not such rare specimens." She spoke before she thought, as she too often did. Now he was studying her intently, with an eagerness in his expression that presaged some brilliant idea. A proposal—though not of marriage. His lips parted, and instinctively she shook her head before he could speak. "Or perhaps not. One such as I would make a poor teacher indeed. Your sister requires a governess who is compassionate, but who can also model proper, ladylike behavior."

Ladylike behavior. The words acted like charm, breaking the momentary spell that had held him. He drew back slightly. "Yes. Yes, of course. I have worried that if she continues in this course, her prospects may be altered…"

"They may well be, Your Grace. But not necessarily for the worse." The prickliness had returned to her voice. "She is, after all, the daughter of a duke."

A whisper of breath escaped his lips, neither a sigh nor a laugh. "She is that."

He rose and lifted the kettle from the hob, where it had been murmuring merrily, not quite to the point of whistling.

"Tea?" she asked, hopeful.

He poured steaming water into a basin, then stepped back to the table to gather the remains of the food and return it to the cupboard. "I'm afraid not—not without waking Mrs. Dean, that is," he added with a smile. "She guards the tea chest more stringently than the silver."

"Then what—?"

But she did not need to finish her question. He had shrugged out of his coat and was rolling up lace-edged sleeves in a manner that would surely give his valet heart palpitations; the view of his corded forearms was having a similar effect on her.

"As I said," he told her, flicking a dollop of soap into the basin, "the army has taught me resourcefulness."

"Surely you must have a servant? Even…abroad," she added, avoiding any mention of where, sensing his discomfort at her earlier mention of France.

"Not always."

He held out his hand for her empty plate, but she rose and brought it to him, snatching a towel from the drying rack near the fire as she passed. She had little familiarity or felicity with domestic tasks, but at least she was wearing an apron.

"I see no need to make more work for my servants." He plunged her plate into the soapy water.

"They will thank you for thinking of them, I'm sure." Though she wasn't quite sure it was true. It required no great stretch of imagination to see him as the servants here must: a stern taskmaster, difficult to please. Would the kitchen staff wake to discover his visit below stairs and think it a criticism of their efforts? A threat to their positions? Perhaps the only person employed at Hawesdale who seemed to look with any particular favor on the advent of the new duke was Miss Chatham, and that did not seem to bode well for anyone.

"Well, anyway," she said, "no one should be surprised. Everyone seems to know that you like things kept orderly." He laughed, the sound full-throated, if not precisely genuine. "Mr. Sturgess thinks that's why you avoid the conservatory," she added, and immediately wished she had not, for at those words, he dunked another plate into the wash water with such vigor she feared it would crack. Desperate for some occupation, she snatched the clean, soapy plate from his hand and dipped it into a second basin of clear water. "I'm sure he only meant..." She made a circle in the air with the plate, searching for the proper description. But wordsmithing was her elder sister's skill, and so she fell back on what the gardener had actually said. "He thinks you must find it too dirty. Too wild."

"Does he, now?" Tristan's voice was soft. Too soft. Another chill tickled down her spine. She waited for him to speak again, but he said nothing more. The remaining items were washed in a moment's time, and once she had dried them, he took them from her and returned them to their proper places. Soon, the only remaining evidence of their late-night feast was the cut loaf. Though it had been put back beside the other loaves, the linen dipped tellingly where the now-missing portion had once held the cloth aloft.

After taking her towel to dry his hands, Tristan knelt to bank the fire again. Mesmerized, she watched the flex of his muscles beneath the thin, silky fabric of his shirt. The flames sank. In another few minutes, the room would return to darkness. Still, the strange intimacy of the place and the moment kept her rooted to the spot. Where was her usual impulse to hurry away?

"And you, Miss Burke," he said at last. "Did you find the glasshouse dirty and wild?"

"Yes, I suppose I did—in the most delightful way. Thank you for sharing it with me. I think...I think it may be the only room in all of Hawesdale

Chase in which I do not feel out of place." In the conservatory, she could be...*herself.*

He continued to stare into the glowing embers and made no reply.

"I should go." Even in the silent room, the sound of her voice was nearly lost.

He cast a look over his shoulder before rising and turning to face her. "I'll escort you back to your room," he said, reaching for his coat.

"I can find it myself." She snatched up her journal from the bench. "I have my map."

The corners of his lips lifted, though she would hesitate to describe it as a smile. "Indeed you do. Good night, then, Miss Burke."

"Good night, Your Grace."

Back in her room, a candle had been left burning, but the fireplace was cold. The clock on the mantel read a few minutes after midnight. She removed the damp apron and wrapped herself in a silk shawl, one of the duchess' many generosities, then sat down on the bed to review the day's sketches, as was her habit. At home, her coverlet was a frequent casualty of just this sort of late-night perusal: wrinkles, a muddy shoeprint, ink stains from a dropped pen or even an overturned bottle. Tonight, however, she was careful to remove her shoes and to use only a pencil, adjusting a line here, adding a note there, most in her own shorthand Latin.

She was tired, but not sleepy, and away from the conservatory, her mind once more darted in a dozen different directions. Cami and Lord Ashborough. The washed-out bridge. Lady Viviane. The characteristics of the star-like blooms that became apples suitable for pie-making.

And the Duke of Raynham, of course.

Out of habit, she began to make lists. Experience had taught her the best way to keep all her worrying and wondering from melting together like different colors of hot wax, making an ugly, insoluble mess. Three columns, each with its heading:

Important things.

Insignificant things.

Things that require further reflection.

Dutifully, she sorted her thoughts into each, feeling a sense of pride at her triumph over the impending chaos. Until she discovered she'd written a certain name three times, once in each column.

As the journal fanned shut around her pencil, it turned the front, back, and side views of the *Passiflora* into a sort of moving picture. After tonight, she could make a similar series of sketches of Tristan in his various moods. A portrait of a duke up to his elbows in a dishpan would surely be a curiosity.

Whatever had possessed her to spout all that nonsense to him, about her mind rattling about like a spineless rider on a trotting horse? He must think her a cork-brained, cotton-headed...*oh*. She squeezed her eyes shut, trying to drive out the memory of his expression as she'd plucked the tufts of cotton wool from her ears. Such disorder, such ridiculousness must be repulsive to a man who'd managed to convey his status as an officer and a gentleman even when covered head to toe with mud.

Yet he had he come to find her. Why? He had even been on the point of offering her a post as Lady Viviane's new governess, she felt sure of it.

But she was foolish enough to want something else.

She wanted to drown in that look he'd had in his eye in the library, to feel the heat of his palm against the curve of her lower back, to hear his voice speak words of passion.

And he was going to marry Miss Pilkington. Cool, elegant, polished Miss Pilkington.

A sob escaped her lips as she flung herself backward into the mound of soft pillows, half laughing, half crying. Afterward, she lay there and listened to the chunter of heavy rainfall against the eaves.

The moment the storm stopped, she would be free of all this. She only hoped it would not be too late.

* * * *

Tristan returned to his chambers by way of the drawing room, wondering whether his guests had retired for the night. Not that he wanted company, precisely. But he did not trust himself to be alone, either.

The footman had not returned to his post, and the door stood partly open, presumably left that way by the last to leave. Voices from within told that the room was not empty, however. Hidden by the stout oak panel, but with a clear view into the room, he paused. The card players had reconfigured themselves. Whitby now partnered Miss Pilkington, who looked more animated than she had at any previous time that day. Beresford and Lady Lydgate were teamed against them, seated on opposite sides of the table; he refused to speculate on what might be going on between them beneath its cover. Sir Thomas faced Lord Easton over the chessboard, the former studying his next move while his opponent snored. Virtually the same dull scene he had left. Only the Newsomes had gone. Guin now sat by the fire in place of the vicar's wife, a book open on her lap.

His mind returned to what had just transpired in the kitchen. How close he had come to offering Erica...what, exactly? Even now, he was not sure. But he'd been momentarily possessed by the certainty that life at Hawesdale, if it must be borne, would be a sight more interesting with her in residence.

Not just interesting. Bearable. She was fresh air and wild energy and… quite possibly a spy.

She was hiding something, certainly. Some part of herself, though he suspected she had come closer than ever to revealing it to him tonight. How desperately he wanted to know more. But the curiosity he felt now was not familiar to him, neither the idle sort that had led him into misery in his childhood, nor the skilled sort that made him an asset to king and country. A curiosity not of mind, nor even—entirely—of body, but of… spirit? Kindred spirits? He laughed to himself. How could that be when they had nothing in common at all?

Though he had not made a sound, his stepmother looked up and caught his eye. When she lifted one hand to wave him in, he held a finger to his lips and shook his head. She and Viv might be the only ones in the house who wanted his company. Even the servants regretted his return, his assumption of his father's title—and on that matter at least, he was inclined to agree. He could see no reason to cross the threshold. With a bow, he bid Guin good night. She nodded her understanding and resumed her reading, turning the motion of her raised hand into a quick smoothing of her hair. No one else knew he had come. Or gone.

Still, he was reluctant to go to bed, fearful of the direction in which his dreams might tend. Would his mind conjure visions of some tropical vine curling sensuously about his limbs, rendering him a willing captive, while an enemy crept through the darkness to carve his secrets from the depths of his soul, like flesh from bone…?

With a shake, he dismissed the disturbing, jumbled image and set off through the dimly lit corridor in the direction of the library and Davies's orderly stack of account books. Nothing like column upon column of figures to keep a man's mind from wandering where it ought not go.

Chapter 11

Lady Viviane laid aside her pencil. "Surely you will want to join the other guests for dinner, Miss Burke."

Startled by the sound of the girl's voice, Erica's normally steady hand sent a line shooting jaggedly across the page. They had spent the day in the conservatory, where Viviane had progressed from fern leaves to a delicate violet with remarkable rapidity, though her mind had a tendency to race ahead of her fingers when she sketched. The only disturbance, the only visitor, had been Mrs. Dean, who had brought them both trays at midday. Barring the rain, it had been a glorious day spent doing exactly what Erica had always wanted to do, and she was determined to think as little as possible about the man who had made it happen.

"No," she demurred, without looking up. "Not really."

Viviane picked up her pencil again, but instead of resuming her sketch, she began to tap one end against her palm. "If you don't, it will seem as if you are hiding."

"Hiding?" Still, she did not meet the girl's gaze. "From whom would I be hiding?"

The duke's guests. The duke. Myself.

"Well, perhaps not hiding, exactly," Viviane conceded. "But I should think at times you'd like more company and conversation than a potted plant can provide. Not," she hastened to add, "that I don't find the study of botany stimulating."

Stifling a sigh, Erica closed her journal. "Of course, Lady Viviane. I forgot myself and kept you at your task too long, today. You may go whenever you wish."

The girl was on her feet so quickly the stool skidded across the flagstone floor. "And you, Miss Burke? You really ought to have a break yourself. Shall I come back and remind you before the dinner hour?"

Erica consented with an absent wave of one hand and went back to her notes. She was perfectly capable of ignoring one reminder. Or ten.

As it turned out, however, she was not capable of ignoring Viviane, who at half-past five drove Erica from the conservatory with all the gravitas of the archangel expelling Adam and Eve from the Garden of Eden, backed by Mr. Sturgess, who had been summoned to douse the lights and lock the door.

So it was she found herself a largely silent participant in another interminable meal—when one did not spill wine and run away, dining went on for hours, it seemed—followed by tea in the drawing room with the other ladies of the party. She drank cup after cup to keep from being expected to make conversation, and also in hopes that she would soon have a plausible excuse to flee in search of the necessary.

"Will you join us in a game of forfeits this evening, Miss Burke?" Caroline Pilkington bravely settled herself on the sofa beside Erica, which required Mrs. Newsome to shift and make room.

"Forfeits?" The vicar's wife had not spoken all evening except to complain about the weather and mutter over whether her children's nursemaid could be trusted to keep her "poor, motherless little ones" sufficiently dry. She sat so stiffly it was not possible for her to stiffen in indignation now, but she sniffed. "I do not approve of wagering."

Erica studied both of them over the rim of her teacup. If she sketched faces, which she never did, she would render Miss Pilkington as an exquisite blossom and Mrs. Newsome as a dried-up twig.

"Nothing too serious, Mrs. Newsome," Miss Pilkington replied with a musical laugh. "I propose a game of charades. The ladies shall ask riddles of the gentlemen, and the gentleman who answers a lady's riddle correctly may request some small favor of her. A kiss, for example."

"A kiss!" The word brought the vicar's wife to her feet. "I'm shocked your mother would allow such a thing. As if wagering with money were not bad enough. To risk something more precious still…"

Across the room, Lady Easton Pilkington turned toward the commotion and cast a languid smile at her daughter, giving the impression of her approval, though Erica doubted she had heard a word of what had been said.

"I most certainly will not participate," declared Mrs. Newsome, who set her teacup and saucer on the table with a clatter. "Nor countenance such indecency with my presence," she added as she marched from the room, apparently recalling that she had not actually been invited to play.

A curve of amused satisfaction on her lips, Miss Pilkington returned her attention to Erica. "What about you, Miss Burke?"

With five siblings, both older and younger, Erica was more than familiar with the forms revenge might take. She knew it would be wisest to decline. But something about Miss Pilkington's coolness made her burn. "Thank you," she said, thrusting her chin upward as she spoke. "I'd be delighted."

And promptly regretted it when the gentlemen filed into the room a moment later led by Tristan, who again this evening had donned his uniform and gleamed in awful scarlet splendor.

The gentlemen were more than amenable to Miss Pilkington's suggestion. Even the vicar had a gleam of regret in his eye when he declined out of deference to his wife. The party thinned further when Lady Easton pleaded another headache and begged her husband to escort her up to their rooms. That left the youthful duchess to chaperone the competition, for neither Sir Thomas nor his wife, the most senior of the guests by age, seemed at all inclined to enforce rules of proper behavior. The baronet even rubbed his hands together in gleeful anticipation, and Erica wondered whether her punishment for the spilled wine was intended to be his wet, whiskery kiss.

The gentlemen disposed themselves around the room: Lord Beresford took the seat Mrs. Newsome had vacated, while Captain Whitby chose the chair beside the duchess near the tea table. Tristan remained standing before the fire, for which Erica could only be grateful, as it made it easier to position herself so that he was not in her direct line of sight.

All eyes were on Miss Pilkington as she leaned forward to explain the rules of her game. "I'm sure you are all familiar with charades. Each lady shall pose a riddle to all the gentleman. The first to solve it shall win the prize."

She did not specify the nature of the prize, but it was clearly understood from the various murmurs and smiles and even laughter that erupted around the room. Nor did it seem that the winners were to be determined entirely by either skill or luck. After a great deal of twittering and fussing, Lady Lydgate recited her puzzle:

> *"I'm a box without hinges, key, or lid,*
> *Yet golden treasure inside is hid."*

Any child could have guessed it. Nevertheless, the gentlemen's answers all fell wide of the mark, as if they deferred by prior accord to...Lord

Beresford? Not her husband? To Erica's shock, it was indeed the earl who pronounced the answer to be "an egg" and claimed his kiss full on the lady's lips.

When Sir Thomas Lydgate answered the duchess' somewhat more challenging riddle, he bowed gallantly and kissed her hand, as if to show how a true gentleman behaved.

Then it was Miss Pilkington's turn. She made eye contact with each of the gentlemen, securing their undivided attention before saying slowly:

> *"My first is aloft in the air;*
> *My second's a path in the ground;*
> *My third may be black, brown, or fair;*
> *And my whole may be hanged, or be drowned."*

As one, all the heads swiveled toward the Duke of Raynham, who leaned with his forearm against the mantelpiece and stared contemplatively into the fire as he worked out the three syllables. An anticipatory silence buzzed in Erica's ears. On the opposite side of the room, the longcase clock cleared its throat and struck the half-hour, making her jump.

"I do not know," Tristan said finally, the hint of a self-deprecating smile playing about his lips as he looked toward Caroline and caught Erica's eye on the way. Though she suspected him of telling an untruth, he did nothing to betray himself. No one would ever know for certain if he lied.

"A highwayman." The voice came from the tea table. A confident Captain Whitby rose and crossed to Miss Pilkington beside her on the couch.

If she had not been seated so close to her, Erica would never have noticed the way Caroline's fingers tightened eagerly in her skirt when Whitby leaned in for a quick buss of her cheek, nor would she have heard his teasing whisper: *"You're welcome."*

Didn't Miss Pilkington want the duke's kiss? Or had she suspected Tristan's reluctance and attempted to test it? What a dangerous game she'd decided to play...

Those thoughts scattered when the company's attention now focused on Erica. It was her turn to pose a riddle. She'd been weighing her options since the game began. To ask something simple and put an end to her misery? Or to rise to the challenge? Perhaps, if she were very clever, she could claim victory without giving away anything at all.

The trouble was, she had never been especially good at wordplay, and now that all eyes were upon her, the only charade she could recall was one she would rather not recite. Though she allowed the silence to stretch longer than was comfortable, no inspiration struck her. At last she sucked in a breath and blurted out the rhyme:

> *"My first is the spirit of life,*
> *From whence all its happiness flows.*
> *'Tis also the center of strife,*
> *The fountain of sorrow and woes!*
>
> *My second, I own, is a pain*
> *In the stomach, the side, or the head;*
> *But if on my first it should gain,*
> *Then pleasure and joy are both fled."*

When she finished speaking, silence fell again. It was not a particularly difficult riddle. Had she truly stumped them?

Or did no one want to kiss her?

Finally, Lord Beresford guessed "toothache" in a reluctant, slightly embarrassed voice. "No, my lord," she replied. Sir Thomas only shrugged and would not make an attempt.

"Beresford was right." Tristan's deep voice sent a quaver through her. "A pain is an *ache*. But I suspect the 'spirit of life' refers to the heart. The answer is 'heartache.'"

Her gaze dropped to the carpet. Once more, she watched his glossy black boots make their way across a room to stop before her, the stride of a man who was sure he was right. "And the forfeit, as I understand it, is a kiss." He held out his hand for hers, and for a moment, she was hopeful that he would follow Sir Thomas's lead.

But with gentle pressure, he drew her to her feet. He meant to kiss *her*, not just her hand. *No. Oh, no.* The air seemed to rush from the room, taking with it all pretense of lighthearted entertainment. Though she'd agreed to play the game, she could not allow this. Even if—especially if—her blood was singing *yes, yes* as it coursed through her body and her nipples had tautened in anticipation, pressing almost painfully against the restraint of yet another of the duchess' tight-fitting gowns.

He must have sensed her hesitation. "Is that not right, Miss Burke?"

Slowly, she lifted her chin and met his dark eyes. Despite the gallons of tea she had drunk, her mouth was dry and she had to wet her lips before she could speak. "No, Your Grace," she insisted, praying she was as good at telling fibs as he. "Your answer was not correct." Tugging her fingers free of his, she gathered up her skirts and hurried from the room.

* * * *

Of course, there could be no escaping the Duke of Raynham in his own house.

She had gone only a little way down the corridor when she heard his footsteps behind her. Still, she pressed on, not exactly sure where she was going but needing to get there all the same. And when she at last reached the door to the conservatory, she fumbled eagerly for the latch.

It was locked.

She leaned against the worn wood, into the warmth that seeped around its edges, longing for the tranquility, the comfort that lay just beyond her reach. Behind her, Tristan came onward at a steady pace, never hurrying to catch up nor calling out for her to wait. As if his success were never in doubt. Her heartbeat ratcheted higher with each step he took, until he stopped, just inches away.

Stretching one arm over her head, he felt along the top of the lintel and retrieved a stout, rusty key. Wordlessly, he inserted it into the lock. With her forehead still pressed against the door, she could feel the grating vibrations as he turned the key. As soon as the door sprang open, she stepped inside.

Moonlight flooded the conservatory, turning spiky leaves and curving vines into a fantastical landscape. Tipping her head back, she looked up, through the glass ceiling, into the expanse of a cloudless night sky.

"Maybe the storm is finally over," Tristan said.

Over? Something very like regret welled within her. But why should that be? Only a moment before, she had been searching for a way to escape Hawesdale. To escape her attraction to him.

When she lowered her gaze enough to meet his, she saw that the moonlight had painted him too, highlighting the sharp angles of his face and turning his scarlet coat charcoal gray. Wordlessly, she stepped deeper into the room, to the ring of orange trees, and settled herself on one of the shadow-cloaked benches beneath them. He followed and sat beside her, at once too close and not close enough.

"Why did you come after me?"

"Why, to claim my prize, of course." He leaned toward her and the safe distance between them evaporated. "Rules are rules, Miss Burke."

She could feel the slight curve of a smile on his lips when they brushed hers. Of course he would be the sort of man who would insist upon following the rules. They'd been written all to his benefit. But she had never learned them.

The soft touch of his mouth on hers was strange. Not unwelcome, though she did not know how, or even whether, she ought to convey her enthusiasm to him. Despite the darkness, she closed her eyes, and for that moment of total blindness, immersed herself in the scents of damp soil, faded blossoms, and the spice of his cologne.

She was still fumbling for a proper beginning when he pulled away and the kiss was over. When she opened her eyes, it was to find him studying her, his eyes glittering, his dark brows knitted together. "It would seem I made a mistake," he said.

The kiss. He means the kiss was a mistake. "The charade? No, you guessed right. The answer was..." She forced the word past lips that longed to be otherwise occupied. "Heartache. I lied because I—" *Because I didn't want you to kiss me.* No, that was a lie too. She searched for some more believable excuse. "Because I—I—"

"Your engagement was not a love match, was it?" He spoke as if he had not heard a word she'd said. As if he were puzzling over some other riddle. Still dwelling, apparently, on their exchange of the day before.

She wished, suddenly, for the thunder of raindrops against the glass roof, something to drown out her tremulous whisper. "Why do you ask?"

"Because if your engagement had been a love match, I very much doubt I would have been the man to give you your first kiss."

Only the fear of stumbling about in the dark kept her in her seat. With a hand on either side of her legs, she gripped the cool, polished iron of the bench. "No," she agreed after a moment. "It was not a love match."

"A marriage of convenience, then?"

"A marriage of mutual benefit," she countered, her voice stronger now, as some of her usual boldness demanded to make itself known. "Henry was always supportive of my work and promised me liberty to continue it. As a married woman, I would have more freedom to travel, to go about my research."

After a pause, he nodded his understanding. "Mutual benefit, you said..." He laid the slightest stress on the first word. No doubt he found it difficult to imagine what sort of profit could accrue to any man who would willingly saddle himself with someone like her.

All her life, people had been urging her to be less selfish. Concentrate. Don't lose track of time. Keep things orderly. Be more ladylike. She had told herself the criticisms were kindly meant. *Don't you want to marry someday?* Mama had been fond of asking.

And the honest, though unspoken, answer had always been *yes*. She wanted companionship, for the world could be a lonely place. And yes, she wanted love. But a conventional marriage...?

What sort of husband do you imagine will be willing to put up with a poorly run household, forgotten meals, overlooked invitations? Not to mention pots of botanical specimens tucked into every corner...

Well, Henry had been willing. "He *wanted* to marry me," she insisted, twenty years of defensiveness coalescing into a bitter kernel of anger she could no longer keep buried. "He cared for me." Her voice dropped once more to a whisper, and despite the protection of the shadows, she could not meet his eyes. "But he was in love with my brother."

Tristan's response was an eternity in coming. "And did your brother... return his affection?"

"My brother is capable of loving no one but himself. I doubt he even knew."

Somewhere in the depths of the conservatory, water dripped, whether the remnants of raindrops in the eaves or condensation falling from the leaf of a plant, she wasn't sure. That inner voice, the one that was rarely quiet and rarely allowed her to be, urged her to seek the source of the sound. Anything but sit here and wait, and wait...

She had not realized his hand lay beside hers on the bench until his little finger brushed against hers. The very slightest of touches, though it sent a spark up her arm that lifted the fine hairs there. A mistaken movement in the darkness, almost surely. She twitched her finger to alert him to his error. But he did not pull away.

"You would have sacrificed yourself." His murmured voice was at once mournful and incredulous. "To a marriage in name only. For such a small freedom..."

"It is not a small freedom to me, Your Grace. Nor was it, I suspect, to him. After all, people are expected to marry, to behave respectably in the eyes of society, whatever their personal inclinations to the contrary. Even if they cannot have the one they love."

Another pause. "What about...?"

It was not difficult to guess the direction of his thoughts. "Children?" She shook her head as matter-of-factly as she could.

The truth was, she quite liked children. They tended to appreciate in her precisely the things with which adults found fault: her willingness to go for a ramble on the spur of the moment, to get prodigiously dirty in the process, to stop for an hour to observe the wonder in the petals of a flower that others dismissed as a weed. But since motherhood, as far as she had ever seen, consisted largely of teaching children *not* to do those things, or scolding them for having done so, she had always known she would not make a very good mother. And so she had refused to allow herself to think of it as a loss.

"With five brothers and sisters, I am sure to have nieces and nephews on which to dote," she added, as much to reassure herself as him.

His finger moved, then, but not away. A slow, careful stroke, up and down the edge of her hand, forcing her to quell yet another shudder of longing. "I confess I had a different sacrifice in mind. Erica?"

When she turned toward the sound of her name, his other hand rose to cup the side of her face, his touch so soft, so gentle, so unlike the man she believed him to be. But, oh, the kiss! This second kiss was all him, firm and demanding, his mouth slanting across hers, compelling an eager moan from her, then swallowing it, only to give it back in the form of a groan of pure need that vibrated against her mouth and made her insides turn to honey.

Was it surrender to part her lips beneath his, to welcome with surprised delight the slick invasion of his tongue? No. This was not conquest, but liberation. Thus freed, she kissed him back. Pressing her lips against his until his own mouth softened, she then dared to touch her tongue to his. On the bench between them, their fingers tangled and curled together too, another link in a chain of desire.

Every inch of her skin craved the feel of his lips, his hands, and the pleasure they promised. But she told herself to be satisfied with his mouth on hers, the way he devoured her every inhibition. With the brush of his thumb along her cheekbone, silk against velvet. With the gentle pressure of his fingertips against her skull and the discovery that even the delicate skin behind her ear could be awakened by his touch.

Anything else, anything more, would be dangerous in the extreme.

And he seemed to know it too, for at last he dragged his mouth away on a sigh, though his fingers tightened on her scalp and neck, holding her prisoner to his heavy-lidded gaze. He was a little breathless, she noted with pride, so she spoke for him. For them both.

"You should go back to your guests, Your Grace. They will understand that you felt yourself obligated to take pity on me and guess my charade when no one else would. They will know that this was only a silly, meaningless forfeit."

"Erica." Half scold, half protest. It was wrong, was it not, to take such delight in the sound of her name on his lips? But she would be a fool to imagine that his kiss meant anything at all.

"I do not blame the other gentlemen, of course," she continued. "Miss Pilkington chose a game best played among intimate friends, and I am a stranger whose motives are unknown..."

At those words, at the mention of Caroline, his softened features transformed almost before her eyes into their customary granite. His hand fell away from her face, and he rose, lifting their still-linked fingers off the bench.

Carefully, she slipped her hand free and curled it in her lap to hide its tremor. "We must all make sacrifices, you see."

With a stiff bow, hardly more than a nod, he turned and left the conservatory.

To the moonlit plants she whispered, "Then pleasure and joy are both fled."

Chapter 12

Tristan returned to the drawing room because he knew Erica was right. To do otherwise would invite uncomfortable speculation about what had transpired between them over the last quarter hour.

And exactly what *had* transpired?

More than a mere forfeit, despite what she'd said. And he was solely to blame. He'd gone after her. He'd asked uncomfortable questions to which he had no right to expect answers. Then he'd kissed her. Really kissed her. Given in to a temptation that had been plaguing him since the storm began.

Now that the storm had ended, however, would he be free of the temptation at last?

Not if the spark of lightning at their touch, the thunder of blood in his veins, was any indication.

Caroline looked up from her conversation with Beresford and smiled gently at him as he crossed the threshold, her expression mild as always. Every inch the duchess she expected to be.

A part of him had been hoping to see a flicker of disappointment at his return, he realized. Or jealousy. Anything that might reveal the depths beneath that placid surface. He was not quite fool enough to believe her as shallow and indifferent as she put on. Of course, if that were his goal, he might've guessed her charade and won the forfeit. Even a brief kiss surely would have told him more than her face seemed inclined to reveal.

"Back so soon?" Sir Thomas teased. "Couldn't you find her?"

"No." More lies. He began to regret that he'd had occasion to grow expert at telling them. "Miss Burke would seem to have asserted her triumph by retiring for the night." Skeptical expressions made their way around the company, but no one challenged his story or disputed Erica's victory at charades. "Another game, perhaps?" he suggested halfheartedly.

"Not for me." Guin shook her head and rose, a gentle signal to all that the evening had come to an end.

Tristan stood at the door and bowed them out. "It would appear that the rain has moved on. In a day or two, when the roads have recovered somewhat, I suppose you'll all be on your way." It was badly done, he knew. Almost a dismissal. But he could not muster an ounce of regret to accompany it.

For their part, his guests exclaimed and began to chatter in what sounded suspiciously like relief. After a fortnight, the odd assortment of ladies and gentlemen had grown tired of one another's company. Except, perhaps, for Lady Lydgate and Lord Beresford, who exchanged a look as the former left the room on the arm of her oblivious—or perhaps apathetic—husband.

Whitby alone sent him a disapproving glance. He had risen out of deference to the ladies but made no move to depart. Something to report, perhaps. Or to protest.

Save his old friend, Guin and Caroline were the last to leave, his stepmother fulfilling her role of chaperone to the end.

"Miss Pilkington." He took her hand and bowed over it, then straightened without releasing her hand.

She made no attempt to pull away, though her eyes widened. She looked up at him expectantly, if not eagerly. "Yes, Duke?"

Percy's perfect bride. A word or two to her tonight, a few more to her father in the morning, and she could be his. *Can you think of any reason why I shouldn't?* he'd asked Whitby. A purely rhetorical question, of course.

But earlier this evening, the answer had become *yes.*

"Good night, Miss Pilkington," he said.

Was that relief in her eyes as she bid him good night in return?

When she and Guin had gone, Whitby sank into his chair, a frown etched onto his brow. "Something stronger than tea, Captain?" Tristan offered as he approached the table.

Whitby shook his head almost absently. "Why did you lie?" he asked after a moment.

"Did I?" Tristan took the chair opposite.

"I don't believe for a moment that Miss Burke escaped your pursuit."

Tristan traced the edge of an empty cup with one finger, choosing his words with care. "I found her in the conservatory."

"And you—" Apparently thinking better of it, Whitby bit off the accusation. "She's *Irish*, Tris. Intimate with men involved in a plot against the British government. A—"

"I do not believe she is a spy," Tristan interjected smoothly before Whitby could lay the charge at Erica's door.

Astonishment, disappointment, mistrust. Emotions slid across Whitby's face and were gone, leaving behind a smooth mask of impassivity. The look of a man who knew how to hide his feelings, for his own safety and that of others. "You like her."

"I do. She is spirited, engaging—"

"Beautiful."

That too, of course, though hers was not the polished, sophisticated style of beauty to which the word was usually applied. The fire that burned deep within her sent its glowing embers into every element of her being. Her speech. Her hair. Her kiss.

Unlike Whitby, he did not trouble to keep his thoughts from his face. Reading them, the captain said, "Be careful, my friend. You cannot afford to make that mistake—or any mistake—right now. Unless you relish the thought of home duty, you must treat every person under this roof with suspicion."

On the night of his arrival, Whitby's story had kindled a flicker of doubt that roared now into flame. Did his friend secretly hope that he would be exposed and forced to stay in England? Tristan had told himself it was understandable: an unspoken, unspeakable wish to return to the way things had once been, the two of them outwitting a common foe. Tonight, however, it smacked of pettiness. Jealousy.

"Even you?" Tristan asked softly.

Whitby pushed away from the table and stood. "The Major Laurens I once knew would not even have had to ask." He strode toward the door, pausing on the threshold. "You told me you desired to return to France out of concern for the greater good, Tris. Lately, I wonder if your motives might not be a bit more selfish."

Tristan rose too. "You presume a great deal, old friend."

"Including our friendship. My mistake." Whitby nodded crisply. "Right, then. Do as you please, Your Grace." The honorific stung, as had no doubt been the intent. "Regarding Miss Burke and…all the rest."

When the door shut none too quietly behind Whitby, Tristan threw himself into a chair before the fire and studied its dying flames. His thoughts were an uncharacteristic jumble, and he found himself recalling

Erica's description of her chaotic mind, a novice rider jounced about on a trotting horse. Exhausting, indeed.

In three days, he'd uncovered no proof of Whitby's allegations, nothing more than the most circumstantial connections—Newsome's brother, Caroline's French gowns. And even if one of his guests *were* desperate for information, which of them would be fool enough to imagine that a man like him left his secrets lying about? No, he kept them close, tucked safely away, like...like...

Like Erica clutched her journal to her breast.

Whitby's accusations. His own suspicions. Everything coalesced around that battered, leather-bound book. If only...

Behind him, the longcase clock struck half-past twelve. By now, everyone would be safely abed. He might investigate certain avenues, and no one the wiser. He might put his intelligence-gathering skills to good use, answer his questions once and for all. And perhaps set himself free of his foolish fascination in the bargain.

Pushing up from his chair, he set off for the south wing and Erica's chamber.

* * * *

Erica pummeled the down-filled pillow with one fist, then tossed herself backward into its cloud of softness. It didn't help, of course. It never did. Stillness and darkness were but excuses for her mind to take its nightly journey down the shadowed, rutted lanes of her memory. Every mistake she'd made. Every misstep. Most from so far back in the past that no amends could be made.

At least tonight, her brain was focused on more recent events. Very recent. The fingers of one hand crept to her lips, wondering if they would feel somehow changed by his kiss. Wondering what might have happened if she had not chased him away.

Another *whomp* to the pillow, and she almost missed the click of the door latch.

Who could be coming into her room at this hour? Even the servants must be asleep. No one here was in her confidence. And until tonight, no man had ever so much as followed her into the next room for the pleasure of her company. She was certainly not so much a fool that she imagined the Duke of Raynham had waited until his other guests had retired before sneaking into her bedchamber to—

Her spinning mind ground to a halt when Tristan's tall, broad-shouldered form slipped through the narrow opening.

Through slitted eyes, she watched him enter and close the door soundlessly behind himself. Somewhere in the furthest recesses of her mind it occurred to her that perhaps she ought to find it alarming to have a man entering her room in the dead of night. But oddly, it didn't alarm her—not this night, not this man. For one thing, if he had wicked business in mind, it would have been foolish in the extreme for him to have waited to enact his plan until she was back in her room, with every one of his guests in easy earshot. She had only to shout to bring half of Hawesdale running to her aid. And for another...well, it was difficult to imagine the officer and gentleman she had come to know plotting something truly wicked.

Perhaps just a little wicked, though.

In the darkness she pressed her lips together, waiting for him to speak to her. But what had he come to say?

Or do?

For a long moment, he stood without moving, presumably allowing his eyes to adjust to the near darkness. She had not drawn the drapes, but the moonlight was feeble, losing its battle with the lingering clouds as it struggled to cast its glow around the chamber.

By its thin, silvery gleam, his shirtsleeves glowed white. He'd shed his coat—and his boots, she realized when he took his first silent steps across the carpet. Strange. Or maybe not. Maybe that was the ordinary way of such things. Though he did not strike her as the sort of man who would have vast experience with midnight assignations, she had even less.

He paused to watch her, and she fought the instinct to hold her breath. Having always shared a bedchamber with her elder sister, she had a great deal of experience in feigning sleep. Slow, even breaths. One, two, three. Eyes closed fully now, lest a glimmer betray her. Surely in a moment, he would speak.

He watched her for an inordinate length of time—or so it seemed to her. Minutes did have a tendency to crawl more slowly in the darkest hours of the night. And she itched, literally itched, with impatience to know what he was thinking, what his expression might be. Nerves fired at random, first on her back, then her shoulder, then the end of her nose, demanding she chase them with a vigorous scratch. In another moment, she would be unable to hold the sensation at bay.

He moved first. She heard the whisper of fabric sliding against itself as he walked. His formfitting breeches...Lord, but she did not need an excuse to be thinking about his breeches just now. *Concentrate.* Was he leaving, disappointed in his hopes of finding her awake and waiting for him? Ought she to stir, ever so slightly...?

Once more, she dared to crack her eyelids. Just enough to pick out his silhouette against the darker shadows of the room's furnishings. He had indeed moved away from the foot of the bed. But not toward the door. He stood beside the vanity table. Its mirror doubled what little light there was and showed her his movements twice. She knew when he passed his fingers over the borrowed hairbrush and a little pot of scented powder the duchess' maid had left behind. Over the inkpot and the quills Miss Chatham had supplied from the schoolroom. Over the cover of her journal...

He paused for a more thorough exploration. She felt his touch as surely as if his fingertips had been caressing her skin, tracing every smooth curve. Too familiar. Too intimate. The nerve endings that only moments before had been demanding she scratch a nonexistent itch began to work in concert, all their energy now focused somewhere near the base of her spine. Desperate to appease them, she wiggled her hips soundlessly beneath the coverlet.

He heard her nonetheless. Or else the movement, though slight, had caught his eye. He turned, the journal in hand, his long fingers pale against its dark cover. She had startled him. Surely he had not meant to pick it up. A soft sound, a murmur of disappointment, slipped past her lips, and she shifted again, hoping these would be mistaken for the noises and movements of sleep.

Though he did not seem to imagine she was fully awake, gone were the leisurely motions, the careful study of moments ago. He turned rapidly toward the door and was to it in half a dozen strides. When he reached for the latch, she saw he still held her journal in his other hand.

The Duke of Raynham was a thief.

Rational thought urged her to speak to him in a low voice, prompt him to drop the book and leave.

Pure instinct ripped a scream of betrayal from her lungs.

She freed herself from the tangle of bed linen and leaped to her feet, racing toward the door. Tristan, frozen in surprise, did not protest when she ripped the journal from his hands and flung it back toward the bed. "How dare you?" she demanded.

"Miss Burke, I—"

His explanation, his excuse—whatever it might have been—died on his lips. Up and down the corridor, beds creaked, footsteps pounded, doors rattled. Up and down the corridor, voices rang.

"What was that?"

"Who—?"

"Is someone hurt?"

"I think it came from Miss Burke's room…"

In another moment, the corridor was filled with people and candlelight. Mrs. Newsome, who had been bustling toward the disturbance, skidded to a stop and stared in horror, scarlet from the ruffled edge of her nightcap to the high collar of her flannel dressing gown. Lady Easton Pilkington, by contrast, was deathly pale. Lord Beresford and Lady Lydgate, suspiciously late to the party, whispered to one another behind her raised hand. Captain Whitby alone did not press forward, but clung to the shadows beyond the nearest sconce, his expression unreadable, his arms folded across his chest. Self-consciously, Erica imitated the pose and recollected belatedly the diaphanous quality of her borrowed sleepwear. Cool night air penetrated the thin fabric and swept along her flushed skin.

From the chamber across the way, Caroline emerged last of all, her eyes awash with something that looked suspiciously like amusement. But it could not be, could it? For there they stood, the center of a circle of otherwise disapproving, disbelieving stares, Erica in a rumpled nightdress and Tristan in his shirtsleeves and stockings, bright spots of color high on his chiseled cheekbones. They would hardly have been worse off to have been caught *in flagrante delicto.*

Caroline's lips pursed, and again Erica had the distinct impression she was fighting back a laugh. "Oh," she said when she had mastered whatever impulse had distorted her lovely mouth.

Tristan, too, was battling some emotion, but it was assuredly not laughter. A muscle ticked along his jaw and his eyes flashed, putting Erica in mind of the way lightning pierced storm clouds, momentarily shifting the sky from black to deepest blue and back to black again. He glanced first at Caroline, then turned toward Erica—no easy task, as his spine appeared to have been replaced with an iron rod, his posture so rigid that even his complete uniform, were he still wearing it, would have been unequal to it.

"Miss Burke," he began, and this time, nothing and no one interrupted him, although Erica felt certain the words he spoke now were not at all the words he had intended to speak two minutes past. "It seems I have the honor of asking you to be my wife."

She understood, suddenly, Miss Pilkington's impulse to giggle. Or perhaps that alarming bubbling sensation in her middle presaged something a bit more dire. Either way, she clamped her jaw tight against it. *No, no, no.* Nothing made any sense. She was the one who spoke wildly, whose thoughts moved with the jerky leaps and wobbly steps of a spring lamb.

Tristan was all cool logic and order. So why was he spouting nonsense now? Why wasn't he explaining to all these people, herself included, the reason he had come to her chamber in the middle of the night? He certainly hadn't compromised her. At least, not in the traditional sense, though when she thought of her journal in his hands she felt undeniably violated. And earlier in the evening there'd been the kiss…well, kisses… but surely even a high stickler like Mrs. Newsome wouldn't require such a dire punishment for mere kisses. And punishment it would be. Of the worst sort. For both of them. Imagine…*her*, a duchess?

And he was imagining it too. Of that, she had no doubt. While she stood there, not speaking, some of the cold fury in his aspect leached away, to be replaced by something very like panic. Probably he was forcing himself to contemplate the years ahead, saddled forever with an unsuitable woman, when he might have had Caroline instead.

A noise grated in Erica's throat then, too rough and too loud to be a laugh. Frankly grateful that only sound and nothing more humiliating had burst forth, she notched her chin a bit higher. Oh, what would her sister say when she heard what had happened? Even though nothing *had* happened, really…

Except that for some inexplicable reason he had tried steal her journal.

"Miss Burke?" he prompted, for all the world as if he had asked a serious question requiring a considered answer.

"*A Thiarna Dia*," she muttered.

"I have not the pleasure of understanding you, ma'am." Not even a glimmer of humor. His voice slid along her spine like icy raindrops.

"I most certainly will not marry you," she said, crisply enunciating each word so that everyone within earshot could hear. And before he or any of the assembled company could recover from the shock of either their discovery or her refusal, she stepped backward into her chamber and slammed the door between them.

Chapter 13

Erica awoke to a tap on her door, surprised to discover she had slept at all. The morning light had a distinctly grayish cast, as if the sky had not yet made up its mind whether the day was to dawn wet or dry. Something firm and sharp-cornered was pressing into her ribs, and when another soft knock came, she raised herself from the bed enough to discover she had collapsed atop her journal.

She rolled onto her back, brushing tangled hair away from her face and rubbing her knuckles into the thin, salty crust of dried tears at the corners of her eyes. Probably some servant, ordered to retrieve the finery that had been loaned to her and then send her on her way in her mud-stained pelisse. Perhaps if she simply ignored the knocking, she'd be left alone, walled into the chamber and never spoken of again. Perhaps that was how one actually died of embarrassment.

"Go away," she muttered, not quite loudly enough to be heard in the corridor.

"Miss Burke?"

The duchess' voice, so unexpected, brought her to her feet. After fumbling to free herself from the bed linens, Erica closed her fingertips around the cool, heavy silk of the dressing gown and drew it about her as she stumbled toward the door. When she reached it, the Duchess of Raynham was lifting her hand to knock again. The Laurenses, even by marriage, were a persistent lot.

Erica made herself open the door wide and invited the duchess into the room with a sweep of one arm. No sense in staging another scene in the corridor for all to hear. And why else would the woman have come but to rail at Erica for having schemed to trap her stepson?

"I'm sorry to have to wake you, Miss Burke," the Duchess of Raynham said gently. Genuinely. "I know you did not have a restful night." Her kind eyes were shadowed with worry, and guilt rolled over Erica. How unjust she had been to this lady, who had been nothing but generous and who evidently had come herself to spare her guest the silent judgment of Mrs. Dean and every maid and footman at Hawesdale Chase.

When she had stepped far enough into the room that the door could be shut behind her, Erica repaid that kindness and generosity by turning to her and demanding an answer only Tristan could give. "Why did he do it?"

Startled, the duchess drew back from the question, straightening her spine and tucking in her chin. "Vivi told me you had a tendency to be forthright."

Lady Viviane. The girl would be sent back to the schoolroom and Miss Chatham, probably not even allowed to say goodbye. The realization left Erica feeling hollower yet. "A flaw, I know," she conceded.

"A quality too few possess, I should say," the duchess corrected. "Especially women." Unbending slightly, she folded her hands in front of her, their pallor stark against her black gown. "If you mean to ask why he offered for you, I can only say that for as long as I have known him, since he was a young man, he has always possessed a strong sense of honor and sought to demonstrate it. He tries to do what is right." Her skirts swayed slightly beneath fidgeting fingers. "And even as I speak those words, I realize how ludicrous such a claim must sound to you, since if it were true, he ought never to have been in such a position to begin with."

Erica let her breath escape. At least the duchess did not intend to accuse her of having invited him to her room. To her bed. But then, the man Tristan's stepmother knew did not sound at all like the sort of man who hid in abandoned cottages rather than going home. Who went sneaking about after dark, prying into things that were none of his business. Whereas the man Erica knew had done exactly that.

Which of them had made the truer sketch of his character?

Tempted to scramble for her journal, she instead walked toward the dressing table and reached for the hairbrush to have something with which to occupy her hands. But as her fingers curled around the cool silver, she remembered that Tristan had been the last to touch it, as his fingers passed over the vanity's contents in the dark. In a flash, the metal grew hot in her hand and she dropped it onto the table with a clatter. "I cannot decide, Your Grace," she said without turning, "whether you are more relieved at my refusal, or surprised by it."

"Why must I be either one?"

Not expecting such an answer, Erica sank down into the chair at the dressing table, meeting the duchess' gaze over her shoulder when she glanced into the mirror.

"There are women who value their reputations above their happiness. And there are women who would angle for a proposal from a duke." The wry edge to her voice made Erica wonder whether the duchess numbered Miss Pilkington among the latter. "I hardly know you, Miss Burke. But from what little I do know, you seem inclined to show better sense than either. Although Tristan is not my son, his happiness means a great deal to me," she continued after a moment. "I would wish for him the sort of match that would make him happy."

Erica dropped her gaze. "And he could not be happy with me."

The words sounded more cutting than she had intended, she realized belatedly. As if she were challenging the duchess' assertion rather than confirming it. But she knew she could not make a man like him happy. Lately, she seemed to be having a great deal of trouble making anyone happy. Including herself.

The duchess' reply, when it came, was measured. "It is, I think, more difficult for a marriage to promote happiness when it has not been freely chosen." She stepped toward the dressing table, picked up the brush, and began to turn it over in her hands. "Though not impossible." Though her movements were unhurried, Erica recognized in them a familiar sort of nervous energy. The type to which she had always assumed real ladies were immune. Particularly duchesses.

She gave the brush an airy wave with a flick of her wrist. "When Vivi was a little girl, I used to brush her hair every night." The slight, faraway smile of memory accompanied the words. "Truth be told…I had little choice. She would never submit to having her nurse do it." Almost absently, she began to run the brush softly over Erica's unruly mass of hair. Her practiced hands made sure, calming strokes, as if Erica were some wild creature capable of being soothed by it. Domesticated. "I think, on the whole, a woman with your spirit would be an equal match for Tristan," she said after a while. Erica's eyes had begun to drift closed, but now popped open, imagining his reaction to his stepmother's pronouncement. "The question, really, is whether you believe he would make you happy." One final stroke, and the duchess returned the brush to the tabletop. "And that question you would seem already to have answered."

Warily, Erica nodded. Oh, yes. She'd left him in no doubt. And if she felt any regret for her hasty reply, what would be the point in wasting energy on the matter? What was done was done.

"Now, wash your face and get dressed, Miss Burke," the duchess ordered as she inspected her own appearance in the mirror, avoiding Erica's gaze. "You have a caller."

"A—a caller?" Erica darted her eyes toward the window, thinking first of her sister. But surely the roads had not yet improved enough for Cami—or anyone else—to travel to Hawesdale.

"Yes. A caller."

Suspecting subterfuge, an attempt to force a meeting with Tristan, Erica sent her a questioning look as she rose. But the duchess would say nothing more.

* * * *

Even before he saw the stranger, Tristan realized that seeking refuge in the library had been a mistake. It was unlike him, unworthy of him, to avoid the breakfast room merely to avoid an uncomfortable scene with his guests. But he'd done it all the same. And for his pains, he was to be treated to uncomfortable memories instead: Erica sweeping from shelf to shelf in search of a suitable volume, his plot to use his poor sister to keep his mysterious guest occupied, and finally, the fateful suggestion to show Erica the conservatory. All of which had led to last night. Charades and kisses and—*Christ*—those heart-stopping moments in her bedchamber, even before he realized he'd been caught.

What he ought to do was write a letter to Colonel Scott and resign his commission. Once, he'd fancied himself a top-notch intelligence officer. Though he'd prayed to never have to put such knowledge to use, he'd learned what to do if he were captured in enemy territory. How to stay silent in the face of threats, even torture. What to say if words must be spoken.

None of that preparation had included blurting out a proposal of marriage.

Nor had he been prepared for the wave of disappointment that had crashed over him when she'd turned him down flat.

He was well aware that throughout Hawesdale at this very moment, people were murmuring about last night, in accents ranging from the servants' northern notes to aristocratic drawls. And every one of those voices was claiming, each in its own way, that Miss Burke must be "tapped." Out of her mind to turn down an offer from a duke.

But if they could see into his mind—or his heart—and if they knew how he had hesitated at the foot of her bed for a moment too long, remembering the feel of her lips and wondering what it would be like to slip beneath the

covers beside her and stay, when all his life he'd only ever wanted to go...
Well, they would have known it was he who'd run mad.

At precisely that moment, he spotted an unfamiliar figure waiting near
the desk and feared he'd added hallucinations to his disorder.

But surely, if his mind were prone to conjuring visions, it would offer
up something more in the line of a certain flame-haired woman? Not a
silver-haired man of medium height, somewhere between fifty and sixty
years, who turned toward the doorway when Tristan made his way deeper
into the room, though he had not made a sound. The carpets were thick as
featherbeds in the library; his father had despised interruptions.

"Good morning, sir," the man said. "I was instructed to wait here for
Miss Burke."

Tristan prided himself on his ability to recognize, on the basis of fewer
words than this man had just spoken, a person's education and origins and
rank. The county he called home—sometimes, even the particular corner
of it. His occupation.

But the stranger remained an enigma. He was not a Londoner, though
he had spent enough time in that city that his birthplace no longer revealed
itself through clipped consonants or rounded vowels. His clothes, his
bearing, all the clues by which people tipped their hands, all the masks
behind which they hid—the collective image formed by these pieces of
evidence was hazy at best. The only sure thing, his unspecified connection
to Erica, raised more questions than it answered.

"Do I have the honor of addressing the Duke of Raynham?" the man
asked, when Tristan did not speak.

Warily, Tristan tipped his head in acknowledgment. "And you are?"

"Arthur Remington, Your Grace." He bowed. "Lord Ashborough's man."

A curious description. Man of business? Manservant? Not a valet, surely,
given his ill-fitting clothes. Yet somehow he carried about him an air of
precision that might, at times, have veered toward the fastidious. Tristan
had the distinct, unsettling impression that Mr. Remington would have
little difficulty assuming whatever role the marquess demanded of him.

"Remy?" Erica's voice came from behind him. Tristan turned to find
her paused on the threshold, as if she too did not trust her eyes.

"Miss Erica." The man's shoulders lowered half an inch, the closest
they likely had ever come to sagging with relief.

Erica hurried to him, skirting past Tristan as if he were no more than
another piece of furniture. "Is Cami here? Is she—?"

"Lady Ashborough is perfectly well, ma'am. In Windermere, with his
lordship."

"He sent you through the storm?" Her gratitude was tinged with a sharper note: annoyance with her brother-in-law for putting another in harm's way. Affronted, the man straightened once more. "He did not. I came of my own free will. Whose fault was it but mine that you were left in Endmoor to begin with?"

"Oh, you dear man." Erica turned on a smile of such radiance that, although not directed at him, it left Tristan almost breathless. "But how did you manage it, through the storms and the flood? The bridge at Kendal—?"

A movement in the doorway caught Tristan's eye. Guin stood framed in the opening, motioning discreetly with one hand for him to come to her side, to afford Erica and Mr. Remington a few moments of quasi-private conversation. Tristan pretended not to see her.

"I had to travel further south and west to cross the Kent," Remington was explaining. "Hence the delay. I should have been back here the next day, otherwise. Despite the rain."

Someone in Endmoor would have directed him to Hawesdale. He might have arrived even before they had. Everything about the last few days would have been different, then.

Tristan stepped toward him. "I was glad to be able to offer Miss Burke my protection."

As if he suspected Tristan's choice of words had not been entirely honest—*protection*, certainly; perhaps even, initially, *glad*—Remington sized him up with a sharp-eyed stare, the likes of which Tristan had rarely known. A softer, worried glance toward Erica, then back again, and his voice when he spoke was hard. "Lord and Lady Ashborough will be obliged, sir."

"Take me to Windermere." Erica stepped closer. "I am ready to leave whenever you say." For the first time, he realized she was wearing her own dress, washed and pressed and almost unrecognizable. She was also carrying her journal. A moment to fetch her pelisse, or have it fetched, and she could walk away from Hawesdale without leaving a trace.

Not a visible one, at any rate.

He parted his lips to say—something. He hardly knew what.

Everyone else believed he had ruined her last night, and he knew of only one way to repair the damage that had been done: repeat his offer, as many times as it took to persuade her of the necessity of accepting it. But he was not entirely convinced he ought to be in the business of persuasion. He despised the sort of man who met a woman's resistance with persistence, who repeated his offers as if her refusal were only a suggestion. She might have grown used to hearing herself called "shatterbrained," but Erica knew her own mind, and he saw no honor in trying to make her doubt it.

Remington too had opened his mouth to reply. But Guin spoke first. "I will not hear of you taking such a risk, Miss Burke. I'm sure Mr. Remington will attest to the poor condition of the roads. I've already arranged with Mrs. Dean for his accommodation. You must both wait until we're certain the rain has stopped for good."

Her tone brooked no argument, but Erica was ready to offer one all the same. "My sister…"

"Would rather see you safe and sound in a few days' time than not at all," Guin replied, clearly intending to close discussion of the matter.

Remington concurred. "I walked every step of more than twenty miles, Miss Erica, through fens that last week were fields." *Of course*, Tristan thought. The man would have arrived at Hawesdale wet and muddy. The clothes he wore now must have been borrowed, likely from Armitage. "And I would not think of allowing a lady to make such a journey. Besides, Lord Ashborough ordered me to stay where I found you and wait for them. This rain can't last forever," Remington added, with a reassuring look for Erica. "Another few days will see the roads passable by carriage, I'm sure."

She set her brow, her lips, her whole body into an answering frown, to which Remington thankfully seemed to be immune. "Now that's settled," Guin announced brightly, "I'm sure Miss Burke will be grateful to hear any report you have to give on her family. I'll send a footman in half an hour to show you to your room. Raynham?"

The peremptory tone in which she spoke his title was more difficult for Tristan to ignore than the wave of her hand had been. And certainly he ought not to expect that Guin's talent for meddling would extend to contriving some scheme in which *he* was to be left alone for a private word with Erica. Still, his answering bow was stiff with disappointment. "Of course. Welcome to Hawesdale, Mr. Remington. Miss Burke."

She had not once so much as glanced his way, and she did not now, though he fancied he glimpsed a slight weakening in her resolve when he spoke her name. As if to be sure of her success, Guin laid her fingertips on his arm to urge him toward the door.

Remington cleared his throat. "Begging Your Grace's pardon, I wonder if I might have a word with the duke first?"

Alone. The unspoken word hung in the air for a moment before Guin grasped it. Her eyes darted toward Tristan, and at his nod, she said, "Of course. Miss Burke, will you walk with me? My daughter has spoken of her botany lessons with such enthusiasm, I am eager to hear your thoughts on her progress."

He fully expected her to refuse. To once more reject the rules society had laid down in the name of "ladylike behavior."

Instead, her shoulders curved inward and her chin dipped. She turned toward the door without a word and was through it so quickly Guin had to scramble to join her. He'd forgotten for a moment how the flare of passion that lit Erica's core sometimes burned itself out. A coal that a moment before had been glowing, now turned pale and collapsed upon itself, hollowed out by the heat that had consumed it, leaving the hearth suddenly cold.

Remington watched her leave, a stern, not-quite-fatherly set to his jaw, but he said nothing, not even when the door closed behind them.

"What can I do for you, Mr. Remington?" Tristan asked after a moment, not troubling to keep the edge of impatience from his voice.

"For me, sir? Nothing at all." Remington seemed genuinely surprised at the notion. He stood with his hands folded behind his back, and again Tristan had the distinct impression that he must know the man, somehow, so familiar did he seem. "I only wished to warn you that your stable hands and your servants seem prone to indulging in gossip."

Tristan had already guessed that rumors were being whispered in Hawesdale's corners, or perhaps shouted from its many ornate rooftops. He knew he had no right to be surprised at this confirmation. Certainly he had no right to be angry at a stranger for supplying it; he had heaped this ignominy on himself. Still, he snapped, "I fail to see what business that might be of yours."

Remington met his heated gaze with coolness, entirely unruffled, not remotely deferential. "None at all, Your Grace. But, as some of what I had the misfortune to overhear concerned Miss Burke and her treatment in this house, I shall feel duty bound to report on the matter to my employer, Lord Ashborough. And I have no doubt he will consider any affront to a member of his family his...business."

Remington's slight hesitation, freighting the word with unsavory connotations, mingled in Tristan's mind with Whitby's description of the Marquess of Ashborough. The accusation of treason in particular. But Tristan was no stranger to unscrupulous characters. "The sort of fellow who'd call me out, I gather," he replied lightly. "Well, I suspect he'll have to wait his turn." At this very moment, Lord Easton Pilkington was probably polishing a pair of pistols, and Tristan was not entirely sure that Whitby didn't mean to take up the matter if Pilkington failed.

Surprise flickered across Remington's face, but before he could give voice to it, someone spoke from the doorway.

"Raynham? A word." As if the mere thought had called him into being, Pilkington stepped across the threshold and strode into the room, either oblivious or indifferent to another man's presence. "I expected to see you at breakfast. I suppose you were too busy thanking your lucky stars that Irish wench refused you."

Out of the corner of his eye, Tristan saw Remington shift ominously. "If you refer to Miss Burke, you would do well to remember that she is a guest of this house."

The man took another step forward, eyes blazing. "As is my daughter, I remind you. *My daughter*, who has borne the affront of your inattention for days, and who last night was forced to witness a shocking spectacle, the likes of which an innocent girl should never—"

"Enough." Tristan paced from the window to the desk and back again, on a spurious quest for calm.

"*Enough?*" Pilkington sputtered. "Oh, I'd say we're at the outside of enough. First your brother, now you. Well, the Laurens family has humiliated my daughter for the last time. I applaud a gentleman who behaves with honor where a *lady* is concerned. In the case of Miss Burke, however—well, we all heard her refusal, though I'll wager it came a bit late," he added in a malicious undertone. "In any case, you're a free man. You'll make Caroline an offer. Today." Beneath the demand, Tristan heard a note of desperation. What exactly lay behind Pilkington's determination to see them wed?

Far below, a movement caught Tristan's eye. Even at this distance, he had no difficulty discerning which of his guests had been desperate for a bit of fresh air, despite the damp. An occasional gust of raw wind twirled the ribbons of Caroline's bonnet and tugged at her normally careful curls. Beside her, Whitby underscored whatever words he was speaking with an agitated wave of his hand.

In his mind's eye, Tristan saw again the flicker of relief cross Caroline's face when he had declined to guess her charade, her momentary hesitation when he'd taken her hand to say good night. He had readily dismissed the notion of Caroline having given her heart to Percy. Only now did it occur to him that she might have given it to someone else.

Perhaps pursuit of a spy was not the only reason Whitby had come to Hawesdale.

Selfish, his oldest friend had called him. Tristan slowly turned to face Pilkington, hands crossed behind his back. "And if I don't?"

Pilkington's chest expanded. But in the time it took for him to draw breath to issue a challenge, he seemed to think better of his words. "You will," he said, his voice flat with anger, and perhaps just an edge of doubt. "You'll find her in the breakfast room."

Though tempted to invite the man to glance out the window, Tristan merely allowed his mouth to curve in a grim sort of half-smile. Pilkington, ready to read the expression as resignation, gave a nod of satisfaction and left the room.

Remington had observed the entire exchange from nearer the fireplace, unremarked and unremarking. Now, amusement glimmered in the depths of the man's eyes. "You offered for Miss Erica," he said, the ghost of a chuckle in his voice. "And she turned you down flat."

Tristan stepped behind his father's desk—an unlikely refuge, but one he'd been forced to seek more than once lately. "I regret that the offer was necessary. It was never my intention to dishonor Miss Burke." He reached out a hand to square Davies's stack of account books. "Will her family have something to say about her refusal?"

"Maybe." He shrugged. "And maybe she'll listen if they do. But I doubt it. She's got more spirit than sense, that one," he added with an affectionate shake of his head.

Instinctively, Tristan rose to her defense. "I'd say Miss Burke appears to be possessed of ample quantities of both."

Remington took the correction in stride. "Based on what I've seen of Lady Ashborough, I'd say they're family characteristics." He paused, obviously considering his next words. "It sounds to me, from what that other fellow said, as if you've already got enough to be going on with. Best to let Miss Erica be. You can thank your lucky stars you fared better than the chap in Endmoor, anyway."

For just a moment, everything went still, quiet enough that he suspected the other man could hear his mind whirr. "Endmoor?" He'd known she'd passed through there, of course. But he hadn't imagined any lengthy encounters. Had Whitby been right about one thing? Had she been lurking around the neighborhood after all?

"She left her journal in the dining room at the inn where we stopped to rest the horses. That was how she got separated from her sister—no one realized she'd gone back inside to get it. Well, a young fellow happened to pick it up. When she caught him poking his nose where it didn't belong, she gave him a wallop with it." Another knowing smile, this one a shade more bloodthirsty. "Poor lad's had naught but gruel since, according to the publican."

Tristan mustered a smile. "I might still end up in worse shape if you recommend Lord Ashborough run me through."

"Oh, as to that, I daresay he's got better things to do too." Remington laughed. "After all, he's a newly married man, Your Grace. Though on occasion," he added, tugging the overlarge waistcoat into place over his surprisingly fit torso, "he does let me take matters into my own hands."

With little other recourse left to him on what was shaping up to be an absurd day, Tristan laughed. He knew, suddenly, why the other man seemed so familiar. "Were you in the army, Mr. Remington?"

"I was. The Fighting Fortieth. Until '77. Injured at the Battle of Germantown and sent home to stay."

Tristan knew the regiment by reputation, fierce men whose service during the war against the American colonies had spanned the Atlantic, from Nova Scotia to the West Indies. No wonder Remington spoke with pride, and a hint of regret at the unwelcome end to his career. "An officer?" he ventured.

"No, sir!"

Only a certain sort of soldier would issue such a vigorous denial of an officer's rank. But Tristan had no doubt the man had held a position of authority. A sergeant, then, probably in command of a platoon. Tough as nails. And far better to have as an ally than an enemy.

Stepping from behind the desk, Tristan offered his hand, which Remington shook firmly. "Welcome to Hawesdale, Mr. Remington." When he released the handshake, Tristan swept his arm toward the door to usher the other man out. Almost to the threshold, though, he hesitated. "May I ask one more question?"

Remington cocked his head. "I won't stop you."

Tristan dropped his voice, hoping to prompt the man's confidence. "What's in Miss Burke's journal?"

The other man rocked back on his heels. "So the fellow down at Endmoor isn't the only curious fool in these parts, eh?" When Tristan made no reply, he shrugged. "Sketches, so she says. Notes about flowers. But I've never seen inside it, you understand." He laughed to himself as he preceded Tristan through the door. "For all I know, it could contain the plans of the entire French fleet."

And that, Tristan thought, a grim smile twisting his lips, *was precisely the problem.*

Chapter 14

Already distracted, even more so than usual, Erica did not immediately realize she was party to a staged distraction. The simple breakfast, enjoyed tête-à-tête in the Duchess of Raynham's private sitting room, was followed by a comfortable coze about family life, educational principles for young ladies, and Lady Viviane in particular. Tristan's name was never mentioned.

Only when the girl failed to appear, despite her mother's repeated insistence on Viviane's enthusiasm for her botany lessons, and the servant who came to clear the dishes was waved away, did Erica begin to suspect that she was being deliberately kept apart.

Did the duchess hope to shelter her from facing the combined scorn of Hawesdale's occupants? Or were those worthies being protected from further exposure to a woman of dubious character?

Erica came to her feet so abruptly her journal slid from her lap, and she had to fumble to keep it from ending up on the floor. Her journal. Her anchor. And Tristan had very nearly succeeded in severing that tie and casting her out to sea.

"Miss Burke?"

Erica hardly heard her. Inside her head, all was chaos, confusion. Of course. Always. Except…mightn't there be times when such confusion was justified? And wasn't this one of those times? Perhaps even the duchess, all smooth good grace in the face of the unexpected, would have met the events of last night with uncertainty. An intruder. A near-theft. An offer. Had she done the wrong thing? Said the wrong thing? Propriety might demand she accept, but didn't good sense dictate she refuse a man she couldn't trust? Besides, Tristan demanded perfection in all things. And no one had ever thought her perfect.

She was at the door before she realized her feet had begun to wander too. "Miss Burke? Are you all right?" The duchess' voice came as if from far away. If she followed Erica to the threshold, she let her cross it unaccompanied. Let her go. Where was she going? *The conservatory, of course.* Its peace beckoned.

Fate smiled on the decision; she met not a single soul in the corridors, and the glasshouse itself was empty.

Deep, desperate breaths. One, two, three. A damp, heavy scent that had no name. The smell of growth and decay combined. Weakly, she sank onto one of the benches ringing the orange trees and wondered where she would find the strength to leave.

She might have been sitting for a moment or an hour when she heard the door open, the protest of its hinges echoing in the glass-ceilinged jungle. He'd found her again. The only real surprise was that he'd been looking. He clearly had not wanted to propose last night and had done so only out of that twisted sense of honor the duchess had described. After his coolness in the library, she had not expected to speak with him again before she left Hawesdale. As she turned toward the sound of his footsteps, the figured metal bench pressed into her skin, giving her back some of its iron resolve.

The visitor was not, however, Tristan.

"Captain Whitby?"

She struggled to rise as he wended his way toward the center of the room. But before she was fully on her feet, he had sunk to the bench beside her, his posture relaxed. A shade too relaxed. The sour odor of brandy mingled with the other scents of the glasshouse.

When he spoke, his voice had lost some of its usual crispness. What had happened to put him into such a state, and the day not half gone? "I wish I knew your secrets, Miss Burke," he mumbled.

Reflexively, she curled her fingers around her journal where it lay on the bench between them.

"Oh, not just those," he said with a laugh, reaching to tap its cover, his index finger brushing the back of her hand in passing.

Given their positions, his touch could not fail to call Tristan's to mind, though the effect could not have been less similar. She drew back, pulling the book more tightly against the side of her leg, braced by the bite of its one remaining sharp corner.

"I thought I knew the game you were playing," he said, "but I can't for the life of me figure out your rules."

"Game?"

"No need to be coy. We're all anglers in the same boat, here."

"I don't—"

"Did you reel him in last night?" He spoke over her, shaking his head, her protests unheard. "A few moments, or an hour, in the darkness—surely you had enough time. Women have ways of making men talk…even the famously tight-lipped Major Laurens, I'll wager." His expression was just shy of a leer.

Although her brain had been primed by a constant stream of disjointed disorder, Erica could make little sense of his rambling speech. "What is it you believe I've done? Of what are you accusing me, sir?"

"It's really too bad you're on the wrong side," he said with another mournful shake of his head. "I've met your brothers in arms, you know. In Paris. A sharp set of fellows, the United Irishmen. Principled, after their way. But none quite as savvy as you…"

Paris. The United Irishmen. Various leaders of the cause had been forced to flee to France. But what had taken the captain into the path of those men? Suddenly she remembered the day of her arrival. Whitby's story about the suspicious poets. Could he be some sort of spy himself? An agent of the British crown?

"The scream was an inspired touch," he continued, sounding reluctantly impressed. "At first I wondered why you'd done it. But what defense could he offer, in the face of all those people? And as for you…well, you got just what you came for. Now when you slip away from Hawesdale, everyone will imagine they know why." His slightly unfocused gaze traveled leisurely down her arm, coming to rest once more on her journal. "What's next, Miss Burke? Oh, how I'd like to know what you've got up your sleeve…"

A chill slithered across her skin, following the same path as his eyes. *We're all anglers in the same boat,* he'd said. "Are you saying you believe me to be—? That the Duke of Raynham is a—?" *No.* Not the Duke of Raynham. He'd called him *Major Laurens.* The officer. The hero. The…

"Shhh…" Whitby lifted one finger to her lips while stifling his own laugh.

She leaped up, journal in hand. "You're drunk, Captain Whitby. I'm not sure you ought to be telling me all this. And I'm quite sure we shouldn't be here alone."

He rose too, steadier on his feet than she expected, and leaned closer. Too close. The stench of liquor overwhelmed every other scent—as if he'd splashed more of it on his clothes than he'd tossed down his throat. Perhaps his drunkenness was an act, an attempt to get her to say something she'd regret, something she hoped he'd forget? But his pale eyes glittered menacingly, and she guessed he'd swallowed a fair share of the brandy too.

"Frightened?" he whispered. "Don't be. We're not really alone." His eyes darted about before coming to rest on her face once more. "This is the proverbial glass house. Any fool should know that someone's always watching."

Ordinarily, she would have looked around her, but instinct told her not to take her eyes off him. Perhaps Mr. Sturgess would come in. Or servants in the kitchen would hear if she—

His bitter laugh sent another puff of brandy-scented breath into her face. "I wouldn't advise screaming. You've used that gambit once, and I don't believe a lady can claim she's been compromised twice."

Oh, what did he want from her? A plea rose in her throat, but she could not shape it into words.

While they had been speaking, the room had been growing steadily dimmer. Whitby glanced upward, and lines of smug satisfaction settled over his face. "You might have got what you came for, Miss Burke. But it doesn't look like you'll get away with it, after all."

With those words, he turned and left as he'd come, each step a shade more deliberate than a sober man's would have been. Just as the door latched behind him, a rumble of thunder rattled the room from floor to ceiling. So that was what he'd meant about not getting away. Rain once more lashed against the glass, and she shuddered as if struck.

But her reasons for wanting to be able to leave Hawesdale were not at all what Captain Whitby had insinuated. Was the man mad? *She*, a spy?

The surrounding greenery absorbed her nervous laughter. She'd heard people call her elder sister a patriot, not always meaning the term as a compliment. And her brothers, of course…along with Henry… Well, if Whitby suspected their connection to the United Irishmen, their involvement in the uprising last May, he was not wrong. But how her whole family would laugh if they ever heard anyone suggest she might be a *spy*. Spies were clever and secretive, while she was famously flighty. Why, forgetting her journal was what had landed her in this mess to begin with, and—

The book tumbled from her suddenly nerveless grasp and landed at her feet, the soft *whap* of leather against stone lost to the tattoo of rain on the roof. Captain Whitby believed she was a spy because…because Tristan believed she was a spy. Or vice versa. Either way, they had convinced themselves that she'd been gathering secrets at Hawesdale. Military secrets. Diplomatic secrets. And recording them in her journal.

Her pulse hammered in her breast, her ears, her…finger? Raising it to her eyes, she watched a perfect, tiny globe of blood form. A page of her journal must have cut her in passing. Salt and a faintly metallic tang greeted her tongue when she pressed the wounded fingertip to her lips, an unwelcome reminder of Whitby's touch, a macabre mockery of the last kiss she'd experienced in this room.

Every look Tristan had given her, every word he'd spoken...their encounters spun across her memory like the distorted scenes cast against the wall by a child's magic lantern. Always, at the back of his mind, he'd been thinking of her as a spy. As the enemy.

He'd even proposed *marriage*. More laughter bubbled to her lips— decidedly manic, this time—but made no escape. Was there no limit to how far he'd go to get what he wanted? To uncover every secret she kept? Even the priceless gift of these hours in the conservatory...

Any fool should know that someone's always watching.

Mr. Sturgess, the duchess, even Viviane... Feeling suddenly exposed, she scrambled for shelter, stumbling toward the door, no more steady on her feet than Whitby had been. No, she'd tripped. Tripped over her journal, which lay abandoned on the damp flagstone where it had slipped from her grasp. Once, the mere sight of its worn leather cover had been calming, the doorway to a place where her weary mind might find respite. But now...?

She turned back, resisted the impulse to kick it away, snatched it up instead. Heat flared through her arm, the same pulse of energy that had laid low the nosy soldier in the pub. So Tristan wanted to know what was inside her journal? Inside *her?* Very well.

After shoving aside a spiky *Agave americana* to clear a space at the nearest table, she sat down, found the pencil stub, flipped to an empty page, and began to write.

* * * *

The gentlemen dined alone—all but Whitby, who was nowhere to be found.

Neither, as it happened, was Erica.

After last night's events, which the other men were pretending not to discuss in his presence, Tristan could hardly blame her for keeping to herself. All day he had done his best to heed Mr. Remington's advice to let her be. Oh, he'd poked his head into the library once or twice, and considered enquiring of Sturgess. Guin had volunteered that she'd last seen Miss Burke late morning and kindly sent her maid to her chamber to check on her, but the maid's knock had gone unanswered. Under ordinary circumstances, Erica's absence would not have occasioned him a moment's worry. She did not set her watch by the rest of the world's clock.

But these were far from ordinary circumstances, and he could not shake his misgivings.

Her nonappearance at dinner went unremarked, and perhaps even unobserved since none of the other ladies were present either. Guin was dining privately with Vivi. Sir Thomas only shrugged when asked after Lady Lydgate, and Tristan declined to enquire of Beresford, though he was as likely to know that lady's whereabouts as the baronet. Mr. Newsome reported that his wife was overseeing the packing of her trunk, despite the resumption of the rain. Thanks to the changeable weather, Lady Easton Pilkington had succumbed to another headache, and Caroline had insisted upon playing nurse to her mother. Pilkington had looked rather sheepish as he had made that announcement, then explained to Tristan in a quieter voice that his conversation with Caroline would have to wait another day. Tristan had only nodded.

Once they were seated, Tristan ran his gaze around the table at five gentlemen who, if they had possessed any interests in common, had exhausted those subjects a fortnight past. Beneath the table, one booted foot tapped restlessly. For all that their numbers were few, the meal dragged on interminably, course after course. When port at last was served, Beresford sipped at his glass, more abstemious than the parson; if Lady Lydgate was somewhere waiting for him, he seemed to be in no hurry to join her. Pilkington had the nerve to call for coffee.

At last, however, the meal came to an end. Someone suggested billiards, but he was already to the door. "Be my guest," he said, only glancing over his shoulder. "I'll join you another night."

Ridiculous, really, for him to worry. He wasn't worried about Whitby's absence, after all, and God knew he was as likely to—

Whitby.

Tristan stopped stock still in the middle of the corridor, closed his eyes, and pulled from the reaches of his mind every word the man had spoken to him since his arrival, every topic they'd discussed. Danger and duty. Rumors and spies. He'd been instantly suspicious of Erica. *She's* Irish, *Tris.* Certainly David Whitby was not the only Englishman who regarded being Irish as crime enough. But surely, surely his oldest friend, his fellow officer, would not have—

Almost before he had opened his eyes, his feet were moving again. Past the empty library, the dark drawing room. He hardly paused. The glasshouse was his destination. He ought to have looked for her there hours ago. Pride had kept him as far from it as the house allowed. Pray God his pride had not been her downfall.

A single candle had been left burning, one flickering flame that sent its hazy glow through the square pane of glass in the unlocked door, deepening the shadows wherever its light was too weak to penetrate.

When he opened the door, the couple seated beneath the orange trees sprang guiltily apart, their hands still clasped as he approached. At last Whitby released Caroline and stood.

"Miss Pilkington." Tristan bowed and instantly regretted his stiffness. She would misread it as jealousy. "Whitby."

Instead of fumbling explanations and apologies, silence hung in the room, louder than the rain against the roof. Caroline, too, got to her feet. "I was—I should go back to Mama. She will be in need of another draught. Excuse me." She started past him, unable to meet his eye.

He wished he could free her, offer his blessing of her choice. But at the moment, Whitby had lost his trust. And Caroline's father, having twice had his appetite whetted by the prospect of wedding his only daughter to the heir to a dukedom, was unlikely to be satisfied with a mere captain.

Whitby hurried forward to curl possessive fingers around her elbow. "I'll walk with you."

"Wait."

They paused in their flight. Caroline's eyes stayed focused resolutely on the ground.

"Has either of you seen Miss Burke?"

She looked up then, neither surprised nor, thankfully, hurt by his question. She shook her head. *The truth.* He felt certain of it. He turned his gaze on Whitby, whose face was a carefully schooled blank. Tristan had worked with him to perfect that expression. "Not recently," the captain murmured, his pale eyes steady and unreadable.

"Then when?"

A pause. "I can't quite recall, Your Grace."

When a man claimed he couldn't recall, it was almost always a lie.

Tristan could demand an honest answer. But a weak, foolish part of him did not want to press for the truth, only to have his friend respond with a sneer: *When? Why, I saw her last night, a little past midnight—as did everyone else.* Nor did he wish to risk hearing something even worse.

As Whitby turned and urged Caroline toward the door, Tristan slammed his palm on the table next to him, nearly upsetting some pointy-leaved plant in a clay pot. But the surface beneath his hand wasn't the tabletop, whose warped, scuffed boards would have felt rough. What lay beneath his fingertips was smooth leather.

He hardly dared look down to confirm his suspicions. It might be any number of things. Vivi had a habit of sneaking novels; she might have brought one to her botany lesson and abandoned it. Sturgess no doubt wrote records or notes in something and might keep such a book at hand. No reason for his mind to leap immediately to...

Erica's journal.

Last night's surge of triumph at having it in his hands had long since fled, to be replaced with unease. The beginnings of terror. *She's left it lying around before.* The memory brought little reassurance. She had, of course, forgotten her journal once or twice, to memorable effect. But this felt somehow different. Call it a hunch. Gut instinct. A good agent relied more often than he'd like to admit on both. And the sight of that journal lying atop the table, half hidden by greenery, was some kind of sign. A message. As if she'd expected him to look for her here. As if she'd wanted him to find it.

Was it a call for help? Had something happened to her?

Or was it a test?

His fingertips still resting lightly on the cover, he looked slowly around the conservatory. Beyond its windows, all was wet and dark. He could see nothing outside. But the single candle burning nearby would ensure that anyone who chose to look in could easily see him. Leaves and limbs, jagged and smooth, cast eerie shadows around the room. The steam that rose from the vents in the floor stirred the air and brought those shadows to life.

"Is anyone there?"

Silence. Not even an echo.

With exaggerated care, as if he feared moving the book would set off an alarm or trigger a blast, he lifted it from the table, tucked it under his arm, and looked around once more.

"Erica?"

Still nothing. He spun on one foot, the rasp of boot leather against the stone floor loud in the stillness, and left the conservatory. He had to find her.

But this search was no more successful than the last. Armitage told him that Mr. Remington had retired early and he'd see no sign of Miss Burke all afternoon. Guin, too, had gone to bed. Outside the billiards room, he could hear the soft clack of ivory balls, some laughter, an oath. Male voices, all. All was quiet in the drawing room, the library, even the schoolroom. He certainly could not tap on her chamber door. Resigned, he descended the stairs to his suite.

The wrinkled pages of the journal whispered to him from the table where he laid it when he went to undress. After he'd crawled into bed, he leaned over the table to snuff the candles. The journal stared up at him, inscrutable. What if she'd wanted him to find it, to read it? What if she were counting on him to discover the truth?

With a muttered curse, he snatched it up.

He studied its binding first, the quality of the leather, the strength of the stitching. When he ran his thumb over the edge of the pages, the contents fluttered to life. Fragments of words and pictures appeared and were gone before he could make sense of them. Before he could rightly be called guilty of reading the thing.

At last, though, there was nothing for it but to open it and find out whether he had been right about Erica Burke. Or dreadfully, dangerously wrong.

For a moment, he weighed the choice of starting at the beginning or opening to a random point. As it was Erica's handiwork, he suspected that a randomly chosen page was as likely to be significant as any. But his mind balked at such a haphazard approach. With a degree of trepidation he tried to dismiss as unreasonable, he peeled back the front cover and saw at the very top of the first page, in a surprisingly ornate hand,

Property of E. Burke

The tails of letters had been turned to branches and leaves, the *E* a fantastical bloom. Beneath her name, in a plainer, masculine hand, were the words

To Erica, from Henry
Christmas, 1797
Dublin

A less lover-like inscription he could hardly imagine. But evidently the journal—and at least some of what it represented to its owner?—had in fact been a gift from the man she had intended to marry. As initial discoveries went, it was almost enough to make him lay the book aside.

Almost.

The second and third pages, spread to the light, revealed what any agent would have recognized immediately as a key. A key to a code he did not know. The symbols were common enough: circles like phases of the moon, empty, half, and full; a leaf; a manicule. And something that looked like a tiny coiled spring. Each symbol correlated to an explanation, a word or phrase—in Latin, if he didn't miss his guess. But not Latin as he'd learned it in school, or as he'd seen spies use the language since. The beginnings of a headache prickled behind his eyes. He had not expected to spend the night translating and code-breaking.

The spelling, the abbreviation, the grammar were all rather...*esoteric*, particularly when combined with a tendency to ornament the letters and margins with botanical flourishes. It might have been a masterful attempt at disguising her intentions. But somehow it felt more like the handiwork of one who'd been inattentive during lessons. Or perhaps had never really been taught? He thought of the conversation with Miss Chatham he'd overheard, about young ladies and ancient languages and Erica's somewhat haphazard education. He'd heard people speak derisively of "lady's Greek," a simplified version, without the accents. Could there be a lady's Latin, too?

More likely, she'd never been offered the opportunity to study the subject properly at all. Suddenly, his mental picture of a girl learning at her father's knee morphed into a girl sneaking peeks at her brother's textbooks, independent and determined and perhaps a little ashamed of her curiosity.

Understanding Erica's journal was going to require him to set aside what he thought he knew. About cryptography. About languages. About her.

All right, then. The circles might indicate…memoranda, of a sort. Tasks to be done, tasks half done, tasks finished. The leaves seemed likely to pertain to botanical observations, ostensibly the primary subject of the journal. Manicules drew attention to something important. And the little spirals? They alone had no description in the key. He'd have to sort it out as he went along.

Slowly he ran his thumb across the edges of the pages again. This time, the symbols, dotting the corner of nearly every page, sometimes two or three to a page, stood out. With the pressure of his thumbnail, he stopped the movement at the drawing of Hawesdale, which looked much as it had when he'd seen it before. A manicule and a circle, filled half with pencil and half with ink, had been added in one corner. At the bottom of the page, a list of names: the upper servants, Guin's maid, the family, the other guests. *P—?* had been crossed out and replaced with *Pilkington. Viviane* was misspelled.

Nothing more devious than a memory aid. He went on.

Next came nearly a dozen painstakingly detailed sketches of the passionflower, its parts carefully labeled, the corner of each page marked with a tiny leaf, confirming his guess about the symbol's meaning. The handwriting here was neater, unembellished, the text a mix of English and passable Latin, the observations precise and scientific. Nothing that seemed out of the ordinary for a botanist.

Following that, a three-part list, the hand rather shaky: <u>Important things</u>, <u>Insignificant things</u>, <u>Things that require further reflection</u>. *Dk of R*— was included beneath each heading. In the upper left-hand corner, she'd drawn a circle and filled in half of it. Which of these items did she consider completed? Which were yet to be done?

He could tell by the smooth feel of the paper beneath his hands that most of the pages after that were empty, so he flipped again to the front to make a more methodical study. The artistry of the flower sketches could not be denied. Indeed, he could have passed a pleasant evening examining them and making more thorough translations of her notes about the plants' attributes and uses. A few had been marked with a dagger, its handle shaped like a capital *P*. *Poisonous*, he presumed.

The pages of pictures and notes were interspersed with more lists. Guests at another dinner party, in order of precedence, the list marked with a half circle. The steps to a dance, with tiny pictures of footprints to accompany them. The variety of things she had hoped—and in many cases, as indicated by heavy *X*s, had failed—to remember brought a wry smile to his lips. Had he really ever believed she might be a spy?

That smile faded when he came to a map, the borders lavishly illustrated with exotic-looking plants, each connected by a dotted line to some tropical land. The places she had hoped to visit when her marriage gave her the freedom to do so? Quickly, he turned to the next pages—several left blank for no rhyme or reason he could discern. But after those came a section of close-written prose in the abbreviated quasi-Latin of the key, the page marked with a spiral—a labyrinth, he'd decided, the wandering path her thoughts took whenever she tried to make sense of herself. For though there were fewer of those mysterious marks than any other, all were appended to what appeared to be diary entries: a complaint about her sister, or some words of mourning for her betrothed.

Over this particular page, however, he hesitated, though the code was not especially sophisticated—something to deter the casual sneak, a younger sibling with prying eyes, perhaps. Leaning on one elbow, he held the book closer to the candle, the better to make out her handwriting. A list of something. Undated. Composed over time, in fact—more than one pen had been used. At times her hand had been firm and steady; at others, considerably less so.

After some effort, he managed to sort out what the page contained: a long catalog of someone's sins and the punishments to be meted out for them. Lateness, slovenliness, forgetfulness. Erica's sins—for such she clearly imagined them to be.

> ~*For a wandering mind during Dr. V's sermon, one hour copying Fordyce*
> ~*For neglecting to reply promptly to C's last, no sugar in tea this fortnight*

*~For missing dinner three times this week— Query: when
mortification inheres to the act itself, may not that prove
sufficient?? (cf., inattentiveness at church—perhaps damned
already?)*

He nearly closed the book at that, jerking his gaze to a spot on the carpet
and sucking in a breath that rattled a bit in the silence of his chamber.
Such ordinary, human failings. And she imagined herself consigned to
hellfire for them.

When his breathing had steadied, he made himself return to the list.

~For sloth...

He made no attempt to decipher the punishment. *Sloth?* How could such
a word even be applied to Erica, whose vibrant energy he had imagined
impossible to contain? But she had tried to contain it. Tried again and
again. The list of infractions filled the page and spilled onto the next; the
punishments grew increasingly dire. He could not go on reading them.
He could not look away.

The journal fanned shut around his first finger, catching where the stub
of a pencil had been wedged deep between the pages. With trepidation,
he opened there to find an unencrypted letter, composed with the dull
implement that marked its place.

Dear Sir,
*You will not, I hope, be greatly offended at my form of
address. I find I have not the slightest notion of the proper
salutation to use when writing to a duke. If such was ever a part
of my education, I have long since forgot it.*
*Thanks to Captain Whitby, I now know what you imagined
my journal contained and why you attempted to steal it from me
last night. Only you can decide whether you have now found
what you sought.*
*You will do me the favor of returning it when you are done. It
contains things of value to me, if to no one else.*

The note was signed with a perfectly ordinary *E.* How ridiculous that
he should spare a pang of disappointment for its lack of embellishment,
when the words of the letter itself were so stark. But it too was a symbol,
like the half-filled circles and spirals and leaves. A symbol of who she had

been when the journal began. And who she had become over the course of filling its pages.

Thanks in no small part to him and what she clearly regarded as his betrayal.

The journal slipped from his hands as he tipped his head back into the pillows and closed his eyes, utterly drained by what could not have been more than an hour's work. In his years as an agent, he'd decoded and read far worse: blackmail, murder plots, brutal acts of war. He'd been deeply invested in uncovering the truth. But he hadn't cared about their senders, he realized belatedly. Hadn't worried for their intended recipients. Not in the way he cared and worried now. Before, he'd relied upon his intellect, his sense of right, his pride. Never before had he ceded any corner of his heart. But the author of this journal had found a place there, that much he could no longer deny.

Was that a sound? He opened his eyes to discover that, for the second time that day, he had called the object of his thoughts into being. Erica stood beside his bed.

Chapter 15

She took unexpected pleasure in the way his gaze cut away and color streaked across the sharp crests of his cheekbones. A visible reminder that he was not actually, entirely in control of *everything*.

"I'd get up," he said, his fingers curling in the bed linens, drawing them higher over his chest, "but…"

But beneath that sheet, he was naked. She knew because she'd watched from behind as he'd walked from his dressing room—his *un*dressing room—to the bed, his figure a marble sculpture come to life, all gleaming muscled curves and intriguing shadowed hollows. Up close now, she found herself unwillingly fascinated by the way candlelight highlighted the slopes and valleys of his broad shoulders, the notch at the base of his throat, the surprisingly dark hair that dusted his chest and led downward in a neat furrow that drew her attention to the very edge of the sheet and even lower.

Determinedly, she dragged her eyes back to his face. "I seem to recall telling you once before that you needn't worry about observing the niceties with me. Standing when I stand and so forth. Now you know why." She nodded toward her journal where it lay in his lap, only the thinnest of barriers between the deepest secrets of her heart and his— Heat crept into her own cheeks. "You're a spy, aren't you? And Whitby said you believed I was too. That's why you came into my room last night. You were looking for my journal. For proof."

He jerked his gaze to hers. "No. I mean, yes. I *was* looking for your journal. Because of my work and what Whitby had said. But the moment I laid a hand on it—no, the moment I set out for your chamber, I knew what I wanted to find. What I *would* find. Proof of your innocence."

Several times, she had caught herself wondering whether he was telling the truth. A man in his position would have ample reason to perfect the art of lying. But his face now was open, his eyes fixed on hers, not trying to hide. She could see the pulse throbbing at the base of his throat. Though perhaps she shouldn't, she so wanted to believe him.

"I suspect Whitby said a great many things," he said after a moment, "or else you would not have"—one hand passed over the cover of her journal without touching it—"left this for me to find." A pause, and now his eyes were searching, as if she had not revealed enough. As if she had not already revealed everything. "That was your intent, was is not?"

At first, she'd been angry, seeing him with it in his hands. When he'd found it lying in the conservatory, he hadn't been able to restrain his curiosity. He'd taken the bait.

Then she'd debated with herself whether she was being reasonable—her barrister brother's influence, no doubt. Tristan was an army officer, devoted to king and country, duty bound to investigate someone he believed to be a threat to either. Knowing as much, she had set out to trap him. The letter she'd written proved as much. Not exactly sporting.

In the end, she settled on *anxious*. Peering from the doorway of the sitting room, desperate to read him, even as he read what was hers. Trying to follow his thoughts as he moved from page to page, forward and back again. Studying the curve of his lips, up or down, watching for the precise moment when the notch of concentration in his brow morphed into a frown.

Now, however, standing inches from him, her anxiety had escalated to fear. Terror. He might be wearing nothing, but she was the one who'd been stripped bare. All her life, she'd worked to hide it, the internal chaos that threatened constantly to overwhelm her. She'd kept secrets from everyone—even the man she'd pledged to marry. But she'd rashly revealed them to Tristan. No secrets anymore.

He said nothing, and the hard bud of her fear split its calyx and blossomed into defiance. Insolence. The jutting chin. The bold words. "You may regret the lost triumph of unmasking a spy, but you must be relieved I did not accept your hasty proposal."

With one long finger, he traced a corner of the cover of her journal, where the leather had softened and curled. She watched the movement stir the fine bones in the back of his hand, then allowed her gaze to travel up his forearm, over the curving bulge of his bicep. When he lifted the book from his lap and extended it to her, she reached to snatch it from him, lest he change his mind. But this time he released it without hesitation.

In that moment of exchange, however, his other hand rose to catch hers. With the lightest of touches, he mapped the sharp angles of her fingers where they gripped her journal, the regrettably tanned skin of the back of her hand, the soft, plump curve at the base of her thumb. He made no attempt to hold her. With the slightest flick of her wrist, she would have been free of his touch. If she turned and walked away, she would be free of him, for he was in no condition to leap up and follow her.

She watched his fingertips skate over her skin. She stayed where she was.

"May I ask one question?" His gaze was fixed where he touched her, and he did not look up as he spoke. She hadn't the strength, suddenly, to do more than nod.

He must have sensed the movement, however, for he lifted his eyes to her face, his expression at once fierce and uncertain, seeking confirmation. She nodded again.

"I wish to know…" The words came with difficulty, and why not? A clenched jaw was hardly conducive to speech. "The course of…correction you undertook." *Revulsion. Anger.* In his voice and in the depths of his blue-black eyes. "Who recommended it to you?" Clearly, he wanted to punish the offending party.

Well, so had she.

"It was my own device," she said. "Henry gave me the journal, to record my botanical observations, he said. But it gave me an idea. You see, I've always been able to recall every flower, every plant I've ever studied, and I thought, perhaps, if I wrote down other things, if I kept a schedule, I might…I might manage almost to be a real wife to him. Not"—heat prickled in her cheeks—"not in all ways, of course, but someone of whom he needn't be ashamed. Surely, I told myself, surely I was capable of organizing a dinner party without forgetting to invite the guests. Or dancing a quadrille without stepping on his toes. So I embarked on a course of self-improvement. I tried…" Her shoulders rose and fell with an unsteady breath. "…everything."

"*Erica.*"

His chiding whisper held a bewildering mix of emotions. His disapproval she understood, even shared. After all, every attempt to better herself had ended in miserable failure. But disbelief? No, he needed to understand that *this*—she tightened her grip on her journal, inadvertently drawing his hand closer to hers—this was exactly who she was.

"Every bit of what you saw in that journal is true. The confusion, the messiness…"

"The artistry, the cleverness," he countered. "The dreams. You might have done yourself real harm, Erica." Mournfully, he shook his head. "All in an effort to eradicate a few trivial faults."

"*Trivial?*" To hear them dismissed as such hurt worse than anything that had gone before. "So they may seem to you, when they affect you not at all. You who have no difficulty concentrating, or composing your thoughts, or—or—remembering when you last ate."

"No," he agreed, a bite of annoyance in his voice, echoed in the press of his fingertips. "Your struggles are not mine. It does not therefore follow that I have no struggles at all. And in a world of men who lie and steal and even kill, I can see no earthly reason for you to—to mortify your flesh like some medieval monk, just because the dinner hour slipped your mind."

Here in his bedchamber, with him stripped of his uniform, it was easy to forget he was a soldier. That he'd surely seen terrible things. And perhaps even done them. She inched toward the bed, hoping to slacken his taut grip. But coming closer did nothing to ease the tension between them.

"You're right," she said, glancing away, no longer able to meet his eye. "A lady's choices are few, her actions often insignificant, for all that she might hope otherwise. Perhaps that's why I never aspired to be a lady."

"Yet you were willing to marry, despite your concerns."

"I did not want to be dependent on my parents for all their lives, and on my brothers thereafter. Nor could I see myself pursuing any of the options open to a young woman in my situation. Can you imagine me teaching?" A ragged, uncertain laugh bubbled from her chest. "I might plan and organize for days or weeks, then forget to give the lesson. Or daydream during the children's recitations. Oh, if you'd taken the measure of my pulse the other evening, when I feared you were about to offer me the post of Lady Viviane's governess, then you'd—"

Whatever words she'd intended to say evaporated into the ether. Slowly, gently, he'd turned her hand and eased his thumb beneath the hem of her sleeve to stroke along her inner wrist where the skin was soft and thin. "It races even now."

Yes, of course, she wanted to say. Her heart often rattled against her ribs, as if trying to keep pace with her thoughts. And *yes, of course* her heart raced now, because she'd cracked open her chest for him and laid everything bare. And *yes, of course* her heart raced now, because he was touching her, and although the last thing she wanted was to bear the responsibilities of being a duchess, that didn't mean she didn't want other things from the duke. Things she'd sworn she would be content never to have. Things she sensed she could have at this very moment if only she were brave.

She held her breath, rose up on her toes, and leaned in to kiss him.

Eyes wide with surprise, he drew back sharply, the back of his head almost striking the ornately carved headboard.

In her life, she'd frequently been troubled by mistakes she'd made. Even in the short history of her acquaintance with Tristan, she'd had ample occasion to feel embarrassment. But never—oh God, *never*—had she wanted to run and hide from what she'd done the way she did now.

She tried to right herself, fumbled for balance, and might have fallen if not for the fact that the journal still linked them. In the split second during which she debated simply letting go of it, his other hand came up and caught her. One strong arm wrapped around her waist, pinning her against the mattress.

She didn't struggle against his hold. All the fight had gone out of her. What a fool she had been. Fixing unseeing eyes on the pattern of the coverlet, she waited for him to release her.

The hand that had been curled around hers let go first...only to slide slowly, lightly up her arm, over her shoulder, to cup the side of her head. "Erica?" A question and not a question. Wonder. Reassurance. The warm pressure of his arm against her hip did not relent. "I'm sorry. You caught me off guard."

She dragged her gaze back to his face. "I should have thought by now you'd have come to expect the unexpected where I'm concerned."

A smile ghosted across his lips, momentarily softening his granite features. "You're right, of course. I only meant...that is to say...after you turned me down..."

Once more her eyes were drawn to the complex geometry of the coverlet. "I turned down your offer *of marriage.*"

"Ah." The almost imperceptible rise and fall of the bed linens attested his breathing. For a long moment, he made no other sound. "And I take it you would not welcome another."

She would have shaken her head if she did not fear it would dislodge his hand. "You've read my journal. You know what I am. I cannot be what the Duke of Raynham needs."

"I see." Another hesitation. "You do not wish to marry me. But if I understand things correctly, you do, however, wish to—"

"Yes." The word swooped in before he could place some terrible name on her desire.

The arm at her hip tightened almost convulsively. With gentle pressure, he lifted her chin. Still, it required every bit of her strength to meet his gaze, dark and raw. "You're a young lady of good family, Erica." She parted her lips, but his fingers curled against her scalp. "You may save your protests on that matter for another day." Reluctantly, she kept her silence. "And I'm no rake," he added.

She'd known as much, instinctively. "A bit of a rogue, perhaps?" she asked, hopeful.

Another almost-smile flickered across his lips and into his eyes, the suggestion of light in the dark pools of his irises. "Perhaps. But on the whole, a gentleman, as I seem to remember telling you once before. And any gentleman who knows that a lady is prone to impulsive behavior ought not to—"

"Impulsive?" she broke in. "I've been waiting for you in your sitting room, in total darkness, for hours." Every time the mantel clock had announced the quarter hour, a bit of her resolve had slipped away, it was true. But it was back in full force now.

One dark brow arced. "Is that right? Then you must be chilled."

She had not imagined, with the high frame of the bed pressed against the front of her legs, that he could somehow pull her closer still. But when the arm around her waist shifted, her spine willingly bent forward beneath its urging. One of her hands caught the edge of the mattress in an instinctive attempt to break her fall. The other settled against his bare chest. Her journal slipped to the floor, forgotten.

She wanted, needed, a moment to absorb the sublime sensations: the hard curve of his muscles, the tickle of silky dark hair between her spread fingers, the searing heat of his skin against her palm. But his voice once more commanded her attention.

"You're in my bedchamber, Erica. Almost my bed. What is it you want? Because if it's only a few more chaste kisses, I would be only too happy to oblige you." *Chaste? Oh, dear God...* The memory of those moments in the conservatory rushed through her veins like heady liquor. "But something tells me you're after something more."

"Yes, more," she murmured, bringing her lips to his. "Everything."

"Promise me," he demanded when she let him have his breath. "Promise me you didn't come here tonight to punish yourself further. To be ruined in earnest simply because a few gossips imagined the worst."

She drew back just enough to allow him to see the puzzlement on her face. "What has punishment to do with pleasure?"

His answering expression...well, she hadn't words to describe it. He might insist he wasn't a rake, but there was something decidedly wicked about the smolder in his eyes. "Ah, love, what an innocent you are..." His next kiss caught her lower lip between his teeth. A nip. A flash of...not of pain, exactly, but of pure sensation that called every cell in her body to attention. "Still, I'll have that promise."

"I give you my word." Anything, *anything*, if he'd only go on kissing her that way.

"Then turn around."

Her disappointment at his growled command lasted only as long as it took for her to follow it. She heard him shift behind her, then his deft fingers went immediately to the row of buttons running up her spine and undid them at a leisurely pace. When she could at last slip free of her gown, he went to work on the strings of her corset. The duchess' maid had been hard pressed to persuade her to wear it, but the unexpected eroticism of allowing Tristan to remove the dreaded garment dissolved any regret Erica felt. With torturous slowness, he drew the cord through the eyelets, first left, then right, then left again. With each hiss of fabric against metal, another inch of her flesh was bared to his gaze. When he reached the end, he paused to wrap the cord around his hand. Out of the corner of her eye, she watched him slide it over his knuckles and lay it on the table beside the base of the candlestick, a silken snake, coiled and waiting.

Waiting for what? The question fluttered through her mind and was gone, chased away by the warm invasion of his hands as they slipped between her corset and shift, first shaping her waist, then rising higher. The corset fell away to join her dress on the floor.

His hands swept lower then, working in tandem, learning the flare of her hips and the curve of her bottom before ascending once more, his thumbs lightly tracing that forbidden cleft before mapping the valley of her spine, climbing to the sharp angles of her shoulder blades. Just another few inches and there would be nothing between his hands and her skin...

She was worrying her lower lip with her teeth. In anticipation, yes. But the little sting of discomfort also made everything else more real. A pinch to make sure she wasn't dreaming. At last, his fingertips reached the gathered edge of her cambric shift and brushed across her bare skin. She couldn't contain the eager quaver that passed through her.

But his voice could. "Settle," he said.

And her body heeded his command.

Despite her obedience, he made her wait. Or perhaps he was weighing his options. At long last his fingers swept around the neckline of her shift to the bow in front and tugged it loose. She longed for him to run his hands over the front of her body as he had her back, unabashedly craving his touch on the aching peaks of her breasts, the curve of her belly, the secrets places below. Instead he brought his hands to her shoulders and slipped her shift down over her arms, over her hips, until the only barrier between them was an old pair of woolen stockings held in place by limp garters. Her toes curled in embarrassment, but the memory of his voice kept her otherwise rooted to the spot.

His right hand stroked up her arm, raising gooseflesh as he passed, then over the sharp peak of her shoulder, along her collarbone, to pause at her throat. His strength, his power—in check now, but undeniable. Saliva pooled in her mouth, and she swallowed hard, knowing he would feel the movement. How could she be so hungry for something she had never tasted? Three fingers crept to the left side of her jaw and urged her to turn her head.

Her body followed. At first, not knowing where to look, her eyes once more took refuge in the patterned coverlet, although he'd cast it aside. But in another moment, instinct—fascination—took over and her gaze roamed at will over his naked body.

In order to undress her, he'd risen from his recumbent position into a sort of half crouch, legs spread. There was something almost feral about the rangy pose, the way his golden brown hair gleamed like a lion's mane in the candlelight. She had no doubt he could devour her, if his control ever snapped. But oddly, the thought produced no fear. He had the tautly sinewed legs of an expert horseman, and between them, his manhood jutted from a nest of dark curls. When it bobbed beneath her appreciative stare, her throat worked up and down again.

For all she knew, he was studying her with similarly lascivious intent. Her eyes only dragged themselves back to his face when the pressure of his hand along her jaw could no longer be denied, and even then, she could not entirely stifle a whimper of disappointment.

He...smiled at the sound. Or maybe not. For if that was a smile, then she'd never seen its like before, except perhaps on a cat. His thumb came up to tug her lower lip free of her teeth, then brushed across its tender fullness.

"Doesn't that hurt?"

"Only a little." Suddenly she wanted to cover herself with her hands, to hide from his knowing gaze. "I think somehow it helps me focus. Most of the time, I don't even know I'm doing it."

The seriousness of his expression seemed to grant the act far more weight than it warranted, in her opinion. Biting her lip was just another bad habit she'd been unable to break.

"Am I interfering with your concentration?"

A nervous laugh caught in her chest. "Oh, yes."

"Well, we'll just have to see what can be done about that."

How he lifted her onto the bed so effortlessly, and without losing his balance, she could not afterward explain. In the moment, it was the most natural movement in the world, the steps of a dance through which for once she did not stumble, and when it was over, she was lying on her back in the middle of the ducal bed. With the duke looming over her.

When he lowered his mouth to hers, she understood at last what he'd meant when he'd called their earlier kisses chaste. What a difference it made when their lips weren't all that touched. The hair on his chest tickled her breasts, and his member was hot where it rested against her hip. She wanted to wrap her arms around him, but somehow, he'd pinned her hands at either side of her head, their fingers tangled, and that was good too, so good that she caught herself wishing he would tighten his grip.

How could possession be a kind of freedom? She only knew that she wanted his weight and his heat, and when he drove his tongue into her mouth, she yearned to take him deeper still. As if he could read her mind, he stretched her arms above her head until he could take both of her hands in one of his. His free hand settled over her throat, stroking along her jaw, coaxing her to open to him fully. She sucked greedily on his tongue, and his answering grunt was accompanied by a sharp thrust of his hips. Reprimand? Or reward? Either way, she did it again.

His hand slid from her throat to her breast, and he traced its curve and cupped its weight before rubbing the flat of his palm over the sensitive peak. That gentle abrasion was the sweetest torture, and her hips rose from the bed, seemingly of their own volition, seeking something to ease the growing ache. He shifted then, lowering his hand to her waist. The kiss grew shallow. "Easy, love," he murmured against her lips. "Your eagerness made me forget myself. But this is new to you. Let's take this slow, shall we?"

"I don't want to go slow." Patience had never been her strong suit.

She felt his mouth curve into a smile as he kissed his way across her cheek to whisper in her ear. "Whatever gave you the idea that you're in charge?"

While he nibbled at her earlobe and traced the whorl of her ear with the tip of his tongue, she took stock of her situation. Naked but for her stockings. Pinned by Tristan's hands and his weight. Entirely at his mercy. A frisson traveled along her spine—not fear. She wanted this, that much she knew, even if she wasn't entirely sure what *this* was, and even if she didn't quite understand why.

He nipped the delicate skin at the base of her throat, and the momentary sting was like an electric charge, snapping her attention back to him. Not unlike the way she bit her lip when something demanded concentration— that prick of sensation drove back the distractions and, for a moment, everything was clear. He'd watched her do it. He knew. He *understood*.

She thought of her journal, lying abandoned on the floor. That awful list of her mistakes, her feeble attempts to correct them. What else did he understand?

Promise me you didn't come here tonight to punish yourself further...

But there was a kind of punishment in the way true pleasure fluttered just out of reach. She closed her eyes and gave herself up to the scent of his skin, the temptation of his mouth, and the frantic scrub of her pulse. Oh, she was tired, tired of trying to maintain control. Let him have it. Just for tonight.

He soothed the tiny bite with his tongue, then brought his lips back to hers, and his kiss was gentler now, and sure, as if she had communicated her resolve to him. The hand that pinned her wrists relaxed, and a whimper of protest rose in her throat. "No. Don't let me go." She needed him to hold her, needed to feel his strength, his power.

"*Shhh,*" he soothed. "I won't."

He shifted, reaching for something, and in another moment she saw the cord of her corset in his hand. "I could tie them. But only if you wish..."

It was nothing she had ever imagined. And yet...didn't gardeners often tie a delicate vine to a trellis, to give it the support, the security it needed to thrive?

Her hair slipped over the smooth linens as she nodded. Carefully, he wound the cool silk around her wrists. When she tugged against it, it did not relent.

Now both of his hands were free to roam. They sought and found her breasts, traced the pebbled edge of her areola. He dragged his mouth down her throat, over her collarbone, then his lips closed around one nipple as he teased the sensitive peak with his tongue. Her spine arched, lifting her chest to him, as if she imagined he could be coaxed into giving her more.

The touch of his tongue became whisper light, the merest flicker of wet heat. At the same time, he ran his palm more roughly over her other nipple before taking it between his first finger and thumb and squeezing lightly.

The pressure shot a charge from her breast to the secret place between her thighs, and tears stung in her eyes.

"Too much?" The words whispered across her damp skin, a cool breeze that stoked the fire higher.

"Yes." More groan than speech. "Please, do it again."

He didn't, though. Not right away. Instead, he brought his lips to the place he'd pinched and began to suck in earnest. One hand ministered to the needy breast his mouth had abandoned, rolling and plucking the taut peak. The other hand slid lower, over her ribs and the sharper bones of her pelvis, pausing to play in her private curls before dipping lower still.

She was already wet and swollen with wanting; the way his fingertips slicked through her folds would have told her as much, if she had not already known. Was there nowhere she wasn't sensitive, no touch he couldn't teach her to crave? His fingers were gentle, teasing, but every bit as focused as the pull of his mouth on her breast. And they were linked, somehow, so that every tug at her nipple sent a ripple of delight into those hidden recesses of her body and back again, until she didn't know where one sensation ended and the other began.

She couldn't move, couldn't *not* move, lifted her hips to his hand merely for the pleasure of having him pin her more securely beneath the weight of his arm. This was madness, utter madness, when she'd so hoped for peace, but she trusted he could give it to her, if only…if only he'd…

"Come," he ordered, his hot breath striking her breast as he pinched her other nipple firmly between forefinger and thumb.

Though the command was unfamiliar, she knew she hadn't the strength to resist it, didn't want to resist it—resist him—anymore. With a choked cry, she gave herself over to the blinding rush of pleasure and release.

Sometime later, he stirred, calling her back from a far off dream, and when she opened her eyes, it was to discover he'd hoisted himself higher in the bed, so that they were lying side by side. "Erica?" His voice was pained. "Touch me." With a tug of his fingers, the corset cord unraveled from her wrists, and her hands were her own again. "*Please.*"

Clergymen, moralists, gossips all spoke of what a woman lost when she went to a man's bed: her reputation, her maidenhead, even her place in heaven. Why had no one ever hinted at the extraordinary power she got in return?

As if trying to make up for lost time, she raced one hand over his shoulder and down his arm to his hip, tracing the muscles, reveling in his hardness. His buttocks clenched and she followed the movement, her fingertips skating into the dimples she'd glimpsed from the doorway earlier.

Then she eased herself apart from him just enough to run her palm over his chest and his abdomen, to curl her fingers in the dark hair that covered him there, and lower...

"Wrap your hand around my cock."

She'd never heard the word before, but some commands were too primal to require explanation. Without hesitation, she curled her small, pale fingers around his dark, hot desire. So firm and proud, its potent shape familiar, like the stamen of a flower. Suddenly the figurative language of every botany text became literal, and she saw the truth they had tried to hide from young ladies' curious eyes. He levered himself above her, and with a swift tilting of her pelvis, she brought his cock to the smooth, silky petals of her body's opening. "Come inside me," she murmured.

A momentary twinge of discomfort told her, *Yes, this is real, this is true.* And then the slick glide of him filling her, the exquisite stretch, the certainty of his possession.

"All right?" he whispered against her hair.

Her arms came around his back. "Never better."

In some corner of her mind, she wondered if perhaps she ought to have known, having so often observed the bees at work in the flowers. But what could have prepared her for the power of his thrusts, the teasing agony of his withdrawal? Slow at first, and steady, then faster, a race toward pleasure, his arms and shoulders taut with strain and her own hunger rising once more.

And with one last, shuddering nudge of his hips into hers, she burst into bloom again.

Chapter 16

Submissive was the last word he'd ever use to describe Erica. And though he wielded a great deal of power over those around him in almost every aspect of his life, he didn't generally expect to do so in bed. But in the army, he'd often seen a longing for support and security in the face of turmoil, the relief in another's eyes when authority was properly exerted. In her journal Erica had recorded her quest for that elusive moment when she could set aside her uncertainties and be herself, and he'd wanted—needed—to give such a moment to her.

He twisted one coppery lock around his first finger while she dozed curled against his side. She'd given him control and then, gloriously, had taken it back again with the brush of her fingers, the surer clutch of her sex. Life would never be boring with her in his bed. In his life. Perhaps next time they'd—

Next time?

The spiral of hair unwound and slipped away. She had no desire to marry him. And beneath this very roof was another woman whose family, at least, anticipated his offer. How could he look forward to any future with the woman beside him now? In addition to being a wealthy aristocrat, he was an officer in an elite corps responsible for protecting British liberties, a hero in many people's minds. He knew ladies generally found his looks satisfactory. But he wasn't vain enough to imagine that one night in his arms had changed Erica's mind.

He needed more time. Time to trace his fingers along the scattered path of her freckles, which hid in the most delightful spots. Time to tempt her with the beauty of Hawesdale's gardens on a sun-dappled afternoon. Time to thank her for the energy and vibrancy and passion she'd brought into his life. He had known them only in other guises: disorder and disarray and loss of self-control. He had not known he needed them. Until now.

But time was not on his side. The storm was weakening. Even at this moment, the silence pressed upon him—no wind battered the eaves, no spit of rain dashed against the windows. In a few days at most, she would leave.

As if his churning thoughts had somehow communicated themselves to her, Erica stirred, made a sleepy murmur, and snuggled closer. Then, on a jerk, her eyes popped open and her body grew rigid. "What if—?" One hand pushed ineffectually at her disheveled hair. "Captain Whitby was wrong about me, but what if he was right in essentials? Could there still be a spy at Hawesdale Chase?"

"I—he—" His thoughts snapped like the lash of a whip. While it was hardly unheard of for an agent to discuss such matters in bed—sometimes, after all, such discussions were the primary object of taking a woman to bed—it was not the conversation he had hoped to have with Erica now. What did it mean that her first thoughts upon waking were of something other than the extraordinary experience they'd just shared? "Perhaps."

With one hand, she scooted herself more upright, while the other tugged the bed linens higher, hiding her rose-tipped breasts from his view. "Doesn't that mean you're in danger?"

"Not immediate danger."

He had known the answer would offer meager reassurance, but he was unprepared for the way it made her curl more tightly within herself. Beneath the sheets, she brought her knees to her chest and wrapped herself into a ball.

"If someone wants something from me, he's unlikely to do anything rash until he has it," he hurried to explain, plucking absently at a wrinkle in the coverlet. "As far as I'm concerned, the greater risk is having my identity as an agent compromised. If it is, I may be unable to return to the field." Speaking those words aloud, facing their reality, was more difficult than he had expected.

She had been watching the movement of his hand as he spoke, but now she lifted her gaze to his face. "You mean to go back? To continue as… mere Major Laurens?"

"Not 'mere,'" he said sharply. "Not to me. It's essential work, though if it's done well, most people will never know it's been done at all."

"But what about…?"

He had not realized he was holding onto a spark of hope until her hesitation breathed life into it and coaxed it into a glowing ember. Was it possible she too had been considering the possibility of a future together?

Then she concluded, "What about your sister?"

The flicker of hope in his chest sputtered. "Vivi will be all right. She has her mother, her—" *governess*, he had been about to say before remembering that he intended to dismiss Miss Chatham. "The familiar faces who've surrounded her since her infancy. She's grown accustomed to my absences, I'm sure."

Doubt crystallized in Erica's amber eyes. "And your other responsibilities here?"

"I never imagined they would be mine," he said after a moment. "I never wanted them."

"But still they're yours."

She was right, of course. He thought of Davies, Guin, and the rest. The neat columns of figures in the account books, not quite as reassuring as he'd hoped. How long did he mean to go on using his father's apathetic management of the estate as an excuse for avoiding his own fears?

"Either way," Erica continued, "I'd say the possibility of a spy at Hawesdale demands your undivided attention."

"Yet it does not have it." He paused before saying anything more. But he could not go on pretending as if nothing had happened between them. "I confess myself distracted by...other things."

But what should he say now that the subject had been introduced? She would not thank him for making her another offer. And he did not know how else to put his own wishes into words. He'd shown her she could trust him with her body, but would she ever trust him with more? Never had he felt so strongly the distinction between the dictates of propriety and the dictates of his heart.

While he was still debating with himself about where to begin, she wrapped the fingers of one hand around her wrist where it lay in her lap, as if she could still feel the snug silk bonds he'd tied. "How did you know?"

A few less-than-honest answers presented themselves, the impulse to feign ignorance of her meaning, but he brushed them aside and reached out to cover her hands lightly with his. "I know you."

"Because of what you read in my journal, you mean." A flush of color crept above the edge of the coverlet where she had pinned it against her chest with her arms.

He shook his head. "You're so much more than what you've written between the covers of that book."

"Am I?" Her hands slipped out from beneath his. "I think perhaps I should go back to my own room."

He could not argue, though he wanted to. He rose instead, wrapping a sheet around himself as best he could, and helped her to dress despite her protests. "You can't very well lace up your own corset," he said.

Though the words were true, he regretted them as soon as they'd passed his lips, for of course then it was incumbent upon him to stand behind her and perform the task himself. The zing of the silk cord through the eyelets was a bittersweet melody now, as the garment once more imposed its rigid order on her delectably soft form.

Last of all, she bent and retrieved her journal from the floor. It hung from her fingers like dead weight, and he had a sudden mental image of her casting it onto the flaming hearth. He walked with her to the door to make sure the coast was clear, grateful suddenly never to have remembered to order Armitage to post a footman there. On the threshold, he reached up to brush a wayward lock from her cheek, then left a soft kiss in its place. The only things he could think to say were so utterly inadequate, he opted in the end to say nothing at all.

As she disappeared into the shadows of the corridor he caught himself wishing that she were a spy, just to give him an excuse to keep her close.

* * * *

Erica bit her lip, hard. Hard enough that for the second time that day, she recoiled at the taste of her own blood. But she couldn't relent. She refused to allow her mind to think of anything but the route back to her room. Refused to allow her stockinged feet to depart from the shortest, straightest path there. Most would say she had wandered far enough astray already.

The corridor was dark. The sconces that had been burning when she was hurrying in the opposite direction had long since been extinguished. In her room, all was dark too. A maid had turned the bedcovers down. With a resigned sigh, Erica laid down on the bed, shifted her hips, tossed her head against the pillow. Tired of answering questions about her frequent sleepless nights, she'd long since learned how to make it appear as if her bed had been slept in.

But she didn't stay there. She extracted herself from the now-tangled linens and went to the windows. All was dark, though the faintest suggestion of dawn separated the sky from the rugged hills and the hulking shadow of the house. Within the hour, servants would be up and at work. She'd made it just in time.

So why did a part of her wish she'd been caught in the duke's bed? There would have been no question then of what their futures would hold. He would have offered, because it was the honorable thing to do and he was, as the duchess had said, an honorable man. And she would not have had the strength to refuse a second time.

Because of all the foolish, careless things to have done…she'd fallen in love with Major Tristan Laurens, the Duke of Raynham.

All along, she had been thinking of him as a rule-maker. And she was the consummate rule-breaker. But after tonight, she understood that he was governed not by mere propriety, but by something much deeper than that.

What other man of her acquaintance, given the choice between a life of ease and a life fraught with danger, would have chosen the latter? Even now, his heart was divided between his obligations at home and his duties elsewhere—and leaning strongly toward the latter. For all his love of order, his determination to maintain control, he was an unconventional duke.

But it did not therefore follow that he would want an unconventional duchess.

If he married her, then *this*—her eyes scanned the shadowy wings of the monstrous house, from the kitchens to the ballroom, from the schoolroom to the ducal suite—would be hers to manage. On her shoulders would rest some portion of the happiness of scores of servants, of Lady Viviane, of Tristan. And she would collapse under its weight and bring everything tumbling down with her.

In the face of those facts, what could it possibly matter what her body wanted? Or her heart?

The fingers of her left hand encircled her right wrist and chafed at the sensitive skin there, feeling again the welcome bite of the bonds he'd tied. She hadn't any word for that…peculiarity, the discovery that pleasure prowled on the very edge of pain. Ought she to add *immodest* and *immoral* to the long list of her sins?

But no. She had promised him she hadn't gone to his bed to punish herself, and she wouldn't do so now. In his dark eyes, she'd glimpsed no judgment. Just the opposite, in fact. *Love*, he'd called her, and while even she wasn't naïve enough to imagine he fancied himself in love with her, she had no doubt he too had taken pleasure in her surrender.

She'd had nearly four and twenty years on this earth to come to grips with who and what she was, to learn what could be changed about herself and what couldn't. And what she'd done with Tristan could not be undone. Self-recrimination would doubtless come creeping along on the nighttime shadows, but now it was nearly dawn, and she refused to waste time on it. The start of a new day was a time to look ahead.

So, what sort of future did she imagine for herself? Quite possibly a lonely one. She would leave here with her reputation in tatters, after all. Even her family might disown her.

But she would also leave with a journal full of sketches of plants she had only dreamed of seeing. She would leave with newfound knowledge about herself. And she would leave with the memory of one night in Tristan's arms. Almost automatically, her chin tilted upward. She had a world to see, didn't she? She curled her journal against her breast, thinking of the carefully drawn map within its pages. She couldn't bear it if all she had for the rest of her life were the rugged landscape of Westmorland and the conservatory at Hawesdale Chase.

Could she?

The tears filling her eyes and coursing down her cheeks she at first mistook for rain. But the day had dawned fair at last. While she had been ruminating, the sun had risen enough to lend its color to the red bricks of the house. The windows of the west wing, including the glasshouse, blazed with reflected light, and already the puddles on the flagstone terrace had shrunk.

With a determined nod, she turned away from the window, swiped away her tears, and laid her journal on her dressing table. After a quarter hour's largely failed effort at taming her tangled hair and her tangled thoughts, she rose again, this time leaving her journal where it lay.

She found Mr. Remington seated at the table in the servants' dining hall, alone. "Do you suppose this change in the weather will alter my sister's travel plans?" she asked.

In the rooms and corridors all around them bustled footmen and maids readying the house for another day. Occasionally she heard the sharper notes of Mrs. Dean's voice above the fray. "Well, Miss Erica," he said after he had contemplated both the question and his cup of coffee. "A sunny day will do wonders for the roads, it's true. But I don't believe Lord Ashborough will be in any hurry to set out until he's certain they're safe. He's got Lady Ashborough's health to consider too."

Erica's jerk of alarm rattled the dishes on the table and nearly upset his cup. Drops of dark liquid leaped into the air; three landed in the saucer, but the fourth settled on the tablecloth and began to spread. "Is my sister ill?"

With calm, deliberate motions, he reached for his cup and used his napkin to blot the stain before taking a sip. She was almost willing to swear his mouth had curved into a grin around the rim. "Mostly just in the mornings," he said as he returned his cup carefully to its saucer.

"I don't understand. What sort of illness would—?"

He cocked one grizzled brow.

"Oh. You mean…you mean she's…"

"*In a delicate condition* is the phrase you're seeking, I believe." Definitely a grin.

Feeling her cheeks pink, she busied herself with squaring the handle of her own coffee cup, the one Remington had insisted upon filling, though she had not yet taken a drink. When she'd told Tristan she would have nieces and nephews on which to dote, she had not anticipated any arriving quite so soon. Truth be told, she'd never even been sure Cami *liked* children—certainly not the messes and noise they tended to make. Always firm with herself, Cami had expected her younger siblings—her sisters especially—to exercise a similar degree of self-restraint. And Erica, at least, had been disappointing her all her life.

Still, it was clear Cami liked her husband a great deal and...well, *they who dance must pay the music*, as the saying went. So—

Beneath the table, her fingers curled in her napkin. *Oh, dear.* Only just this moment had it occurred to her that after last night, she too might be...

Her mind shied from even the polite euphemism. *No. Impossible.* Well, not *impossible*. But unlikely, surely?

"I shouldn't worry if I were you, Miss Erica. It's the most natural thing in the world."

Erica jumped up from the table before realizing that of course he spoke of her sister's condition, not her own. To cover her reaction, she wandered to the window and discovered it too high in the wall for her to see out. Her heart was racing. A child. Tristan's child.

Was she really fool enough to *hope?*

"Are you all right, Miss Erica?"

She nodded, a shade too quickly, and her eyes darted toward the door. "Never better," she insisted, before remembering that she'd spoken those same words to him as he'd... *Oh, dear.* At what point did the heat in her cheeks put her at risk for going up in flames?

"This wouldn't have anything to do with the rumors I heard yesterday, would it? About you and the Duke of Raynham?"

With anyone else, she might have demurred. But thanks to his notorious employer, Remy had seen a deal too much of the world to be put off. "Yes and no," she explained, dropping her voice and returning to her place at the table. "Captain Whitby, another of the guests, believes there's a spy at Hawesdale Chase. The fact that I am a stranger here, combined with my... family connections"—Remington gave a knowing nod—"rendered me an object of suspicion at first. The duke, however, was persuaded that the contents of my journal would prove my innocence. Believing—rightly—I would be reluctant to show it to him, he came to my room the night before last looking for it."

"Ah." His voice held the merest hint of skepticism. "And did you give him what he wanted?"

"Mr. Remington!" she gasped. But her affront did not budge the questioning look from his face. With trembling fingers, she picked up his discarded napkin and began to pleat it. "Yes."

If he suspected the weight of meaning behind that simple word, his face did not immediately show it. He drained his cup and rose to pour another from an urn on the otherwise empty sideboard. The servants would eat later. "I understand he offered you marriage. And you refused."

"If you're going to tell me that I ought to have accepted him—"

"It wouldn't be my place. Though as a general principle, I see no harm in changing your mind."

He wasn't probing. He hadn't even asked a question. And yet there was something about his calm demeanor, his ability to understand what she couldn't say, that made her want to tell him everything.

But she didn't. "Me, a duchess?" She laughed, a shade too brightly. "In any case, he holds out some hope of returning to—"

"The army?" he supplied when she hesitated. Her eyes widened with surprise. "I can spot an officer a mile away—even without his red coat."

She mustered a weak smile. "It is not, I suppose, the choice most men in his position would make," she said, hoping to temper what sounded like Remy's annoyance.

He had lifted his cup halfway to his lips, but at her words, the cup paused in midair. "Oh, I understand his decision. I'm an old military man myself."

A military man? Suddenly, any number of things snapped into place. Arthur Remington's erect posture, the carefulness with which he always acted, the extraordinary trust Lord Ashborough placed in the man. And in the back of her mind, a plan began to form…

He spoke before she could put it into words. "But I begin to think he might have a few things to learn yet." Pausing to take a drink, he grimaced and reached for the sugar bowl. After stirring vigorously, he tapped the spoon on the side of his cup and let it clatter into the saucer. Every noise jangled against Erica's frayed nerves and made her jump. "You didn't exactly answer my question about why you're in such a hurry to leave," he pointed out, eyeing her once more. "One sunny morning won't shrink a swollen river or mend a road that's washed away. You know that."

She weighed her answer. Because he had it entirely wrong, of course. She didn't want to run away. She wanted to run to Tristan with every fiber in her being.

"I suppose you're right," she agreed, mustering what she hoped was a look of disappointment. "And since we're stuck here, mightn't you go to him and see what assistance you could offer? One military man to another."

"The duke doesn't strike me as the kind of man who welcomes interference," Remington said with a sharp shake of his head. "And if it's help he wants, why not turn to Captain Whitby?"

"I believe the captain has lost his confidence." She clenched her teeth against the memory of her encounter with the man. "He has certainly lost mine."

Remington frowned. "I see." With one hand he pushed away from the sideboard. "Well, I suppose I might just speak with him about one thing and another." As he moved toward the door, she rose to follow him. "And just where do you think you're going?"

"With you."

"Oh, I think not. Stay and drink your coffee," he insisted, gesturing toward her abandoned cup with a jerk of his chin.

She feigned a shudder of distaste. "Doubtless it's passed tepid and moved on to cold."

"A book from the library, perhaps? Some flower to sketch?"

She shook her head. "Come, Remy. Did you really expect me to sit here waiting with my hands folded in my lap like a lady?"

Remington laughed, but crossed his arms over his chest all the same, making it clear that he did not intend to budge. "If anything happens to you, Lady Ashborough will have my head."

"Oh, you needn't have any fear on that score," she replied airily. "It really only hurts the first time she takes it off."

He frowned. "Miss Erica, you're—"

Words tumbled through her mind, all the usual cruelties and criticisms. *Shatterbrained, careless, selfish…* She batted them away like a swarm of gnats while she plowed ahead, seeking something truer. "Brave," she finished for him.

Brave enough to master her fears. And brave enough to take what she wanted, just as she'd done last night.

To her shock, he didn't disagree.

"Remy." Her voice dropped to a whisper then. How to make him understand that the only real danger here was the danger to her heart? "Please."

With one foot poised on the threshold, he turned and gave her a sidelong, assessing look. "All right, Miss Erica," he relented with a sigh. "Come along."

Chapter 17

"It's a generous offer." Tristan crossed his hands behind his back and walked from one window of his private sitting room to the next. The view showed him nothing of the devastation the rain must have brought to Hawesdale: flooded fields and cottages, drowned animals, even people. From this vantage point, it would be easy enough for the Duke of Raynham simply to bask in the sun's warmth as it spread from the eastern horizon and ignore the rest. "But I cannot accept it."

When a footman had woken him to deliver the message that Miss Burke wished to speak with him in private, he'd hardly dared to let himself wonder what she had to say. The hurried moments he had spared to dress—he hadn't taken time to shave or even tie back his hair—had nevertheless been sufficient to leave room for speculation.

He had been unprepared for Mr. Remington's addition to the meeting, however. Even less prepared for the man's offer to assist him in catching the spy at Hawesdale Chase.

"Why not?" Even tired, Erica sounded ready to fight if she had to. "I assure you, Remington is up to the challenge."

Tristan turned his head just enough to catch a glimpse of the man over his shoulder. "You have experience in such matters, do you, Mr. Remington?"

"Oh, things have come up. Now and again."

"He's very trustworthy," Erica interjected. "And clever. Why, this past spring, he helped Lord Ashborough—"

"Whisht, Miss Erica. His Grace won't care about that."

Tristan had heard countless men praised for their honesty and bravery. Remington's laconic reply told him more of what he needed to know. Too few, in his experience, knew when to keep their mouths shut. "Perhaps," he said, turning his back on the rugged, sun-kissed landscape, "the rumors are only that: rumors. Perhaps there never was a spy."

"You don't believe that."

The confidence with which Erica contradicted him ought not to come as a surprise. And as she had a habit of speaking hastily, he also knew he ought to exercise caution in drawing conclusions from what she said. Still, he could not help but wonder whether he was slipping, losing the essential ability to mask his thoughts. Or whether, as he feared, the mask was still firmly in place, but she now possessed the ability to see through it.

"Whether I do or not, Miss Burke, it does not change my decision. I cannot allow Mr. Remington to run such a risk on my behalf."

Her eyes blazed like cut topaz. "Then I'll do it."

"Miss Erica—"

"No." He spoke more softly than Remington, but he had no fear of making himself heard.

"Why not?" she demanded.

"Because I—" He snapped off the first words that rose to his tongue, startled:

Because I love you.

He tested the idea like a man drawing his thumb across a blade to test its sharpness, knowing one careless slip would leave him with a wound. But even the possibility of pain—and it was real, for he doubted she would be eager to hear him make such a declaration—did not diminish the fierce truth of those three words.

"If I may, Your Grace." Remington's voice jerked him back into the moment. How long had he been standing there with his mouth agape, while they waited for him to finish his sentence? "You do not strike me as a hasty man. But another day or two of deliberation, and it will be too late. Now is the time to act, before the weather makes it possible for your guests to scatter. If the truth is uncovered, Miss Erica can be cleared of any wrongdoing before the gossip spreads beyond the walls of this house."

Exasperation puffed from Erica's lips. "I don't care about—"

"I do," Tristan said flatly. *Despite all appearances to the contrary.* With a wave of his hand, he invited both of them to sit before sinking with surprising weariness into a chair. What a hash he'd made of things. "Continue, Mr. Remington."

"Miss Erica mentioned a Captain Whitby." The man still sat with the straight-backed posture of a soldier that clearly conveyed he'd rather be doing than sitting. "I wonder if you are certain he's not the culprit."

"If he's the real spy," Erica interjected, astonished by the notion but obviously willing to consider it, "he had some nerve cornering me in the conservatory to accuse me of the crime."

Though her words contained no details of the encounter, Tristan could easily picture it. A screen of leaves and branches for cover. A few well-chosen innuendos. A threat. As if it were a thing disconnected from him, he watched his hand curl around the arm of the chair. *A loyal betrayal.* The most perverse sort of contradiction he could imagine. Persuaded of Erica's guilt, had Whitby imagined himself acting to protect his oldest friend? If so, he'd failed, for by frightening the woman Tristan loved, Whitby had earned his disgust and distrust instead.

That did not, of course, make him the culprit they were seeking.

Nor did it make him innocent.

"I believe it would be best if we proceeded without alerting Captain Whitby to our scheme," Tristan said quietly. "Whatever it may be."

Remington nodded once. "Understood."

Silence reigned for some time as he considered how best to proceed. Every plan that presented itself, he dismissed as relying too heavily on evidence acquired from Whitby, the veracity of which he had neither the means nor the time to prove. Remington might be some help below stairs, but he was one man. A stranger. And Erica...

"Tell them all that Whitby was right about me," she blurted out.

Of course she had been using those quiet moments to form her own absurd plan. "The hope, my dear," he said, "is to reduce the speculation surrounding you, not increase it."

At the wry edge to his voice—or perhaps the endearment—her eyes narrowed. "The *hope* is to catch a spy whose very existence is a threat to your work, and by extension a threat to us all. Is it not?"

To his right, Remington discreetly turned a snicker into a cough.

"Whitby told you of his suspicions." She leaped to her feet and both he and Remington moved to follow, but she waved them down even as she paced. "You...you believed my journal contained secret information and went to my chamber to find it. Its contents confirmed your hunch." She paused to look between them, never quite making eye contact. "Spread that story among the guests—Remington must do the same for the staff."

"How does that help?" Tristan asked. "The real villain will know we've got it wrong."

"Exactly."

"He—or she—will relax," Remington explained with a nod of understanding and the beginnings of a grin. "Feel secure. Make mistakes. And you needn't worry about tipping your hand in the process," he added.

"I daresay no one will be surprised to learn that a high-ranking officer is possessed of privileged information—*how* privileged need never enter into it."

"Yes," agreed Erica. "You'll simply explain that you've..." She tapped a finger against her lip as she considered. "Oh, I know. You've left a sensitive document lying about, hoping to catch me red-handed."

"And hope the real spy takes the bait," Tristan finished, catching up with her thoughts at last. It wasn't a terrible plan. But it was the sort of plan over which he'd have very little control, and that unsettled him. "Absolutely not."

This was not one of the occasions on which Erica crumpled when she met resistance, however. Piercing him with the gem-like intensity of her gaze, she strode forward until she stood before him. "It will work."

"I won't do anything to put you in danger—*greater* danger," he corrected, seeing her poised to remind him that no one at Hawesdale was entirely safe.

"You won't be. It will only be confirming their suspicions. Telling people what they expect to hear." Despite the tilt of her chin, the gleam in her eyes, he could see the soft, vulnerable place at her core. The place in which she believed that all those critics and all those skeptics might not be entirely wrong about her.

He wanted to fold her into his arms, to be the shield she needed when her own grew thin or weak. And to draw her tight against him because then she would be too close for him to see into her soul. This beautiful, terrifying transparency that he could never have imagined—this, this was what it meant to look on another person with the eyes of love. It frightened him as nothing ever had. And he could not look away.

He rose to his feet, but he did not step closer. Because she was watching him, and he could tell from the catch in her breath, the slight widening of her eyes, that she had seen it too.

His heart thudded out its alarm at discovering its unexpected vulnerability. His head, meanwhile, was cataloging the dangers—to her most of all. But there were others. Despite Remington's assurances, would uncovering the guilty party compromise his identity as an agent? A true villain, caught in the act, might be desperate enough to expose Tristan for what he really was—a fellow spy.

How much was he willing to risk?

Everything. Because he knew that all Erica had ever really wanted was someone who believed in her. Someone who loved her just as she was.

"It's brilliant," he said and nodded his acquiescence to her scheme.

Bright spots of color appeared in her cheeks, and her lips curved into a smile he had only begun to learn. But in that moment he knew he would fight for the chance to put that expression on her face again. And again. And again.

Remington cleared his throat as he stood. "I'd say it's a sound plan. I'll set about spreading the word."

"And you can begin by forging a suitably interesting document," Erica said to Tristan before excusing herself with a curtsy. Remington wavered for a moment, loitering on the point of saying something more, before nodding to Tristan and following her out the door.

The mantel clock chimed eight. An hour or perhaps two until he could expect to find the others at breakfast and begin to sow the seeds of Erica's misdirection plot. But time enough to begin the document she'd asked him to create.

Not that he needed to fabricate such a document. He could doubtless find something that would suffice among his papers. Nevertheless, he seated himself at the secretary, remembering as he did so the sight of Erica in her dressing gown examining the antique desk, looking for her journal. How much had changed since that moment. And how little.

A private smile lifted his lips. He dipped a pen and set its tip to a blank sheet of foolscap, knowing exactly the letter he needed to write. Not to catch a spy. To catch Erica.

* * * *

When he entered the breakfast room, he found it unoccupied except for Caroline and a footman, who slipped out a side door when Tristan nodded his dismissal.

"Good morning, Miss Pilkington," he said and bowed. She looked cool and elegant in a blue morning gown, her smooth brown hair carefully arranged. Still, it was clear she must have passed a largely sleepless night. The shadows beneath her eyes, the lines of exhaustion on her face, could not hide from the morning sun. "May I enquire after your mother? Is she improved?"

"How thoughtful of you to be concerned," she said, rising only to curtsy. "She is resting comfortably. I believe the worst has passed."

"I am glad to hear it." He glanced past her at the window and back again. "Perhaps the improvement in the weather will give her some reprieve."

Caroline nodded, though a hint of skepticism flashed through her eyes. "One may hope." She returned to her place, a half-empty plate before her and a coffee cup that had already been drained. "She's suffered from these headaches as long as I can remember, but sadly, her condition has been severe and worsening since the spring, in fair skies or foul."

"To what does her physician attribute such a change?"

"Papa—" She pressed her lips together and swallowed, as if she wished to take back the word. "Mama has not consulted one."

Tristan wrinkled his brow but said nothing. Why hadn't Pilkington insisted that his wife be seen by a competent medical man?

As he stepped to the sideboard, Caroline resumed pushing her food around her plate. Wordlessly, he filled a clean cup with coffee and brought it to her. She looked up. "You are too kind."

"Sugar? Milk?"

"Yes, thank you."

She was still stirring when he said, "I am fortunate to have found you here this morning. I have been hoping for a few moments of private conversation."

The spoon slipped from her fingers and rang against the thin china of the cup. "My father told me. I am sorry that my mother's health prevented us from speaking yesterday, as you requested."

He had taken the chair opposite her when he returned to the table, but she did not meet his eyes as she spoke. Her much vaunted poise and good breeding seemed to have deserted her, as she resumed toying with the spoon. A sign of discouragement, as plain as she knew how to make it. "Miss Pilkington," he said, "do not be alarmed. I only wanted to—"

"I hope you will wish me joy," she spoke across him, then looked up, a slight tilt to her chin. She had not quite mastered Erica's defiant expression, but with a little practice she would do very well. "Captain Whitby and I are to be married."

He parted his lips to speak, but found no words at the ready. It was not exactly surprise that stopped his speech, for after yesterday afternoon's encounter in the conservatory, he had been all but certain of the way things tended between the two. Once, he would have declared Whitby the best of men and deserving of her favor. Now, however, such praise did not rise easily to his tongue.

Again, she misread his reaction. "I *am* sorry. Papa ought never to have told you... That is, I certainly never expected..."

"I understand." She had not expected, nor wanted, his offer, and while perhaps such words ought to offend him—the second rejection in as many days—this time he felt nothing but relief. "My felicitations to you both, of course."

She hesitated. "I do not wish to be the cause of a breech between you and Captain Whitby."

He tried to wave her concern away with a flick of his hand, but as the gesture managed to send his own empty cup spinning in its saucer, it failed to convey a convincing dismissal. Settling his palm over the cup, he stopped its motion with an alarming crunch of china against china. "I hardly know, Miss Pilkington, how to explain the case without giving offense. You will naturally assume that jealousy lies at the root of my displeasure, but I find I must beg your pardon and say that it has played no part."

Her eyes widened. "Do you mean to say that you did not want—?"

"In the matter of your father's expectations, and perhaps your own," he said, choosing his words with care, "I find that what I *would* have done and what I *wished* to do were not perfectly aligned."

"Oh," she said, and this time her eyes sparkled. "Oh, I see." Amusement played around her lips. "One's inclination is not always at the service of one's better judgment, is it?"

He cut his gaze away—answer enough, he supposed. "Does your father know?"

Hurriedly, nervously, she shook her head, then drew in a firm breath that lifted her shoulders. "But it does not matter. I am of age. And according to the arrangements set down at my parents' betrothal, half of what Mama brought to her marriage will be settled upon me at mine, whether he likes my choice or not."

"Whitby is a fortunate fellow," he said, not thinking particularly of the money. He only hoped his oldest friend would prove worthy of such good fortune. Once, he would have had no doubt.

To paper over what might have been an awkward silence, he rose and filled a plate from the sideboard. When he returned to the table, Caroline set aside her coffee. "If you did not come to ask…" With one fingertip, she drew a line across the table linens, connecting the two of them. "What *was* the matter you wished to discuss?"

"It is time, I believe, to make clear to my friends that I do not intend to resign my commission." With studied calm, he paused to take a bite of eggs, as if such an announcement were an ordinary one for a man in his position to make and easy enough for those around him to understand. "I will return to my regiment in the new year."

He had managed to keep his voice firm, although in truth, neither staying nor going was the simple choice it had once been. But if everyone at Hawesdale imagined his military connections unbroken, the better chance the villain would be tempted by the promise of valuable information.

Before Caroline could react to his shocking revelation, he heard the bustle of another guest entering the breakfast room. Rising, he bowed to Lady Lydgate. "Good morning, ma'am. Allow me to ring for fresh coffee."

"Never mind that," she insisted with a dismissive flutter of her beringed hand. "I came to find out if it's true."

"If what is true, ma'am?" Caroline asked.

"My maid told me that it's being whispered about the servants' hall that Miss Burke is a..." She paused to glance theatrically from one corner of the room to another, as if she feared being overheard, then dropped her voice to an exaggerated whisper. "A *spy.*"

Mr. Remington was a fast worker, he'd say that much for the man.

"Preposterous." Caroline's brows dove downward and she looked to him to contradict the rumor.

Amateur theatricals had never been among his favored pastimes, and for a moment he doubted his ability to play his part. But Caroline's worried expression, combined with Lady Lydgate's voracious curiosity, left him little choice. The first bit was easy enough, he found, passing so near the neighborhood of the truth. "I'm afraid it is true, Miss Pilkington. Captain Whitby first suspected it and conveyed his suspicions to me. I went to her chamber in search of proof, and...well, you know how close to disaster I came."

"But if she caught you at it, why offer her marriage?" Lady Lydgate exclaimed. "Why not expose her?"

"Very likely because he had not yet found the necessary evidence, ma'am," Caroline interjected, "and did not want her to guess the real reason for his intrusion."

By God, it was as if someone had handed her a script. Tristan managed to nod.

"And have you got what you wanted from the girl now?" the other lady demanded.

He set his teeth into the soft flesh of his inner cheek to fight down the grin that seemed determined to rise to his lips. "Not quite. It is my hope—" He pretended to break off, as if he feared he'd said too much.

True to form, Lady Lydgate was ready to coax the details from him. "Have you some plan to catch her?"

It was his turn to send a surreptitious glance around the room and lower his voice. "I've been expecting an important packet from my colonel, and I have hopes that with this change in the weather, it will be delivered today. Rather tempting bait to leave lying around tonight in...say, the library, wouldn't you agree?"

"Official military correspondence?" Caroline's eyes were wide with surprise, her lips creased with disapproval. "I should think you would not wish to risk—"

He heaved a reluctant sigh. "I know what you are about to say, Miss Pilkington. But I cannot expect to catch someone as clever as Miss Burke—oh, she *is* clever, have no doubt about that—with anything less valuable. Now," he added, looking from one to the other with his sternest expression, "I must ask you not to say one word more of this." Such a request would ensure that Lady Lydgate, at least, would retail the rumor far and wide. When his gaze fell on that woman, however, he found that she had anticipated him. She squeaked. "Ma'am? You have not already...?" He raked his eyes over her face, studying for signs of guilt.

"I wouldn't dream of it," she insisted. "Although...it's just possible Sir Thomas might have overheard what Higgs said to me while she was dressing my hair. And, well...I did mention it to the earl when we passed in the corridor just now... And come to think of it, Mrs. Newsome was leaving her chamber as Lord Beresford and I were speaking, and she does seem to take a rather untoward interest in our conversations, so I suppose she could have overheard..."

Excellent. That was very nearly every guest accounted for, except Caroline's parents. Unfortunately, he did not take her for a gossip.

"Well," he said, unbending slightly toward Lady Lydgate, though not so much that she would doubt his sincerity, "I suppose it won't do any harm, so long as that's as far as the story goes."

"The essential matter, I gather," Caroline put in, looking thoughtful, "is that Miss Burke hears of the delivery of the letter without learning what you suspect."

"Precisely. And that should be an easy matter to convey. Over dinner, perhaps." A step in the corridor drew his notice before he could say more. He looked up to discover Whitby entering the breakfast room with Tristan's stepmother on his arm.

David's handsome face, carved in a deep smile as he laughed down at some amusing remark Guin had made, froze. Gradually, it melted into wariness as he watched Tristan, apparently expecting a confrontation. But over what? Whitby's treatment of Erica? His proposal to the woman Tristan was supposed to marry? Or the possibility that he was in fact the spy?

Tristan nodded coolly and tried not to think about how many plots the two of them had hatched together, or what Whitby might say when Lady Lydgate spilled the "secret," as she undoubtedly would. Nodding to them both, he said, "I wish you good morning. Regrettably, I cannot stay." A flicker of concern crossed Guin's face, but he pretended not to notice.

In the corridor, he paused only long enough to hear Lady Lydgate say to Caroline in a carrying voice, "I for one suspected something from the first. Don't you, of all people, recall her behavior that first evening?" Caroline made some inaudible response, to which Lady Lydgate replied, "Pishposh, my dear girl. You heard what he said. It's hardly spreading gossip. Why, I daresay the tale might even serve to amuse your poor sick mother."

And Caroline, who must at that moment be desperate for something to divert either or both of her parents' attention, said with a bit more firmness, "Perhaps you're right."

He pulled his watch from his waistcoat pocket and flicked the catch with his thumb. Half past ten. By the dinner hour, every person under Hawesdale's roof would surely know of the expected packet and the plan to use it to catch a spy. He snapped the watch shut again and set off to send Mr. Davies a note.

He was not quite to the study when he saw Armitage bearing down on him from the opposite direction, accompanied by the man himself.

"We'll met again, Mr. Davies," Tristan said as Armitage bowed and excused himself, his mission accomplished. "I was just on the point of sending you a message—"

"To enquire about the state of the farms?" Davies finished for him as Tristan showed him into the study. "Dreadful, Your Grace. Dreadful. 'Tis glad I am that you're here now." The strength of his Scottish burr grew with his agitation. "'Twill make it easier to learn your wishes about repairs and the like, and quicker to get the work done."

Earlier, as he'd stood looking out the sitting room window, Tristan had imagined the devastation that must lie just beyond his view. Now, he thought of how blithely he'd once dismissed the importance of his role as duke in making things right again. He nodded, half expecting his man of business to berate him soundly for his ignorance, his arrogance. Whatever happened tonight, he understood at last how much he was needed here too. He had a decision to make—a decision that had once seemed simple, but which grew more difficult with every passing hour.

Thankfully, Davies was not the sort of man prone to waste time in recriminations. "But I'm forgetting what brought me," he said as he reached into his coat and withdrew a stack of folded parchment. "No word yet on Lady Ashborough's return. But the mail coach came through Endmoor late last night. I wanted to get these to you as soon as possible, in case there might be important business in't." He held out the handful of letters.

Tristan took them without any particular interest in their contents. Until he saw a familiar hand on the outer sheet of the one uppermost. He blinked to clear his vision and looked again to be sure.

The letter had been sent by Colonel Zebediah Scott.

Chapter 18

Having been left alone by Remington as he went about his gossip-mongering, Erica had spent the rest of the morning in a dream-addled sleep that did little to make up for the night before or to prepare for the night ahead. Again and again, she saw Whitby's leering face accuse her; now, however, he was joined by the whole leering company, pointing and laughing and saying they had always suspected the worst, while Tristan stood to the side, arms crossed over his chest, and declared in her defense that such a shatterbrained creature could never be a spy.

In the afternoon, she made up her mind to visit the conservatory. Why should she squander an opportunity to study and sketch, merely because of what else had transpired beneath its glass roof, the competing memories of Whitby's words and Tristan's kisses? Clutching her journal and a freshly sharpened pencil, she pushed herself across the threshold. It was just a room.

Under the sun's brilliant rays, the glasshouse fairly steamed. Absent the clatter of rain, she would have been willing to swear she could hear the sounds of growing and blooming and ripening, an erotic symphony that filled her ears and her mind with the groaning, aching pleasures of the night before. Groping in the pocket of her sturdy work apron, she found the cotton wool, stuffed it in her ears, and worked until the pages of her journal were limp.

At last, when the sun was low on the horizon and the trickle of sweat down her spine had left her chilled, Remington came into the room, bearing a folded, unsealed note.

Swiping the back of one dirty hand over her damp forehead, she reached with the other to take it from him. *The trap is set. When you come to dinner*, it read in a bold, dark hand—Tristan's hand, *behave as if nothing has changed.*

She refolded the note, tucked it between the pages of her journal. Could she do it? Go into a crowd of strangers? Ignore the judgment in their eyes? She'd done it often enough, it was true, but she was no actress. What had she been thinking when she agreed to play this part? She looked into Remington's face. "What if I fail?"

"You won't, Miss Erica." His voice sounded far away, muffled by the cotton wool. "You can't. Otherwise, the real culprit may suspect what's afoot."

With a sigh, she plucked the cotton from her ears, then reached behind her back and tugged loose the apron strings, slipped the garment over her shoulders, and laid it carefully on the bench. Finally she rose, gathered her journal, and nodded once. She had promised herself she would be brave. She would do this for him.

* * * *

In some ways, the dinner itself was worse that all her lurid, distorted nightmares, for no amount of fidgeting or pressing her fingertips to her eyelids or pinching her thigh through the layers of her skirts could dispel it or give her a moment's peace. For the most part, the other guests moved and spoke and ate as if she were utterly invisible—a prospect that, while pleasing in theory for one who generally felt awkward in company, turned out to be miserable in practice. Tristan held himself aloof, neither polite nor impolite. No one seemed to remark his behavior to her either way. The matter of their midnight escapade had, it seemed, been pushed aside by the greater thrill of a spy in their midst, although no one spoke of it.

Except, that was, Lady Lydgate. "Did you hear the news?" she asked Captain Whitby in an overloud voice. "The Duke of Raynham received a confidential missive from his colonel just this day and repaired *to the library* to pore over it for hours." A glance over her shoulder at the last, to confirm Erica was in earshot. "I wonder what news it contained." Erica pointedly looked the other way before the woman was tempted to say more.

Only the duchess behaved with kindness toward her. More than her usual kindness, in fact. So much so that Erica caught herself wondering whether she too was only playing a part. When they approached the table, she discovered the duchess had gone so far as to have the seating irregularly arranged. Erica sat down at her right hand.

"Are you feeling quite well, Miss Burke?" the duchess inquired over soup.

"Yes, Your Grace. Perfectly well."

While the fish was being served, she said, "I worry that you spend too much time in the heat of the conservatory."

"Undoubtedly, Your Grace. I have a regrettable tendency to lose track of time."

"You need a good night's rest," she declared later as she drove her spoon into a mound of frothy syllabub, her brow creased with concern. "The house will, I hope, be perfectly quiet tonight. No storms, no…disturbances. Nothing at all to draw you from your bed."

"No, Your Grace."

"Allow me to send my maid to you. She prepares a sleep tonic that has always worked without fail."

Oh, dear. The duchess, disinclined to think ill of anyone, seemed determined to do everything in her power to put Erica beyond the power of suspicion, even if it required drugging her into a stupor. Next she would suggest setting a guard outside Erica's chamber door to ensure an unbroken night's rest, and if she did that, the whole plan would be ruined, for everyone must believe she was free to roam.

With very little hope of aid, given that Tristan had hardly looked her way all evening, she sent a desperate glance twenty feet down the table. He gave no sign of having seen her silent plea.

"Or perhaps a—" the duchess began. But before she could complete the suggestion, Tristan laid his palm flat against the table and gave a nod in his stepmother's direction. Immediately, she rose and laid aside her napkin. "Shall we leave the gentlemen to their port, ladies?"

Amid the scrape of chairs, the rustle of silk, and the murmur of conversation as the women rose as one to withdraw, Erica longed to slip from the room. But to do so would disrupt all their careful plans. So she waited, sipped tea, pretended not to hear Lady Lydgate's speculations.

After some time, the gentlemen joined them. All but Tristan. "The butler came bearing an urgent missive from Mr. Davies and he left," Mr. Newsome explained in answer to the duchess' query.

At first, Erica's heart fluttered in alarm. An emergency? Something to do with her sister? But of course it must be a ruse, a further attempt to assure the spy in their midst that Tristan had left his papers—and the house itself—unguarded.

No one suggested cards or forfeits tonight. While the evening was yet young, they retired to their separate chambers, curious glances darted among the company. "Good night," Erica said firmly as she closed her door.

But before many moments had passed, she opened it again. In the corridor all was silent. No one watched as she made her way to the library.

Every pair of draperies but one had been tightly drawn, and the sliver of light that passed between those, red with the setting sun, only made the rest of the room darker in comparison. Dark, and silent as the grave she discovered as she stepped across the thick carpet toward the desk. Papers had been scattered across its otherwise empty top with apparent carelessness. A circle of wax on the edge of one sheet marked it as a letter, a long letter. Three sheets, at least, and no doubt a masterful imitation of what it pretended to be: confidential correspondence between Major Laurens and his colonel. Without a candle, she could not hope to make out a word. She walked on.

Three sides of the library were lined with bookshelves, surrounding the doorway and running up both sides of the twin fireplaces that stood at either end of the long room. Near the middle of the room stood the desk, neither facing the wall of windows nor turned away from it, as if the one who had positioned it had feared the tempting view but not enough to shut it out entirely.

She oughtn't to be here, she knew. Her presence might upend everything. But fatigue had made her more restless than usual and she could not keep away, though she doubted her ability to sit still long enough to catch a spy. She was frightened. Frightened for Tristan. Frightened of what failure tonight might mean for them both.

What of success, though? What would it look like? Each of them going their separate ways, their separate dreams still firmly grasped, unaltered by what was really, when all was said and done, nothing more than a few days trapped under the same roof by a bit of rain?

Well, more than a *bit* of rain…

Water moved ships. It wore away mountains. Surely, it could soften a stony heart, too?

If it had not been fear she'd glimpsed that morning in Tristan's eyes, then what was it?

As her wandering steps wove among the groupings of furniture—sofas, tables, high-backed chairs—she considered where she might best secret herself. Then a warm hand grasped her ankle.

She did not scream. Three silent breaths left her lightheaded but proved insufficient to slow her frantic pulse.

"Erica?" Tristan's voice. He hadn't left after all. With a sharp tug he brought her to her knees beside him. "What are you doing here?" His whisper was laced with a mix of fear and fury.

The sun had set, leaving no light by which to read his expression. "No one saw me leave my room," she whispered back. "And I—I needed to be here. I had to know."

She expected him to argue. Instead, she could hear the sound of his coat sliding against the fabric of the sofa as he settled back into his hiding place. "Sit with me," he murmured, and in the darkness, she let his hands guide her to the floor beside him, shoulder to shoulder, thigh to thigh. She had not realized she was cold until she felt the heat of his body against hers, and she turned toward him like a heliotrope following the sun.

He lowered his head to hers and his breath puffed across her lips when he spoke, more sensation than sound. "If I kiss you now, Erica, all our plans will be for naught."

"Why?"

"Because I won't be able to stop at kisses."

A whimper of longing rose in her throat at his words.

"Shh..."

Only a fraction of an inch separated their lips. The effort required to close the gap was far less than the effort required to keep herself still. To cede control to him once again.

Her reward—and a dubious reward it seemed to be—was to feel him slip his hand into his coat, then search for her hand and press a folded square of paper into her palm.

"What's this?"

"A coded missive."

Had there been some misunderstanding? "Then what's on the desk?"

"New orders from my commanding officer."

"Forged?"

"Real."

"But—I don't understand—"

"We have much to discuss." His hand circled hers and squeezed, and the stiff paper crumpled and curved into her palm as she curled her fingers more tightly around it, as if she could absorb its contents that way. "Later."

She nodded, and the scrub of her hair against the silk damask of the sofa must have been sufficient to convey her assent, for he said nothing more. She freed a hand to tuck the note into her bodice, but as soon as she was done, he laced his fingers through hers and rested their joined hands on his hard thigh. After last night's intimacies, it should have been the merest nothing. Yet it was...*something*. Something extraordinary. And when his thumb stroked idly across her palm, a sound rose again in her throat. Had it escaped, it would have sounded much like the last, needy and hungry.

But what she needed, what she hungered for, was *them*—not just the joining of their bodies, but the joining of their souls, the clasp of support and reassurance that would always be there, whenever, wherever one of them needed it, together or apart, public or private, weak or strong. She returned the pressure of his fingers. He was nothing she'd ever wanted and everything she'd ever needed, and she would be a fool to let him go.

That knowledge, the certainty that she was his and she would find a way to make him hers, made it somewhat easier to release his hand when, an eternity later, the door creaked open and clicked shut again and his arm went rigid with anticipation. They were about to catch the spy in the act.

Despite the darkness, she squeezed her eyes shut, the better to concentrate on sounds. The carpet was too think to register a single footfall, but wasn't that the rustle and scrape of paper across the polished desktop? And a little gasp of surprise—a woman's voice, surely—when the library door opened once more?

A man's voice this time, though only a whisper. "Have you got it? Good."

Erica swore she could hear Tristan's heartbeat as he leaned closer and spoke into her ear. "Pilkington."

But who was his accomplice? Opening her eyes, she discovered that all was not in total darkness. The man had left the door ajar, allowing light from the corridor to leak into the room. She leaned away from Tristan in hopes of peering around the edge of the sofa, but he caught her hand again and would not let her move.

"I expected to have to handle matters myself, this time," Pilkington said, an edge of annoyance in his voice. "I feared you would not get word of the delivery of that letter. Now, give it to me."

Who was she, the woman who, from the sound of things, was still scrabbling to gather the papers strewn across the desk? Who on earth did Pilkington imagine might have failed to hear the rumors that had swept through Hawesdale Chase like fire? One of the lower servants, perhaps, though he did not strike her as the sort of person who entrusted important matters to scullery maids.

"Give it to me," Pilkington repeated, his voice rising above a whisper for the first time.

"No. Not this time."

Erica very nearly cried out, for Tristan had squeezed her hand to the breaking point at those words. That voice, though…rough and shrill with fright…almost familiar…

"Hold!" Tristan shouted, dragging Erica to her feet beside him before releasing her. Remington appeared in the doorway with a lantern in one hand and a pistol in the other. Pilkington threw up one arm to shield himself from the light, and behind him, cowering in the shadow of his body, stood… *Lady Viviane?*

"For God's sake, don't shoot Vivi," Tristan ordered hoarsely as he vaulted over the sofa and landed only a few feet from an astonished Lord Easton, and rather too close to Remington's line of fire for Erica's comfort.

"Don't shoot anyone," Erica said, hurrying forward.

"I won't," Remington ground out, his eyes fixed on Pilkington. "Yet."

"That's right," Tristan agreed. Cold resolve settled over him, until all that was left was a stone statue of man, something that might break but would never, never bend. "Not until I find out what the hell is going on."

Viviane's face was a mask of pure terror and tears streamed down her cheeks. Erica stepped to her side and would have pulled the papers from her shaking hands, but the girl would not, or could not, relent. "I'm sorry, Tris," she sobbed.

But his eyes were only for Pilkington. "So help me God, if you've hurt my sister…"

Remington came forward, his stride smooth, his hand steady, his aim unwavering, even when he bent to deposit the lantern on a low table. "I'd say you've got two minutes at most, Your Grace, before we have an audience."

"I'm not sure I care." And with remarkable speed, like the strike of asp, he drew back his fist and punched Lord Easton in the face. Pilkington, whose entire attention had been focused on the pistol in Remy's hand, hit the carpet with a thud. Bewildered, Erica watched as Remington handed his gun to Tristan, knelt to search the unconscious man's pockets, and finally tied Lord Easton's wrists with his own cravat.

Meanwhile, Tristan came closer to his sister, and when her eyes shifted nervously toward the pistol in his hand, Erica stepped nimbly between them. At the movement, something snapped inside him and some of the tension eased from his body. His complexion warmed and his eyes showed fear. Carefully, he laid the pistol on the desktop and extended an empty hand. "Oh, God, Vivi. No. It's all right. Tell me you're all right."

She snuffled loudly, and Erica turned just in time to catch her as she fainted. The papers she'd been clutching fluttered to the floor. Together, she and Tristan carried the girl to the sofa.

"Burn those," Tristan ordered Remington, and when he'd completed his other tasks, Remy did not hesitate to gather up the fallen pages, open the little glass door on one side of the lantern, and touch them to the flame.

"But—" Erica exclaimed as Remington strode to the fireplace and dropped the burning letter onto the hearth.

"I know what it said," Tristan said, bending over his sister's pale, still form.

Viviane moaned and blinked and in a moment was struggling to sit up. Erica sat beside her and wrapped one arm around her thin shoulders while Tristan knelt at their feet. "He—he p-p-promised—"

"Promised what?" Erica prompted when Tristan couldn't seem to form words.

"He t-told me you were in danger. He said everything I c-could tell him would help to keep you safe."

Tristan's throat worked. "How long?"

"M-m-months and months. Since right after Papa and Percy died. I didn't know m-m-much, tried to remember what I'd heard them say, about where you were and what you might be doing. When your t-t-trunks came, I f-found a couple of letters, but I couldn't b-b-break the code, and I—" Her teeth chattered in earnest then and she broke off.

"Shh," he murmured as he rose and came to sit on her other side. When he wrapped his arms around her, he caught Erica in his embrace too. Their eyes met over Viviane's dark head, and she could see by his distracted gaze he was trying to piece together the information that had been stolen, how much damage had been done.

They were still seated that way when the others began to arrive, Lady Lydgate leading the way in a violently purple silk wrapper, both her husband and her lover at her heels. The duchess came next and flew to her daughter; Tristan surrendered his place to her and went immediately to the door to speak to Whitby. The captain turned but was too late to prevent the next arrivals from seeing into the room. Caroline shrieked, Lady Easton fainted, and the commotion made Pilkington stir at last.

Erica caught herself instinctively counting off the room's occupants. Who was missing? Ah, the vicar and his wife. A nervous hiccup of laughter burst from her as she imagined Mrs. Newsome barring their chamber door to keep her husband from indulging in the sin of gossip.

Lord Beresford and Sir Thomas carried Lady Easton to the sofa on the opposite side of the room, and Caroline knelt on the floor and chafed her mother's hands while Lady Lydgate plied her with a makeshift fan that Erica feared might in fact be one of the late duke's priceless medieval manuscripts.

Then Captain Whitby stepped to the center of the room, surveyed the chaos around him, and said, "I owe Miss Burke an apology. I was the one who told the duke she was a spy. I was wrong. She had no hand in any of this."

"Except," Remington pointed out, one hip propped against the desk and the pistol pointed once more at Pilkington, "for unmasking the real villain." Whitby nodded. "I owe you an apology too, Raynham, for—"

Though she wasn't quite sure how it happened, the next moment Tristan was hugging him and Whitby returned the gesture, two friends reunited after a long and difficult journey. "That's Major Laurens to you," Tristan said gruffly when they broke apart. "But if anyone other than this man"—he jerked his chin in Pilkington's direction—"is to take a share of the blame, it must be me. Captain Whitby warned me there was trouble at Hawesdale." His gaze darted around the room, pausing longest over the odd collection of his sister, his stepmother, and Erica. "I didn't want to hear it."

"My father couldn't possibly be a spy," Caroline cried, in the sort of voice one uses when trying to convince one's self as much as others.

"No," Vivi declared, her own voice firm again. "He's a traitor. He started in at Percy's funeral, trying to get information from me. He told me I would be helping Tris..." She glanced toward her mother and said, more quietly, "I'm ashamed to admit how much I told."

At Whitby's hiss of indrawn breath, Tristan said sharply, "She believed she was doing it to keep me safe."

But it couldn't have done, of course, and every shocked face in the room seemed to know it. Every detail Viviane had gleaned and passed along to another would only have put her brother in greater danger.

From the floor came a groggy mumble. "The girl lies," Pilkington rasped out, having roused himself enough to struggle against his bonds and attempt to rise. Remington pushed him back down with the toe of one boot. "I say," his prisoner protested, "I'll not have this fellow—"

"Oh, do shut up, Easton." His wife, whom no one had realized was awake, sat up with her daughter's assistance. As she spoke, she held one hand to her temple, her eyes narrowed against the beam of Remington's lantern as if the light gave her pain, though the room was actually quite dim. "Can't you see no one believes you?"

Caroline, who had been looking from one parent to the other with a frown notched between her delicate brows, gasped. "Mama?"

"Why did you do it?" the lady demanded of her husband in a surprisingly firm voice.

For a long moment, he appeared to ignore the question. Then, with an awkward, resigned lift of one shoulder, he said, "Why do people do most things? We needed money."

"I brought you a fortune—"

"You brought me *half* a fortune, long spent. The rest is to be Caroline's. By law, I could not touch it, though we needed it desperately. I hoped, after she married, she might prove generous. In the meantime, however, I hardly knew where to turn. Then one night I ran into Lord Hawes in his club. He was in his cups and happened to let a few tidbits slip."

"Percy?" Vivi gasped.

"I found his information…valuable. On that occasion, and others. When he died, I was frantic." He paused, a distant look in his eyes. "We were in the carriage on the way to the late duke's funeral when your mother sighed and said that it was a pity you couldn't simply marry Hawes's brother instead."

"I surely wasn't serious," Lady Easton protested.

"I was." His voice was flat. "And so were our creditors. Still, I knew such an arrangement would take time—time for Major Laurens to return, a period of mourning before a marriage could take place… Then I saw Lady Viviane, who seemed to know a surprising amount for a little girl."

Tristan lunged forward; Captain Whitby held him back.

"Oh, dear child." Lady Easton looked first at Lady Viviane and then toward her daughter. "Please believe I had no idea. Perhaps I might have been more clear-sighted if it weren't for these headaches…"

"Headaches?" Tristan echoed. A pause. "Miss Pilkington, didn't you tell me just this morning that your mother's headaches have been steadily worsening since the spring?"

Caroline nodded. "Around the time of—" The flush of embarrassment warred with a sudden pallor, leaving her face splotched. "Oh."

"Good God, Pilkington," Tristan thundered. "Have you been poisoning your wife to keep her from finding out you'd turned traitor?"

Lord Easton shook his head sharply, though he groaned at the effort. "Not…*poison*, exactly."

On Erica's other side, the duchess lifted her hand to her mouth to stifle a cry, and across the room, Lady Lydgate stopped fanning. "I have a bottle of laudanum in my room. I keep it for the toothache. Shall I fetch it for you, ma'am?" the baronet's wife asked solicitously.

"No." Every eye turned to Erica. "She needs to rid herself of whatever toxins she's been ingesting. A tisane of red clover will help more. It grows wild, of course, but I believe I saw some potted in the conservatory."

Caroline's smile was weak, but genuine. "Thank you, Miss Burke."

After that, the various groups around the room splintered into separate conversations, and with Vivi a warm, drowsy weight against her shoulder, Erica's attention inevitably began to drift. Across the room, Captain Whitby was calling Miss Pilkington "Caro" and being slapped heartily on the back by Sir Thomas, while Lady Lydgate turned a cold shoulder to Lord Beresford and devoted her attention to the pallid but determined Lady Easton. Tristan and Remington discussed something with great animation, occasionally pulling Captain Whitby aside to join them. And the duchess did as she always did, organizing and comforting, though with tears in her eyes. Tea appeared, and more candles, and at some point, footmen who carted Lord Easton away, accompanied by Remington.

Before she quite knew what had happened or how much time had passed, Tristan was kneeling once more at her feet.

"Time for bed, Viv. We'll deal with the rest in the morning," he said to his stepmother, though he looked far from sleep himself.

"C-can you forgive me, Tris?" his sister asked with a yawn.

"There's nothing to forgive."

The duchess rose and went to the door. "She'll sleep in my room tonight. I've already rung to have a bed made up."

When Tristan bent to lift his sister in his arms, he fixed Erica with feverish eyes, long past fatigue. "Don't forget the note, love," he said, his voice low, more seductive than a whisper.

Suddenly Erica was alone again in the library, its book-covered walls illuminated by the flickering light of Remington's abandoned lantern. A moment before, she had been considering whether it would be altogether too indecorous to curl up on the sofa and sleep right there. Now, however...

She pulled the folded paper from her bodice and sat with it on her palm for a long while. Apprehension swept through her, and excitement, and— Flooded with all the possible things the note might contain, both good and bad, her mind bounded from one idea to the next and her pulse began to flutter to keep up with its frantic pace.

"Oh, just read it." Her voice, loud in the quiet room and slightly breathless, cut through the clutter of her thoughts.

Rising, she approached the desk, unfolded the note, and laid it flat in the lantern's light. The decisive strokes of Tristan's pen leaped to life and danced across the page. Why, it wasn't written in English! What on earth...?

Then she remembered he'd described it as a coded message. And she recognized the code. Her code. How quickly he'd mastered it. In the upper right-hand corner of the little square of paper, he'd drawn a circle and filled in half of it. A half-completed task. And beneath that, he had written a line that might have appeared on a certain list in her journal...if she'd dared.

For defiance, an hour in the conservatory with Dk of R—

A tremor of excitement passed through her. Surely, though, after all that had happened, he didn't mean tonight?

But she'd seen his burning eyes, knew that strange energy when a discovery drove sleep away. And when she recollected the circumstances under which the note had been given, those moments in the darkness, the touch of his hand and his whisper against her lips...

She folded the note again and, as Mr. Remington had done, opened the lantern to expose the flame and set the paper alight. When that single, scandalous line was reduced to ash on the hearth, she picked up the lantern and made her way to the conservatory.

Chapter 19

When Tristan looked through the small window in the door of the conservatory and saw Erica, calm eased into his veins, the first calm he had experienced in hours. *She'd come. She'd stayed.*

She was striding between the rows of tables and talking animatedly as she did so. Occasionally, she would pause, gesticulate with her hands, then shake her head. Quickly, he scanned the room for the person to whom she spoke. Mr. Sturgess, perhaps, though the hour was late. But he saw no one else. As he watched for a moment longer, he could draw no other conclusion than that she was talking to the plants.

At the sound of the door opening, she stopped and looked up at him. He gave her a wry smile. "Do they make any answer?"

For a moment, she looked bewildered at his question. Her lips formed the word *who?* before lapsing into an echoing smile of chagrin as she glanced about her. "None that I have been able to make out."

He took a step closer. "That's probably for the best."

She made no move to close the remaining gap between them, and he did not press her. "I was debating with myself whether I ought to return to my chamber," she said quietly. "Whether you would come."

"I said I would."

"But you didn't say *when*. I've been telling myself it was only my foolish hope that you meant tonight…" She trailed her fingertips through a mound of glossy green leaves and set them trembling. "You must be exhausted."

"Yes."

"Furious."

He considered for a moment, wary as always about admitting that heated emotion. "*Frustrated*, I should call it. I blame myself for not assessing the situation more carefully. But when I think about what Pilkington did, what he might have done..." He nodded. "Yes. Furious."

At last she ventured closer, though still separated from him by the breadth of one plant-covered table. "I can wait. This"—she flicked one wrist, gesturing from herself to him, unwilling to assign a label to whatever stood between them—"can wait."

"I cannot."

Something flared in her eyes—surprise? excitement? trepidation? What an astonishing variety of emotions he had seen written there this past week, both light and dark.

Surrounded by greenery, her coppery curls springing free in the warm, damp air, she was like a wild thing in her element...and yet, not. For when all was said and done, the conservatory was only a simulacrum of nature. He remembered once, when he was a very small boy, a bird had found its way inside that pristine garden and then been unable to find its way out, trapped by glass walls that offered only the illusion of freedom.

"Will you sit?" he asked, tipping his chin in the direction of the orange trees. A genuine question. He knew she too was tired, yet she radiated that peculiar energy that had driven her through the storm the afternoon they'd met. The last thing he wanted to do was try to contain it. Try to contain her. But he was dangerously close to vaulting across the table, gathering her into his arms, and spouting poetry—flower poetry, if that was what it took to win her.

With a nod, she turned and made her way toward the iron benches. He followed and seated himself beside her, determined to keep a proper distance between them.

To his surprise, however, her hand crossed that divide and reached for his. Her fingers were cold despite the warmth of the room.

"You forgot *frightened*," he said after a moment. "In your list of the things I have been feeling tonight. I have never been so frightened in all my life."

She studied him with curious, luminous eyes. "For your sister?"

"Yes. If I—if *we* had not been there, God knows what Pilkington might have resorted to when Vivi refused him." A shiver passed between them, and whether it had started in Erica's spine or his own, he couldn't entirely be sure. "Frightened too for my fellow intelligence officers," he went on. "Men who perform delicate work by taking enormous risks, risks that my carelessness has made greater still. The coded letter of which she spoke was a cypher—an old one, it is true, but still of some value. I shall never forgive myself."

He might have made some excuse for having allowed the pages to make their way into his things as he packed for a journey no man wanted to take. He could still see the news of his father and brother's deaths, written in Guin's shaking hand. Or perhaps it had been his own hand that had shook as he read her words, accompanied by a trenchant order, scrawled onto the sheet that enclosed her letter. Colonel Scott had anticipated Tristan's reluctance, his divided sense of duty. *Go anyway*, he had written. And so, after a few ineffectual protests, Tristan had agreed to come home. In a fit of frustration, he had thrown his things into a trunk and sent it on ahead. And at its arrival, his eager sister had seen to its unpacking...

"And frightened for you," he continued after a moment, cupping one hand beneath her jaw and tilting her face to his. "You who insisted on inserting yourself into the fray, though I distinctly remembering telling you, 'Absolutely not.'"

"I suppose that was the defiance to which your note referred?" She met his eyes readily, and the familiar sparkle lit hers. "Well, I think you were frightened for yourself. Because you are terrified at the thought of surrendering even a little bit of control."

Oh, yes. She knew him. Too well, perhaps.

"But I did it anyway," he said, and found his breathing curiously labored, fighting its way past some obstruction in his chest. "I let myself fall in love with you."

"*Tristan.*"

There was wonder in the sound of his name on her lips. And pleasure. And resistance too. As he had expected. He met them all with a whisper of kiss, imagining her unready to make any other reply, or perhaps unready himself to hear the reply she would make.

When he drew back, he let his hand slip from her cheek. "I came here feeling that Hawesdale Chase had less claim on me, less use for me than the British Army. And I think it's time I explained why." He paused, uncertain despite his determination. So many years he'd spent learning how to make others divulge their secrets, how to keep his own. But the gentle pressure of her fingers, tangled with his atop the seat of the iron bench, gave him the strength to continue.

"I grew up knowing it was possible—likely—that my father was not the Duke of Raynham, but rather a man with whom my mother had indulged in a liaison. The head gardener, in fact."

He saw, rather than heard, her sharp intake of breath. "Mr. Sturgess?"

"No, the man who held the post thirty years ago. In whose cottage you found me...hiding. The fact that the cottage has remained uninhabited all this time always struck me as confirmation of the truth of the tale. And because the rumor has never been far from my thoughts," he went on, "I chose to believe it must have a similar prominence in others' memory. I read Davies's careful respect as reluctance. I saw impertinence in a servant's momentary indecision. And worst of all, I refused to recognize what was real." He tightened his grip on her fingers. "After tonight, though, I see that I am needed here. For the sake of the tenants whose livelihood has been threatened by this storm. And for my sister most of all."

She took in all of it with remarkable calm. "When my mother married an Irishman," she said after a moment, "her father, the late Earl of Merrick, refused to see her again. He went to his grave believing that the circumstances of a man's birth mattered more than anything else he did with his life. You are a good man. A good brother. And you will be a good duke."

God, he hoped she was right. "You're forgetting one thing, though," he reminded her. "My colonel's letter."

"The one you told Remington to burn. What was in it?"

"A dismissal, of sorts. After reviewing the information about my work that had been stolen and sold—by Pilkington, as we now know—it was his assessment that it would be too risky for me to return to France and resume my post there." At her quick intake of breath, as if she sensed his disappointment, he hurried to add, "His letter also acknowledged that I had no doubt discovered myself glad to be home, despite my initial reluctance to return, and therefore tempted to stay."

This time, she was not so quick to react, though at last she ventured a cautious nod of agreement. "But...?" she prompted.

"But the letter also contained an offer, if I might be willing to consider it. An assignment of a temporary nature, to begin in six months and last roughly a year. Training new agents."

"Where?"

"In the West Indies."

For a moment, her eyes lost focus, and he wondered if she were thinking of that exquisitely drawn map in her journal. "And what have you decided?" she asked at last.

"It is, of course, a complicated situation. Even now, after all that has happened, I have been trying to imagine a way in which I might have both—have everything I want, in fact."

"What *do* you want, Tristan?" she whispered.

The answer was clear—had been clear for quite some time, if he had not been too blind to see it.

"Come with me. See the places and the plants I know you've dreamed of seeing. Make a brilliant discovery—a dozen discoveries—a hundred. And then come home. Help me make Hawesdale the very best it can be. Teach my sister whatever she wants to learn. We'll go to London, hear lectures—no. No, you'll *give* the lectures. Any dream of yours...*every* dream of yours...let me help you make it real."

She drew three careful breaths, in through her nose and out through her lips. He'd watched her do it before, but he had no idea what it presaged, what words she might speak when she was done. Once more she was opaque.

"And *your* dreams?" she asked at last.

"They've all become dreams of you."

"Oh, Tristan," she said, choking his name past something that sounded suspiciously like a sob. "Those do sound like lovely dreams. But you must know I'd make a terrible duchess."

"I'm not asking you to be my duchess, love..."

Every muscle in her body, even the blood in her veins, appeared to have turned solid as mortification overspread her face.

Hurriedly, he finished his sentence. "I'm asking you to be my *wife*."

Warily, she unbent the tiniest degree. "But you're a duke. Which means your wife will be..."

"*You*, I hope. Just as you are." Her lips quivered at that, and the pink came back into her cheeks. "I cannot blame you for not wanting to be the Duchess of Raynham," he said, "for I certainly never wanted to be the Duke. But these last few months—no, this *week* has reminded me how little of the world I really control, whether as a duke, a major, or simply a man. And when I think of all your supposed 'flaws,' well... It seems to me you're far better prepared for this messy, uncertain life than I am." He brought his hand to her face again, stroked his thumb along her cheekbone. "Will you share the ups and downs of this journey with me, love?"

She hesitated. "What will your colonel say about you marrying an Irish rebel?"

"He might just consider you an asset," he answered with a teasing half smile. But her expression did not soften and he realized the question had been sincere. And something in the nature of a confession? Perhaps Whitby's suspicions about her family hadn't been wrong after all. *Damn.* Releasing her other hand, Tristan pinned her face between his palms, so that she could not avoid his eyes. "He'll come around. Because you're not just any Irish rebel. You're mine."

She melted then, into his arms, into him, her hands sliding up his shirtfront and wrapping around his neck, while her lips traced a fiery path along his jaw to his ear, all the time whispering, "Yes. Yes. Yes."

. He tried unsuccessfully to shift and gather her into his arms, but the bench was narrow and unforgiving. "I wish now I'd given in to temptation in the library. That's the softest carpet in the house."

"Hardly a proper place for you to punish my defiance, Your Grace." Her laugh tickled against his throat, where her tongue was doing marvelously naughty things.

Ah, yes. The note. "I was thinking of it more in the nature of a reward."

"The floor in here is warm," she suggested.

"But deuced...*hard*." The groan slipped from his lips as one of her hands made its teasing way to his lap.

Once before in this room, he had wondered what it would be like to find himself the sole focus of her attention. Now he knew. Her curious fingers lightly traced his erection through the woolen breeches; he made no attempt to deter her when, some minutes later, she sought the buttons of his fall and slipped them free, one by one. Then it was more of the same pleasant torture through the thin barriers of his shirttail and his drawers, her light touch learning him with slow deliberation. It would, at this rate, be another hour before she ventured beneath the linen. Anything like gratification hovered far in the distance, almost a mirage. He gritted his teeth and let her play.

His turn would come.

In assessing that he had more patience than she, he was correct. He underestimated her persistence, though, and very nearly to his peril. He had not anticipated that her mischievous exploration would bring him almost to the point of pain, so near crisis that his body trembled with the effort of holding it at bay. His breath was ragged when he told her to stop. Or at least, those were the words he had meant to say. What passed his lips was something closer to a curse, a plea, garbled and desperate for release, and he caught her wrists and pulled her hands away a moment before he embarrassed himself.

Lifting those wicked hands to his lips, he kissed each finger, and each brush of his lips produced a corresponding catch of breath. Ten times he watched her eyes widen, her gaze darken a fraction more, until he held her spellbound. With deceptive lightness, he laid her hands down, one on either side of her hips, palms flat against the bench. Obligingly, she curled her fingers into the iron scrollwork and left them there as his mouth came to meet hers and his hands settled elsewhere, one against her waist, the other cupping the curve of her breast. So many layers between his touch and her skin, yet he could feel her impatience, the rise and fall of her ribcage and the flutter of her heart.

Her kiss, too, was eager and openmouthed. Deliberately, he denied her at first, tracing the very edge of her lips with his own, eluding the darting tip of her tongue. But only at first. Desire could be kept at a simmer for only so long before it began to burn.

Still, for a time he contented himself with kisses, her soft mouth so inviting, the taste of her so sweet. Then he let his lips drift to her throat, the wings of her collarbone, pausing to give a gentle nip to the slope of her breast where it rose above the edge of her dress, pushed to prominence by her corset. He could sense how desperately she wanted to be free of it, bare to his touch as she'd been the night before.

"We're in the glasshouse," he reminded her. "And we've left the lantern burning. Anyone might see us."

A tremor passed through her. "Let them see."

My God. Her reckless passion would be his undoing. And he would have no regrets.

But he didn't undress her. He made do with sliding one hand beneath her skirts, over her knees, to the hot silk of her thighs. When her legs parted, he traveled higher, inch by careful inch. Her crisp curls were damp already, and she hissed with pleasure when he drew his fingers lightly through them, once, then twice.

"You're going to make me sorry for teasing you, aren't you?" she cried softly.

"Yes." He slipped one finger deeper, just brushing her bud. "And no."

What he really wanted was to set his mouth to her there, taste the dew that coated his fingers, feel her tremble against his tongue. But there would be a time for that, and a place more comfortable than this. Here, on this unrelenting iron bench and behind these glass walls, she was a prisoner of a different sort. Tonight, he wanted to be able to watch her face, as she had no doubt watched his. See the flush, the glitter of perspiration rise to her skin, the desperate agony of pleasure as he touched her, bringing her again and again to the very brink of release.

He would teach her something about patience.

"Stand up," he ordered long moments later, rising himself and shoving his breeches to his knees.

She was trembling, weak with desire, but with his help she got to her feet, and once more her trust was a gift unlike any other he had ever known. With gentle pressure, he turned her to face the bench and bent her over it, placing her hands to support her weight. Dragging her skirts upward, he bared her backside to his gaze, welcome curves of creamy flesh over which he swept his eyes and hands before stepping closer. With one quick thrust, he was inside her.

Her head came up with such force her hair came free of its pins in a flash of silken fire; he heard them skitter across the flagstone floor. Three slick strokes would finish him, he had no doubt, but it was time enough to slip his hand around her hip, to flick one fingertip across her swollen bud. She shattered with a scream that rang from the walls, and his seed sprang from him, filling her.

Sometime later, when they were collapsed together on the bench and he'd tidied their clothes as best he could, he let a wry laugh escape. "*Wild*, did Sturgess say?"

She snuggled closer. "Don't forget *dirty.*"

"Oh, I hadn't." With one hand, he smoothed her tumbled hair. A hum of pleasure vibrated through her. "He was wrong about one important thing, though."

"What was that?" she asked absently, distracted by his touch.

"I love it here." At Hawesdale. In the conservatory. With Erica.

Like a cat, she tipped her head into his soothing stroke. "And I love you."

Chapter 20

Three days later, after bidding adieu to the Lydgates and Newsomes, Erica found herself standing in the high-ceilinged entry hall, arm in arm with the Duchess of Raynham, the sole remaining guest at Hawesdale Chase.

"Though a *guest*," the duchess reminded her, patting her hand, "you will not be much longer. We shall switch places, you and I."

"You mustn't say such things, Your Grace," Erica insisted. Despite her general state of elation at discovering herself loved and in love, she'd also experienced a corresponding increase in anxiety. At times, she still wondered whether she had made a mistake by agreeing to this rapid and radical change of circumstances. Because all Tristan's reassurances did not change the essential truth of the matter: once she'd spoken her vows and signed the register, she would be the Duchess of Raynham. "Surely your stepson has warned you, and you have seen with your own eyes, how ill-prepared I am to fill your shoes?"

The duchess tipped her head, studying Erica as she considered her words. "Then don't," she said at last with a shrug. "You must make the title, and the role, your own. Who could fail to be charmed by your delightfully easy manner?"

"*Delightfully easy manner?*" Erica couldn't prevent the chortle that rose to her lips. "You needn't persist in claiming my faults are virtues, Your Grace. We all know I haven't the first notion how to act like a duchess."

Her lips curved in a knowing smile. "But you have every notion how to make Tristan happy. I've seen more smiles on his face in the last week than I have in the last ten years. His happiness—and yours—matter far more than anyone else's stuff-and-nonsense idea of what a duchess must be." At Erica's skeptical expression, the duchess' face settled into more serious lines. "I will not pretend that everyone shares my philosophy of the matter. I wish, however, that you would consider adopting it all the same. Hold your head up—I've seen you do it—and you will have mastered the essentials, my dear. After all, if a duchess is not permitted her eccentricities, who is?"

"But Hawesdale is so vast, and…" Erica could feel the familiar panic rising in her chest.

"I will help and advise you as long as you wish it, in the management of the household and whatever other assistance you believe you require. If," she added, fixing Erica with a firm look, "you will promise me two things."

"Yes?"

"You must do me this courtesy: treat me as a friend and tell me honestly when you are ready to stand on your own—and you will be one day," she added pointedly when Erica opened her mouth to protest, "so you may say your breath."

Erica managed a wobbly nod of agreement. "And the second?"

"Be true to yourself. Do not judge yourself against some imagined, and imaginary, paragon. It is you Tristan loves, not—forgive me—that rather dull person you've set up in your mind for an ideal."

It was, she recalled with a blush, not unlike the promise Tristan had extracted. If he had learned to love her for who she was, then surely she could learn to love herself. "Yes, Your Gr—Guin," she agreed, forcing herself to shape the name by which she'd been invited to address her future mother-in-law. "I can be forgetful, sometimes, but I do try to keep my promises."

"I'll attest to that," Tristan said with a wink as he reentered the hall.

"Are the Lydgates and the Newsomes safely away?"

Erica had expected Lady Lydgate to be mournful today. Lord Beresford had departed early the day before, without ceremony, and also without settling his debts of honor to the other gentlemen. But in the earl's absence, the baronet himself seemed once more to have claimed his wife's affection. The two had left arm in arm, smiling at one another. Sir Thomas had even forgone any mention of prolonging their visit for another day's shooting, although the weather continued fine.

"*Happily* away, I'd say, as I overheard Mrs. Newsome tell her husband more than once how glad she was to be leaving 'this den of iniquity.' But I cannot vouch for their continued safety. I greatly fear she may yet climb upon the coachman's box and insist on taking up the reins herself."

It was, all in all, a considerably merrier leave-taking than the day before, when Miss Pilkington and her mother, both pale and silent, had set off in one direction, while Captain Whitby and Lord Easton, accompanied by the magistrate and several members of the Endmoor militia, headed in another. But the captain had announced his intention to be with Caroline again in a fortnight, Lady Easton had given her heartfelt blessing to the match, and Erica had hope that the promise of future joy would overcome their present misery.

At that moment, Lady Viviane burst through the door that had only moments before been closed behind her brother. Since the night on which all had been revealed, she had been alternating in her moods between disconsolate and jubilant—in the way of all girls who are almost thirteen, perhaps. Disconsolate when she remembered the danger into which she had unwittingly put her brother and so many others, jubilant when she learned that Tristan would be home until spring and that she would have a sister at last, "and one whose bonnet is not stuffed with straw," as she was fond of saying.

"Shouldn't you be in the schoolroom, Viv?" Tristan asked with a mock frown.

Viviane tossed her head. "You dismissed my governess, Tris—if I turn out ignorant and ill-mannered, you'll have only yourself to blame."

"I declare, Viviane, you are sadly near it already," said her mother. "Come along and I'll hear your geography lesson."

"But there's a carriage on the drive..."

"Of course there is, Viv," Tristan teased. "Despite Mrs. Newsome's dearest wish, the Lydgates's carriage cannot actually fly."

"Another coach," she insisted with an exasperated sigh as her mother led her away. "A crested one. Headed toward the house, not away."

"A crested coach." Erica swallowed around the knot that had formed in her throat. "Do you suppose...?"

Tristan motioned to the footmen to open the doors again. "Only one way I know of to find out."

She preceded him down the steps and onto the drive; there was no portico. With agitated, erratic steps, she paced a few strides in the direction of the distant coach, then back again. The third time she approached Tristan, he held out his arm, and with a ragged sigh, she let her hand rest on his sleeve.

"If you're nervous, love," he said, covering her hand with his own, "may I suggest ringing for Remington to join us in welcoming Lord and Lady Ashborough? He might provide a worthy distraction."

With a questioning glance, she tilted her face toward his.

"He asked me yesterday evening whether I thought I would have any need of a personal secretary, an aide of sorts, on our voyage," Tristan explained, his own gaze still on the approaching conveyance. "I said yes."

She pursed her lips to keep from laughing. "You're stealing Lord Ashborough's manservant?"

His broad shoulders lifted and fell. "It would seem that a man who has grown accustomed to London and a life of activity takes exception to the idea of spending his remaining years holed up in Shropshire with what I believe must be some sort of...dog? I'll admit, his description of the beast left me a little unsure."

With that, her laugh could no longer be contained, and once it was set free, a bit of her nervousness flew with it. "Poor Elf. She's very fond of Remy—or at least his shoes."

The carriage wheels rattled over the quaint stone bridge that crossed the stream in front of the house, no longer a raging river. The sound once more jarred her pulse into a frantic rhythm. In another hundred yards, she would be able to see into the coach, catch her first glimpse of Cami's disapproving frown.

Tristan tightened his grip on her hand. "You're worried about what your sister will say about this, about us. But I think she may be more understanding than you expect. From what you've told me, there were more than a few irregularities in Ashborough's courtship of her," he reminded her, returning his eyes to her face.

She recalled the day Cami and Lord Ashborough had arrived in Dublin, totally unchaperoned. Cami's last letter had painted a less than flattering portrait of the man, but even Erica, who was sometimes oblivious to what others might be thinking, could see something had happened to alter Cami's opinion. Now, she had some idea what it might have been. "I'm not sure it could properly be called a courtship at all, in fact. Like you, he was intended for marriage with another. But at least"—she arced her brow in a playful scold—"he did not suspect my sister of being a spy, then use every means at his disposal to get his hands on her journal to prove it."

Tristan's expression remained perfectly serious. "What matters is whether he captured her heart."

She turned to give him a swift kiss before the coach was near enough to see them. "As you have mine?"

His other hand came up to curve against the side of her head, his eyes brighter than she had ever seen them. Her thoughts flickered in a dozen directions. A proper lady would be wearing a bonnet on this sunny day. A proper lady wouldn't dream of his touch every night. Then the gentle pressure of his fingertips against her scalp, the security she would always feel in his embrace, pushed everything else out of her mind.

"Likewise," he whispered near her ear.

Now the carriage wheels crunched on the crushed stone of the drive. Cami's profile appeared in the frame of the coach window, the edge of her bonnet, her raven black hair, the rims of her silver spectacles.

Erica dug her ungloved fingers into Tristan's arm. "My sister is a marchioness."

"I—er, yes?" His brow creased in a baffled frown.

"Still unaccustomed to *non sequitur* in my conversation, Your Grace?" She smiled. "My sister is a marchioness, and I…I'm going to be a duchess."

He laughed softly. "That you are."

"I'll outrank her." She made no attempt to disguise the glee she felt, childish though it might be.

Another laugh. And another kiss, swift and sure and true. His eyes sparkled. "I knew you'd come to see the value of that lofty title, love."

THE END

Author's Note

In the Georgian era, charades were rhyming riddles; each line of the poem referred to a syllable of a word or the name of a famous person (the more familiar acting game known as *charades* comes along a little later). All but one of the charades in Chapter 11 of *The Duke's Suspicion* came from *Amusing Recreations; or a Collection of Charades and Riddles on Political Characters and Various Subjects* by Mrs. Pilkington (a happy coincidence, and no relation to Caroline, I assume), published in 1798 (the year in which the events of the story take place).

Keep reading for a sneak peek at

THE LADY'S DECEPTION

The next book in the

Rogues & Rebels series

And don't miss the first book in the series

THE COMPANION'S SECRET

Available now from

Susanna Craig

And

Lyrical Books

The Lady's Deception

If it was blasphemous to swear at the knelling of church bells, Paris Burke was surely doomed.

He paused to shake the sound from his head. The call to Evensong at Christchurch? Surely not. The waters of the Liffey must be making the bells echo, doubling their peals. It could not possibly be as late as...

He pulled his watch from his waistcoat pocket, tilted its face toward the fading sunlight, and swore again.

During the years of his life when he might have offered ample excuses for running late—the combined and sometimes competing demands of the law and his hopes for Ireland's liberation—only once had he failed to keep an assignation. The disastrous effects of that mistake would haunt him for the rest of his days. Fortunately, the consequences of missing an appointment with Mrs. Fitzhugh were not so dire. Nonetheless, he regretted what it said about the kind of man he'd become.

Tucking the watch away, he glanced over his shoulder in the direction of King's Inns—not with longing, precisely. Oh, the dinner in the commons had been good enough, and the wine had flowed freely. Time was, the company alone would have been enough to call him back. The brotherhood of jurisprudence. The discussions, the debates.

Tonight, though, he had felt certain absences too strongly. The faces that could no longer join them. The voices that would never be heard again. No matter how many times he had signaled for his cup to be filled, their ghostly shadows had refused to be dispelled.

For the first time, he was not sorry he'd given up his lodgings closer to the courts. The walk across the city would afford him ample time to clear his head. And to concoct some explanation for his lateness, though whatever he produced would do little to blunt the disappointment with which he was bound to be greeted.

He took another half-dozen strides, rounding the corner of Church Street to pass in front of the Four Courts. The last of the daylight cast a jagged chiaroscuro across the ground, the building itself too new for its shadows to have grown familiar to his eyes. From the gloom, something slipped into his path. What sort of claret had they been pouring, that it continued to conjure these spectral apparitions, this one with pale hair and paler skin? He swore a third time.

"You ought to mind your tongue in the presence of a lady," the wraith said primly, resolving itself into the perfectly ordinary figure of a blonde woman wearing a pelisse the color of Portland stone.

No, not *perfectly ordinary*. Perfectly ordinary women did not materialize on the King's Inns Quay. They did not have hair the color of summer butter, spilling from beneath a ridiculous frippery of a hat that looked a little worse for wear. Nor did they have eyes the color of—well, no sea he had ever had the pleasure to know. With another shake of his head, he stepped closer, finding himself in need of the support of hewn granite.

"I'm looking for someone," she said, watching his every move. Her brows knitted themselves into a tight frown. "A lawyer. You see, I'm a governess and this morning I—"

"You're English." Part observation, part accusation. She wasn't the first beautiful woman his fancy had invented, but never before had his imagination betrayed his politics so thoroughly.

"I'm Miss Gorse," she replied, as if that decided the matter.

Oddly enough, it did. Because only a real woman could have such a prickly name. And such a prickly voice. Which, heaven help him, was still speaking.

"…in my previous post, I had charge of the two children of Lord—"

Two children. *Damn it all*. His sisters. He'd promised them, when the last interview had turned up no likely candidate, that Mrs. Fitzhugh would surely know of someone suitable. And now he'd have to confess that he'd—

A tongue of wind licked along the river, rippling the water before gusting up the imposing edifice in whose shelter they stood. The wind stirred Miss Gorse's skirts, too, revealing something at her feet. A valise? The sort of women who strolled the streets of Dublin at twilight did not usually, in his experience, tote luggage.

He pushed himself up a little straighter, bolstered as much by the cool breeze as by the cornerstone's sharp edge where it fitted neatly along the groove of his spine.

"A governess, did you say?"

Her mouth was already forming other words. It hung open a moment before shaping the one he hoped to hear. "Yes."

Was it possible? He'd understood the meeting with Mrs. Fitzhugh to be preliminary, but perhaps she'd not needed to speak with him before deciding on the perfect person for the job.

"And you're looking for a lawyer?"

"A solicitor, yes. I thought—"

"She told you that you'd find Mr. Burke at King's Inns, I gather."

"Er—"

"My father is the solicitor, though. Rowan Burke. I'm a barrister, in point of fact. But Mrs. Fitzhugh is right in thinking that you'll really be in my father's employ. A man without children isn't likely to need a governess, now is he?" His wry laugh ricocheted off the stone walls, startling a flock of drowsy rooks who cawed their disapproval.

Her lips were parted once again, but this time no words came. She was watching him with wide eyes that did not narrow, even when she at last closed her mouth and jerked her head in some uncertain motion, neither disagreement nor agreement.

"My sisters will be delighted to meet you, Miss Gorse. I am surprised, though, you didn't go directly to Merrion Square."

"Is it—?" She paused, wetted her lips, and began again. "Is it far?"

"No more than a mile. An English mile, to be precise," he added, curving his mouth into a sort of smile. He would not have guessed that Mrs. Fitzhugh had a sense of humor. To send him, of all people, an Englishwoman... "At least we've a fine night for a stroll."

Alarm flared in her eyes when he bent to pick up her valise, and he thought for a moment that she meant to stop him. Instead she dipped her head in a nod. "Indeed, Mr. Burke. I had no thought this morning that the day would turn out so fine."

"Ah, well. It mightn't've, you know." Turning, he set off along the quayside. "An Irish spring is not to be predicted."

"This is my first," she said. "My first Irish spring, that is."

Last spring, then, she'd been elsewhere. In England, presumably. Far from the turmoil that had enveloped Dublin and the surrounding countryside. Far from the rebellion that had taken the lives of so many. And for what? For naught, for naught...

The warm glow of the claret sputtered like a candle, struggling to withstand the damp, clammy mist rising from the Liffey. He had not realized he had lengthened his stride until he heard the sounds of someone struggling to keep up.

"Mr. Burke?" She had one hand pressed to her side and a hitch in her gait. "I wonder if we might walk a bit more slowly."

When she reached his side, he held out his free arm and she took it, not with the perfunctory brush of her fingertips, but with her whole hand, leaning heavily against him. *Odd.* She didn't look frail. "Shall I hail a sedan chair, Miss Gorse?" Though truthfully, this was an unlikely spot to hail anything but trouble. And the more he thought of Mrs. Fitzhugh sending this woman to him here, in this fashion, the less he liked it. Why, he might have been detained at commons for hours, and she left alone as darkness fell…

Her touch lightened as she bristled. "I can walk." Her step was almost brisk as they crossed the Carlisle Bridge. "Perhaps you would do me the kindness of telling me something of my pupils?"

"My sisters. Daphne and Bellis. Ten and eight, respectively. As ignorant as most girls their age, I daresay."

She drew back her shoulders at that description. "Their previous governess was not firm enough with them?"

"I'm almost embarrassed to admit it, but they haven't any previous governess. They are the youngest of the six of us and shockingly spoiled. My father in particular has always been prone to indulgence where they were concerned."

Disapproval—or was it disbelief?—sketched across her face. "Whatever made him decide to hire a governess now?"

"He knows nothing of the matter, Miss Gorse."

Those words brought her up short. "You have hired me without reference to his authority? Will he not be angry?"

"My parents are in London. You need concern yourself with no one's authority but mine."

A group of young men, Trinity students, passed in a noisy gaggle and were gone. Beneath the high walls surrounding the college, the evening shadows were deeper still. But not too deep for him to read a question in her eyes. A question for which he had never yet determined a satisfactory answer.

He'd already done a masterful job of proving himself unequal to the responsibilities of an eldest son and brother. Why in God's name had his parents entrusted him with the care of two young girls?

"Not much farther now," he said brusquely. Obligingly, Miss Gorse resumed walking, though her pace had slowed and she was limping noticeably now. But she made no complaint, and he had the distinct impression she would not thank him for enquiring about it.

To cover the sound of her shuffling, irregular footsteps, he passed the last quarter mile regaling her with stories about the girls: Daphne's interest in learning the harp, which he attributed to Cami's unfortunate book—although he omitted that particular detail from his account. And Bell's fondness for a game of cricket, in which both he and Galen had been wont to indulge her.

On the north side of Merrion Square, he stopped. "And here we are."

She climbed the steps as if they were mountains, tottering a bit at the end while he fished for his key and opened the door to let them in. It hardly seemed possible for two girls, both slight of build, to make as much noise as Daphne and Bell as they thundered down the stairs from the drawing room to greet them on the landing.

"Did you see Mrs. Fitzhugh?" demanded Bell.

At the same time, Daphne asked, "Is she our new governe—?"

Miss Gorse looked from one to the other, gave a wan smile, and collapsed on the floor.

Bell's eyes grew round with disbelief and her lower lip quavered. "I didn't mean to frighten her to death, Paris. Honest I didn't."

"She isn't dead, *eejit*," Daphne declared, nudging her younger sister with an elbow.

"*Silence.*"

Years of training had given Paris exceptional control over his voice. It could command a crowd. It could compel a confession. But never in all his life had it actually managed to quiet his youngest sisters.

They were both staring at him now, wide-eyed and wobbly-lipped, and he knew in another moment there would be tears. *Oh God, anything but tears.*

"She's just fainted. Bell, run downstairs and tell Molly to make us a pot of tea, will you?" Bellis nodded. With one backward glance at the woman at his feet, she was gone. "And Daphne? If you could…" *Could what?* The clarity that had come with the cool evening air had flown, and the lingering fumes of claret in his brain showed very little interest in forming themselves into a coherent request. He knelt beside Miss Gorse, who was deathly pale but breathing easily.

"I'll see if I can find a vinaigrette," Daphne offered.

"Yes. Thank you. And I'll take Miss Gorse upstairs." Because he couldn't very well leave her in a heap in the foyer, though if this was the sort of weak-willed governess Mrs. Fitzhugh recommended…

He slipped his hands beneath her and rose, expecting to stumble beneath her weight. But she was no burden. Tucking her against his chest, his ascended the stairs, thinking first of the sofa in the drawing room, then bypassing it in favor of a proper bed in the chamber that Cami and Erica had once shared. As he laid her atop the coverlet, she stirred and murmured but did not wake. His fingers fumbled to unpin her hat. More golden locks sprang free, tumbling over the pillow and across her brow. He brushed them carefully from her eyes. She wasn't feverish, at least. Pray God, it was nothing contagious. Perhaps he ought to send Molly for the physician who lived across the square.

He turned his attention next to unbuttoning her gray pelisse with swift, businesslike motions. Then his hands traveled to hers, tugging free her gloves and pausing to note with relief the steady drum of her pulse in one fine-boned wrist. At last, he removed her shoes and found the hem of her dress damp, stained with grass and fresh mud. The shoes themselves were shockingly worn down. On the sole of one was a hole the size of a three shilling piece—no wonder she had limped. It looked as if she'd walked considerably farther today than the distance from Four Courts to Merrion Square.

Where had she come from? Far enough that she could have fainted from the fatigue of her journey?

When Daphne returned holding out a vinaigrette, he shook his head. "I think perhaps we'd best let her rest."

"But what about her dress?" Daphne's cheeks pinked. "And her—her…?"

"Her stays?" His arms retained a memory of the young woman's soft curves. "She isn't wearing any, Daph."

Before his too-precocious sister could ask how he knew about such things, he waved her from the room, pausing on the threshold for one last look.

She looked like the princess in some fairy tale, imprisoned by some wicked spell. In repose, her expression had lost its wariness, its prickliness, and he realized for the first time how young she was. Twenty, if he had to guess. Hardly the woman of experience he'd requested.

Silently, he closed the door behind them. The mystery of Miss Gorse would have to wait until morning.

About the Author

Photo Credit: Vicky Lea, Hueit Photography

A love affair with historical romances led **Susanna Craig** to a degree (okay, three degrees) in literature and a career as an English professor. When she's not teaching or writing academic essays about Jane Austen and her contemporaries, she enjoys putting her fascination with words and knowledge of the period to better use: writing Regency-era romances she hopes readers will find both smart and sexy. She makes her home among the rolling hills of Kentucky horse country, along with her historian husband, their unstoppable little girl, and a genuinely grumpy cat. Visit her at www.susannacraig.com.

In this tempestuous new series, rebellious hearts prove hard to tame—but can England's most dangerous rake be captured by a wild Irish rose?

They call him Lord Ash, for his desires burn hot and leave devastation in their wake. But Gabriel Finch, Marquess of Ashborough, knows the fortune he's made at the card table won't be enough to save his family estate. For that he needs a bride with a sterling reputation to distract from his tarnished past, a woman who'll be proof against the fires of his dark passion. Fate deals him the perfect lady. So why can't Gabriel keep his eyes from wandering to her outspoken, infuriatingly independent Irish cousin?

Camellia Burke came to London as her aunt's companion, and she's brought a secret with her: she's written a scandalous novel. Now, her publisher demands that she make her fictional villain more realistic. Who better than the notorious Lord Ash as a model? Though Cami feels duty-bound to prevent her cousin from making a disastrous match, she never meant to gamble her own heart away. But when she's called home, Ash follows. And though they're surrounded by the flames of Rebellion, the sparks between them may be the most dangerous of all…

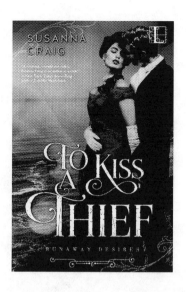

In this captivating new series set in Georgian England, a disgraced woman hides from her marriage—for better or worse...

Sarah Pevensey had hoped her arranged marriage to St. John Sutliffe, Viscount Fairfax, could become something more. But almost before it began, it ended in a scandal that shocked London society. Accused of being a jewel thief, Sarah fled to a small fishing village to rebuild her life.

The last time St. John saw his new wife, she was nestled in the lap of a soldier, disheveled, and no longer in possession of his family's heirloom sapphire necklace. Now, three years later, he has located Sarah and is determined she pay for her crimes. But the woman he finds is far from what he expected. Humble and hardworking, Sarah has nothing to hide from her husband—or so it appears. Yet as he attempts to woo her to uncover her secrets, St. John soon realizes that if he's not careful, she'll steal his heart...

**Susanna Craig's dazzling series set in Georgian England sails to the
Caribbean—where a willful young woman and a worldly man do
their best to run every which way but towards each other...**

After her beloved father dies, Tempest Holderin wants nothing more than
to fulfill his wish to free the slaves on their Antiguan sugar plantation.
But the now wealthy woman finds herself pursued by a pack of unsavory
suitors with other plans for her inheritance. To keep her from danger,
her dearest friend arranges a most unconventional solution: have Tempest
kidnapped and taken to safety.

Captain Andrew Corrvan has an unseemly reputation as a ruthless,
money-hungry blackguard—but those on his ship know differently. He
is driven by only one thing: the quest to avenge his father's death on the
high seas. Until he agrees to abduct a headstrong heiress...

If traveling for weeks—without a chaperone—isn't enough to ruin
Tempest, the desire she feels for her dark and dangerously attractive
captor will do the rest. The storm brewing between them will only gather
strength when they reach England, where past and present perils threaten
to tear them apart—even more so than their own stubborn hearts...

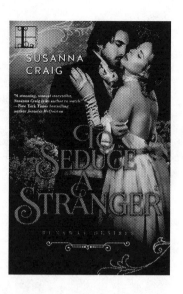

Desire waylays the plans of a man with a mysterious past and a woman with an uncertain future, in Susanna Craig's unforgettable series set in Georgian England.

After her much older husband dies—leaving her his fortune—Charlotte Blakemore finds herself at the mercy of her stepson, who vows to contest the will and destroy her life. With nowhere to turn and no one to help her, she embarks on an elaborate ruse—only to find herself stranded on the way to London...

More than twenty years in the West Indies have hardened Edward Cary, but not enough to abandon a helpless woman at a roadside inn—especially one as disarmingly beautiful as Charlotte. He takes her with him to the Gloucestershire estate he is determined to restore, though he is suspicious of every word that falls from her distractingly lush lips.

As far as Charlotte knows, Edward is nothing more than a steward, and there's no reason to reveal his noble birth until he can right his father's wrongs. Acting as husband and wife will keep people in the village from asking questions that neither Charlotte nor Edward are willing to answer. But the game they're each determined to play has rules that beg to be broken, when the passion between them threatens to uncover the truth— for better or worse...